THE CITY AND THE STARS

BY ARTHUR C. CLARKE

HARCOURT, BRACE AND COMPANY
NEW YORK

PRINTED IN THE UNITED STATES OF AMERICA

TO VAL

For the benefit of those who have read my first novel, [illegible] of Night, and will recognise some of the material [illegible] work, a few words of explanation are in order.

Against the Fall of Night was begun in 1937 and, after four or five drafts, was completed in 1946. Though for various reasons [illegible] thor's ego, book publication was delayed [illegible] though this work was well received, it has not [illegible] novel, and my initial dissatisfaction with it [illegible] years. Moreover, the progress of science since the [illegible] story was first conceived made many of the [illegible] opened up vistas and possibilities quite unimaginable when [illegible] originally planned. In particular, certain developments [illegible] ory suggested revolutions in the human way of [illegible] than those which atomic energy is already introducing [illegible] incorporate these into the book I had [illegible] write.

A sea voyage from England to Australia [illegible] to grips with the [illegible] out to the Great Barrier Reef [illegible] months diving among [illegible] to action. It may [illegible] ing settles a man's mind [illegible] in the morning, [illegible] returning from the [illegible] pleted at that particular [illegible] almost twenty years [illegible]

About a quarter of the present work appeared [illegible] Night; it is my belief [illegible] will find that this is virtually a new novel. [illegible] will grant an author the right [illegible] that this is any [illegible] twilight of Earth.

[illegible]

London, September, 1954—[illegible]
Sydney, March, 1955

PREFACE

For the benefit of those who have read my first novel, *Against the Fall of Night*, and will recognize some of the material in the present work, a few words of explanation are in order.

Against the Fall of Night was begun in 1937 and, after four or five drafts, was completed in 1946, though for various reasons beyond the author's control, book publication was delayed until some years later. Although this work was well received, it had most of the defects of a first novel, and my initial dissatisfaction with it increased steadily over the years. Moreover, the progress of science during the two decades since the story was first conceived made many of the original ideas naïve, and opened up vistas and possibilities quite unimagined when the book was originally planned. In particular, certain developments in information theory suggested revolutions in the human way of life even more profound than those which atomic energy is already introducing, and I wished to incorporate these into the book I had attempted, but so far failed, to write.

A sea voyage from England to Australia gave an opportunity of getting to grips with the uncompleted job, which was finished just before I set out to the Great Barrier Reef. The knowledge that I was to spend some months diving among sharks of doubtful docility was an additional spur to action. It may or may not be true, as Doctor Johnson stated, that nothing settles a man's mind so much as the knowledge that he will be hanged in the morning, but for my part I can testify that the thought of not returning from the Reef was the main reason why the book was completed at that particular time, and the ghost that had haunted me for almost twenty years was finally exorcised.

About a quarter of the present work appeared in *Against the Fall of Night*; it is my belief, however, that even those who read the earlier book will find that this is virtually a new novel. If not, at least I hope they will grant an author the right to have second thoughts. I promise them that this is my last word on the immortal city of Diaspar, in the long twilight of Earth.

Arthur C. Clarke

London, September, 1954–S.S. Himalaya–
Sydney, March, 1955

Like a glowing jewel, the city lay upon the breast of the desert. Once it had known change and alteration, but now Time passed it by. Night and day fled across the desert's face, but in the streets of Diaspar it was always afternoon, and darkness never came. The long winter nights might dust the desert with frost, as the last moisture left in the thin air of Earth congealed—but the city knew neither heat nor cold. It had no contact with the outer world; it was a universe itself.

Men had built cities before, but never a city such as this. Some had lasted for centuries, some for millenniums, before Time had swept away even their names. Diaspar alone had challenged Eternity, defending itself and all it sheltered against the slow attrition of the ages, the ravages of decay, and the corruption of rust.

Since the city was built, the oceans of Earth had passed away and the desert had encompassed all the globe. The last mountains had been ground to dust by the winds and the rain, and the world was too weary to bring forth more. The city did not care; Earth itself could crumble and Diaspar would still protect the children of its makers, bearing them and their treasures safely down the stream of time.

They had forgotten much, but they did not know it. They were as perfectly fitted to their environment as it was to them—for both had been designed together. What was beyond the walls of the city was no concern of theirs; it was something that had been shut out of their minds. Diaspar was all that existed, all that they needed, all that they could imagine. It mattered nothing to them that Man had once possessed the stars.

Yet sometimes the ancient myths rose up to haunt them, and they stirred uneasily as they remembered the legends of the Empire, when Diaspar was young and drew its lifeblood from the commerce of many suns. They did not wish to bring back the old days, for they were content in their eternal autumn. The glories of the Empire belonged to the past, and could remain there—for they remembered how the Empire had met its end, and at the thought of the Invaders the chill of space itself came seeping into their bones.

Then they would turn once more to the life and warmth of the city, to the long golden age whose beginning was already lost and whose end was yet more distant. Other men had dreamed of such an age, but they alone had achieved it.

They had lived in the same city, had walked the same miraculously unchanging streets, while more than a billion years had worn away.

ONE

It had taken them many hours to fight their way out of the Cave of the White Worms. Even now, they could not be sure that some of the pallid monsters were not pursuing them—and the power of their weapons was almost exhausted. Ahead, the floating arrow of light that had been their mysterious guide through the labyrinths of the Crystal Mountain still beckoned them on. They had no choice but to follow it, though as it had done so many times before it might lead them into yet more frightful dangers.

Alvin glanced back to see if all his companions were still with him. Alystra was close behind, carrying the sphere of cold but ever-burning light that had revealed such horrors and such beauty since their adventure had begun. The pale white radiance flooded the narrow corridor and splashed from the glittering walls; while its power lasted, they could see where they were going and could detect the presence of any visible dangers. But the greatest dangers in these caves, Alvin knew too well, were not the visible ones at all.

Behind Alystra, struggling with the weight of their projectors, came Narillian and Floranus. Alvin wondered briefly why those projectors were so heavy, since it would have been such a simple matter to provide them with gravity neutralizers. He was always thinking of points like this, even in the midst of the most desperate adventures. When such thoughts crossed his mind, it seemed as if the structure of reality trembled for an instant, and that behind the world of the senses he caught a glimpse of another and totally different universe. . . .

The corridor ended in a blank wall. Had the arrow betrayed them again? No—even as they approached, the rock began to crumble into dust. Through the wall pierced a spinning metal spear, which broadened rapidly into a giant screw. Alvin and his friends moved back, waiting for the machine to force its way into the cave. With a deafening screech of metal upon rock—which surely must echo through all the recesses of the Mountain, and waken all its nightmare brood!—the subterrene smashed through the wall and came to rest beside them. A massive door opened, and Callistron appeared, shouting to them to hurry. ("Why Callistron?" wondered Alvin. "What's *he* doing here?") A moment later they were in safety, and the machine lurched forward as it began its journey through the depths of the earth.

The adventure was over. Soon, as always happened, they would be home, and all the wonder, the terror, and the excitement would be behind them. They were tired and content.

Alvin could tell from the tilt of the floor that the subterrene was heading down into the earth. Presumably Callistron knew what he was doing, and this was the way that led to home. Yet it seemed a pity. . . .

"Callistron," he said suddenly, "why don't we go upward? No one knows what the Crystal Mountain really looks like. How wonderful it would be to come out somewhere on its slopes, to see the sky and all the land around it. We've been underground long enough."

Even as he said these words, he somehow knew that they were wrong. Alystra gave a strangled scream, the interior of the subterrene wavered like an image seen through water, and behind and beyond the metal walls that surrounded him Alvin once more glimpsed that other universe. The two worlds seemed in conflict, first one and then the other predominating. Then, quite suddenly, it was all over. There was a snapping, rending sensation—and the dream had ended. Alvin was back in Diaspar, in his own familiar room, floating a foot or two above the floor as the gravity field protected him from the bruising contact of brute matter.

He was himself again. *This* was reality—and he knew exactly what would happen next.

Alystra was the first to appear. She was more upset than annoyed, for she was very much in love with Alvin.

"Oh, Alvin!" she lamented, as she looked down at him from the wall in which she had apparently materialized, "It was such an exciting adventure! Why did you have to spoil it?"

"I'm sorry. I didn't intend to—I just thought it would be a good idea . . ."

He was interrupted by the simultaneous arrival of Callistron and Floranus.

"Now listen, Alvin," began Callistron. "This is the *third* time you've interrupted a saga. You broke the sequence yesterday by wanting to climb out of the Valley of Rainbows. And the day before you upset everything by trying to get back to the Origin in that time track we were exploring. If you won't keep the rules, you'll have to go by yourself."

He vanished in high dudgeon, taking Floranus with him. Narillian never appeared at all; he was probably too fed up with the whole affair. Only the image of Alystra was left, looking sadly down at Alvin.

Alvin tilted the gravity field, rose to his feet, and walked toward the table he had materialized. A bowl of exotic fruit appeared upon it—not the food he had intended, for in his confusion his thoughts had wandered. Not wishing to reveal his error, he picked up the least dangerous-looking of the fruits and started to suck it cautiously.

"Well," said Alystra at last, "what are you going to do?"

"I can't help it," he said a little sulkily. "I think the rules are stupid. Besides, how can I remember them when I'm living a saga? I just behave in the way that seems natural. Didn't *you* want to look at the mountain?"

Alystra's eyes widened with horror.

"That would have meant going outside!" she gasped.

Alvin knew that it was useless to argue further. Here was the barrier that sundered him from all the people of his world, and which might doom him to a life of frustration. He was always wanting to go outside, both in reality and in dream. Yet to everyone in Diaspar, "outside" was a nightmare that they could not face. They would never talk about it if it could be avoided; it was something unclean and evil. Not even Jeserac, his tutor, would tell him why.

Alystra was still watching him with puzzled but tender eyes. "You're unhappy, Alvin," she said. "No one should be unhappy in Diaspar. Let me come over and talk to you."

Ungallantly, Alvin shook his head. He knew where *that* would lead, and at the moment he wanted to be alone. Doubly disappointed, Alystra faded from view.

In a city of ten million human beings, thought Alvin, there was no one to whom he could really talk. Eriston and Etania were fond of him in their way, but now that their term of guardianship was ending, they were happy enough to leave him to shape his own amusements and his own life. In the last few years, as his divergence from the standard pattern became more and more obvious, he had often felt his parents' resentment. Not with him—that, perhaps, was something he could have faced and fought—but with the sheer bad luck that had chosen them from all the city's millions, to meet him when he walked out of the Hall of Creation twenty years ago.

Twenty years. He could remember the first moment, and the first words he had ever heard: "Welcome, Alvin. I am Eriston, your appointed father. This is Etania, your mother." The words had meant nothing then, but his mind had recorded them with flawless accuracy. He remembered how he had looked down at his body; it was an inch or two taller now, but had scarcely altered since the moment of his birth. He had come almost fully grown into the world, and would have changed little save in height when it was time to leave it a thousand years hence.

Before that first memory, there was nothing. One day, perhaps, that nothingness would come again, but that was a thought too remote to touch his emotions in any way.

He turned his mind once more toward the mystery of his birth. It did not seem strange to Alvin that he might be created, in a single moment of time, by the powers and forces that materialized all the other objects of his everyday life. No; *that* was not the mystery. The enigma he had never been able to solve, and which no one would ever explain to him, was his uniqueness.

Unique. It was a strange, sad word—and a strange, sad thing to be. When it was applied to him—as he had often heard it done when no one thought he was listening—it seemed to possess ominous undertones that threatened more than his own happiness.

His parents, his tutor, everyone he knew, had tried to protect him from the truth, as if anxious to preserve the innocence of his long childhood.

The pretense must soon be ended; in a few days he would be a full citizen of Diaspar, and nothing could be withheld from him that he wished to know.

Why, for example, did he not fit into the sagas? Of all the thousands of forms of recreation in the city, these were the most popular. When you entered a saga, you were not merely a passive observer, as in the crude entertainments of primitive times which Alvin had sometimes sampled. You were an active participant and possessed—or seemed to possess—free will. The events and scenes which were the raw material of your adventures might have been prepared beforehand by forgotten artists, but there was enough flexibility to allow for wide variation. You could go into these phantom worlds with your friends, seeking the excitement that did not exist in Diaspar—and as long as the dream lasted there was no way in which it could be distinguished from reality. Indeed, who could be certain that Diaspar itself was not the dream?

No one could ever exhaust all the sagas that had been conceived and recorded since the city began. They played upon all the emotions and were of infinitely varying subtlety. Some—those popular among the very young—were uncomplicated dramas of adventure and discovery. Others were purely explorations of psychological states, while others again were exercises in logic or mathematics which could provide the keenest of delights to more sophisticated minds.

Yet though the sagas seemed to satisfy his companions, they left Alvin with a feeling of incompleteness. For all their color and excitement, their varying locales and themes, there was something missing.

The sagas, he decided, never really got anywhere. They were always painted on such a narrow canvas. There were no great vistas, none of the rolling landscapes for which his soul craved. Above all, there was never a hint of the immensity in which the exploits of ancient man had really taken place—the luminous void between the stars and planets. The artists who had planned the sagas had been infected by the same strange phobia that ruled all the citizens of Diaspar. Even their vicarious adventures must take place cozily indoors, in subterranean caverns, or in neat little valleys surrounded by mountains that shut out all the rest of the world.

There was only one explanation. Far back in time, perhaps before Diaspar was founded, something had happened that had not only destroyed Man's curiosity and ambition, but had sent him homeward from the stars to cower for shelter in the tiny closed world of Earth's last city. He had renounced the Universe and returned to the artificial womb of Diaspar. The flaming, invincible urge that had once driven him over the Galaxy, and to the islands of mist beyond, had altogether died. No ships had entered the Solar System for countless aeons; out there among the stars the descendants of Man might still be building empires and wrecking suns—Earth neither knew nor cared.

Earth did not. But Alvin did.

TWO

The room was dark save for one glowing wall, upon which the tides of color ebbed and flowed as Alvin wrestled with his dreams. Part of the pattern satisfied him; he had fallen in love with the soaring lines of the mountains as they leaped out of the sea. There was a power and pride about those ascending curves; he had studied them for a long time, and then fed them into the memory unit of the visualizer, where they would be preserved while he experimented with the rest of the picture. Yet something was eluding him, though what it was he did not know. Again and again he had tried to fill in the blank spaces, while the instrument read the shifting patterns in his mind and materialized them upon the wall. It was no good. The lines were blurred and uncertain, the colors muddy and dull. If the artist did not know his goal, even the most miraculous of tools could not find it for him.

Alvin canceled his unsatisfactory scribblings and stared morosely at the three-quarters-empty rectangle he had been trying to fill with beauty. On a sudden impulse, he doubled the size of the existing design and shifted it to the center of the frame. No—that was a lazy way out, and the balance was all wrong. Worse still, the change of scale had revealed the defects in his construction, the lack of certainty in those at-first-sight confident lines. He would have to start all over again.

"Total erasure," he ordered the machine. The blue of the sea faded; the mountains dissolved like mist, until only the blank wall remained. They were as if they had never been—as if they were lost in the limbo that had taken all Earth's seas and mountains ages before Alvin was born.

The light came flooding back into the room and the luminous rectangle upon which Alvin had projected his dreams merged into its surroundings, to become one with the other walls. But were they walls? To anyone who had never seen such a place before, this was a very peculiar room indeed. It was utterly featureless and completely devoid of furniture, so that it seemed as if Alvin stood at the center of a sphere. No visible dividing lines separated walls from floor or ceiling. There was nothing on which the eye could focus; the space enclosing Alvin might have been ten feet or ten miles across, for all that the sense of vision could have told. It would have been hard to resist the temptation to walk forward, hands outstretched, to discover the physical limits of this extraordinary place.

Yet such rooms had been "home" to most of the human race for the greater part of its history. Alvin had only to frame the appropriate thought, and the walls would become windows opening upon any part of the city he chose. Another wish, and machines which he had never seen would fill the chamber with the projected images of any articles of furniture he might need. Whether they were "real" or not was a problem that had bothered few men for the last billion years. Certainly they were no less real than that other impostor, solid matter, and when they were no longer required they could be returned to the phantom world of the city's Memory Banks. Like everything else in Diaspar, they would never wear out—and they would never change, unless their stored patterns were canceled by a deliberate act of will.

Alvin had partly reconstructed his room when a persistent, bell-like chime sounded in his ear. He mentally framed the admission signal, and the wall upon which he had just been painting dissolved once more. As he had expected, there stood his parents, with Jeserac a little behind them. The presence of his tutor meant that this was no ordinary family reunion—but he knew that already.

The illusion was perfect, and it was not lost when Eriston spoke. In reality, as Alvin was well aware, Eriston, Etania, and Jeserac were all miles apart, for the builders of the city had conquered space as completely as they had subjugated time. Alvin was not even certain where his parents lived among the multitudinous spires and intricate labyrinths of Diaspar, for they had both moved since he had last been physically in their presence.

"Alvin," began Eriston, "it is just twenty years since your mother and I first met you. You know what that means. Our guardianship is now ended, and you are free to do as you please."

There was a trace—but merely a trace—of sadness in Eriston's voice. There was considerably more relief, as if Eriston was glad that a state of affairs that had existed for some time in fact now had legal recognition. Alvin had anticipated his freedom by a good many years.

"I understand," he answered. "I thank you for watching over me, and I will remember you in all my lives." That was the formal response; he had heard it so often that all meaning had been leached away from it—it was merely a pattern of sounds with no particular significance. Yet "all my lives" was a strange expression, when one stopped to consider it. He knew vaguely what it meant; now the time had come for him to know exactly. There were many things in Diaspar which he did not understand, and which he would have to learn in the centuries that lay ahead of him.

For a moment it seemed as if Etania wished to speak. She raised one hand, disturbing the iridescent gossamer of her gown, then let it fall back to her side. Then she turned helplessly to Jeserac, and for the first time Alvin realized that his parents were worried. His memory swiftly scanned the events of the past few weeks. No, there was nothing in his recent life that could have caused this faint uncertainty, this air of mild alarm that seemed to surround both Eriston and Etania.

Jeserac, however, appeared to be in command of the situation. He gave an inquiring look at Eriston and Etania, satisfied himself that they had nothing more to say, and launched forth on the dissertation he had waited many years to make.

"Alvin," he began, "for twenty years you have been my pupil, and I have done my best to teach you the ways of the city, and to lead you to the heritage which is yours. You have asked me many questions, and not all of them have I been able to answer. Some things you were not ready to learn, and some I did not know myself. Now your infancy is over, though your childhood is scarcely begun. It is still my duty to guide you, if you need my help. In two hundred years, Alvin, you may begin to know something of this city and a little of its history. Even I, who am nearing the end of this life, have seen less than a quarter of Diaspar, and perhaps less than a thousandth of its treasures."

There was nothing so far that Alvin did not know, but there was no way of hurrying Jeserac. The old man looked steadfastly at him across the gulf of centuries, his words weighed down with the uncomputable wisdom acquired during a long lifetime's contact with men and machines.

"Tell me, Alvin," he said, "have you ever asked yourself *where* you were before you were born—before you found yourself facing Etania and Eriston at the Hall of Creation?"

"I assumed I was nowhere—that I was nothing but a pattern in the mind of the city, waiting to be created—like this."

A low couch glimmered and thickened into reality beside Alvin. He sat down upon it and waited for Jeserac to continue.

"You are correct, of course," came the reply. "But that is merely part of the answer—and a very small part indeed. Until now, you have met only children of your own age, and they have been ignorant of the truth. Soon they will remember, but you will not, so we must prepare you to face the facts.

"For over a billion years, Alvin, the human race has lived in this city. Since the Galactic Empire fell, and the Invaders went back to the stars, this has been our world. Outside the walls of Diaspar, there is nothing except the desert of which our legends speak.

"We know little about our primitive ancestors, except that they were very short-lived beings and that, strange though it seems, they could reproduce themselves without the aid of memory units or matter organizers. In a complex and apparently uncontrollable process, the key patterns of each human being were preserved in microscopic cell structures actually created inside the body. If you are interested, the biologists can tell you more about it, but the method is of no great importance since it was abandoned at the dawn of history.

"A human being, like any other object, is defined by its structure—its pattern. The pattern of a man, and still more the pattern which specifies a man's mind, is incredibly complex. Yet Nature was able to pack that pattern into a tiny cell, too small for the eye to see.

"What Nature can do, Man can do also, in his own way. We do not know how long the task took. A million years, perhaps—but what is that? In the end our ancestors learned how to analyze and store the information that would define any specific human being—and to use that information to re-create the original, as you have just created that couch.

"I know that such things interest you, Alvin, but I cannot tell you exactly how it is done. The way in which information is stored is of no importance; all that matters is the information itself. It may be in the form of written words on paper, of varying magnetic fields, or patterns of electric charge. Men have used all these methods of storage, and many others. Suffice to say that long ago they were able to store themselves—or, to be more precise, the disembodied patterns from which they could be called back into existence.

"So much, you already know. This is the way our ancestors gave us virtual immortality, yet avoided the problems raised by the abolition of death. A thousand years in one body is long enough for any man; at the end of that time, his mind is clogged with memories, and he asks only for rest—or a new beginning.

"In a little while, Alvin, I shall prepare to leave this life. I shall go back through my memories, editing them and canceling those I do not wish to keep. Then I shall walk into the Hall of Creation, but through a door which you have never seen. This old body will cease to exist, and so will consciousness itself. Nothing will be left of Jeserac but a galaxy of electrons frozen in the heart of a crystal.

"I shall sleep, Alvin, and without dreams. Then one day, perhaps a hundred thousand years from now, I shall find myself in a new body, meeting those who have been chosen to be my guardians. They will look after me as Eriston and Etania have guided you, for at first I will know nothing of Diaspar and will have no memories of what I was before. Those memories will slowly return, at the end of my infancy, and I will build upon them as I move forward into my new cycle of existence.

"That is the pattern of our lives, Alvin. We have all been here many, many times before, though as the intervals of nonexistence vary according to apparently random laws this present population will never repeat itself again. The new Jeserac will have new and different friends and interests, but the old Jeserac—as much of him as I wish to save—will still exist.

"That is not all. At any moment, Alvin, only a hundredth of the citizens of Diaspar live and walk its streets. The vast majority slumber in the Memory Banks, waiting for the signal that will call them forth onto the stage of existence once again. So we have continuity, yet change—immortality, but not stagnation.

"I know what you are wondering, Alvin. You want to know when you will recall the memories of your earlier lives, as your companions are already doing.

"There are no such memories, for you are unique. We have tried to keep this knowledge from you as long as we could, so that no shadow should lie across your childhood—though I think you must have guessed part of the truth already. We did not suspect it ourselves until five years ago, but now there is no doubt.

"You, Alvin, are something that has happened in Diaspar only a handful of times since the founding of the city. Perhaps you have been lying dormant in the Memory Banks through all the ages—or perhaps you were created only twenty years ago by some random permutation. You may have been planned in the beginning by the designers of the city, or you may be a purposeless accident of our own time.

"We do not know. All that we do know is this: You, Alvin, alone of the human race, have never lived before. In literal truth, you are the first child to be born on Earth for at least ten million years."

THREE

When Jeserac and his parents had faded from view, Alvin lay for a long time trying to hold his mind empty of thought. He closed his room around him, so that no one could interrupt his trance.

He was not sleeping; sleep was something he had never experienced, for that belonged to a world of night and day, and here there was only day. This was the nearest he could come to that forgotten state, and though it was not really essential to him he knew that it would help compose his mind.

He had learned little new; almost everything that Jeserac had told him he had already guessed. But it was one thing to have guessed it, another to have had that guess confirmed beyond possibility of refutation.

How would it affect his life, if at all? He could not be sure, and uncertainty was a novel sensation to Alvin. Perhaps it would make no difference whatsoever; if he did not adjust completely to Diaspar in this life, he would do so in the next—or the next.

Even as he framed the thought, Alvin's mind rejected it. Diaspar might be sufficient for the rest of humanity, but it was not enough for him. He did not doubt that one could spend a thousand lifetimes without exhausting all its wonders, or sampling all the permutations of experience it could provide. These things he could do—but if he could not do more, he would never be content.

There was only one problem to be faced. What more *was* there to do?

The unanswered question jolted him out of his reverie. He could not stay here while he was in this restless mood, and there was only one place in the city where he could find some peace of mind.

The wall flickered partially out of existence as he stepped through to the corridor, and its polarized molecules resisted his passage like a feeble wind blowing against his face. There were many ways in which he could be carried effortlessly to his goal, but he preferred to walk. His room was almost at the main city level, and a short passage brought him out onto a spiral ramp which led down to the street. He ignored the moving way, and kept to the narrow sidewalk—an eccentric thing to do, since he had several miles to travel. But Alvin liked the exercise, for it soothed his mind. Besides, there was so much to see that it seemed a pity to race past the latest marvels of Diaspar when you had eternity ahead of you.

It was the custom of the city's artists—and everyone in Diaspar was an artist at some time or another—to display their current productions along the side of the moving ways, so that the passers-by could admire their work. In this manner, it was usually only a few days before the entire population had critically examined any noteworthy creation, and also expressed its views upon it. The resulting verdict, recorded automatically by opinion-sampling devices which no one had ever been able to suborn or deceive—and there had been enough attempts—decided the fate of the masterpiece. If there was a sufficiently affirmative vote, its matrix would go into the memory of the city so that anyone who wished, at any future date, could possess a reproduction utterly indistinguishable from the original.

The less successful pieces went the way of all such works. They were either dissolved back into their original elements or ended in the homes of the artists' friends.

Alvin saw only one *objet d'art* on his journey that had any appeal to him. It was a creation of pure light, vaguely reminiscent of an unfolding flower. Slowly growing from a minute core of color, it would expand into complex spirals and curtains, then suddenly collapse and begin the cycle over again. Yet not precisely, for no two cycles were identical. Though Alvin watched through a score of pulsations, each time there were subtle and indefinable differences, even though the basic pattern remained the same.

He knew why he liked this piece of intangible sculpture. Its expanding rhythm gave an impression of space—even of escape. For that reason, it would probably not appeal to many of Alvin's compatriots. He made a note of the artist's name and decided to call him at the earliest opportunity.

All the roads, both moving and stationary, came to an end when they reached the park that was the green heart of the city. Here, in a circular space over three miles across, was a memory of what Earth had been in the days before the desert swallowed all but Diaspar. First there was a wide belt of grass, then low trees which grew thicker and thicker as one walked forward beneath their shade. At the same time the ground sloped gently downward, so that when at last one emerged from the narrow forest all sign of the city had vanished, hidden by the screen of trees.

The wide stream that lay ahead of Alvin was called, simply, the River. It possessed, and it needed, no other name. At intervals it was spanned by narrow bridges, and it flowed around the park in a complete, closed circle, broken by occasional lagoons. That a swiftly moving river could return upon itself after a course of less than six miles had never struck Alvin as at all unusual; indeed, he would not have thought twice about the matter if at some point in its circuit the River had flowed uphill. There were far stranger things than this in Diaspar.

A dozen young people were swimming in one of the little lagoons, and Alvin paused to watch them. He knew most of them by sight, if not by name, and for a moment was tempted to join in their play. Then the secret he was bearing decided him against it, and he contented himself with the role of spectator.

Physically, there was no way of telling which of these young citizens had walked out of the Hall of Creation this year and which had lived in Diaspar as long as Alvin. Though there were considerable variations in height and weight, they had no correlation with age. People were simply born that way, and although on the average the taller the person, the greater the age, this was not a reliable rule to apply unless one was dealing in centuries.

The face was a safer guide. Some of the newborn were taller than Alvin, but they had a look of immaturity, an expression of wondering surprise at the world in which they now found themselves that revealed them at once. It was strange to think that, slumbering untapped in their minds, were infinite vistas of lives that they would soon remember. Alvin envied them, yet he was not sure if he should. One's first existence was a precious gift which would never be repeated. It was wonderful to view life for the very first time, as in the freshness of the dawn. If only there were others like him, with whom he could share his thoughts and feelings!

Yet physically he was cast in precisely the same mold as those children playing in the water. The human body had changed not at all in the billion years since the building of Diaspar, since the basic design had been eternally frozen in the Memory Banks of the city. It had changed, however, a good deal from its original primitive form, though most of the alterations were internal and not visible to the eyes. Man had rebuilt himself many times in his long history, in the effort to abolish those ills to which the flesh was once heir.

Such unnecessary appurtenances as nails and teeth had vanished. Hair was confined to the head; not a trace was left on the body. The feature that would most have surprised a man of the Dawn Ages was, perhaps, the disappearance of the navel. Its inexplicable absence would have given him much food for thought, and at first sight he would also have been baffled by the problem of distinguishing male from female. He might even have been tempted to assume that there was no longer any difference, which would have been a grave error. In the appropriate circumstances, there was no doubt about the masculinity of any male in Diaspar. It was merely that his equipment was now more neatly packaged when not required; internal stowage had vastly improved upon Nature's original inelegant and indeed downright hazardous arrangements.

It was true that reproduction was no longer the concern of the body, being far too important a matter to be left to games of chance played with chromosomes as dice. Yet, though conception and birth were not even memories, sex remained. Even in ancient times, not one-hundredth part of sexual activity had been concerned with reproduction. The disappearance of that mere one per cent had changed the pattern of human society and the meaning of such words as "father" and "mother"—but desire remained, though now its satisfaction had no profounder aim than that of any of the other pleasures of the senses.

Alvin left his playful contemporaries and continued on toward the center of the park. There were faintly marked paths here, crossing and crisscrossing through low shrubbery and occasionally diving into narrow ravines between great lichen-covered boulders. Once he came across a small polyhedral machine, no larger than a man's head, floating among the branches of a tree. No one knew how many varieties of robot there were in Diaspar; they kept out of the way and minded their business so effectively that it was quite unusual to see one.

Presently the ground began to rise again; Alvin was approaching the little hill that was at the exact center of the park, and therefore of the city itself. There were fewer obstacles and detours, and he had a clear view to the summit of the hill and the simple building that surmounted it. He was a little out of breath by the time he had reached his goal, and was glad to rest against one of the rose-pink columns and to look back over the way he had come.

There are some forms of architecture that can never change because they have reached perfection. The Tomb of Yarlan Zey might have been designed by the temple builders of the first civilizations man had ever known, though they would have found it impossible to imagine of what material it was made. The roof was open to the sky, and the single chamber was paved with great slabs which only at first sight resembled natural stone. For geological ages human feet had crossed and recrossed that floor and left no trace upon its inconceivably stubborn material.

The creator of the great park—the builder, some said, of Diaspar itself—sat with slightly downcast eyes, as if examining the plans spread across his knees. His face wore that curiously elusive expression that had baffled the world for so many generations. Some had dismissed it as no more than an idle whim of the artist's, but to others it seemed that Yarlan Zey was smiling at some secret jest.

The whole building was an enigma, for nothing concerning it could be traced in the historical records of the city. Alvin was not even sure what the word "Tomb" meant; Jeserac could probably tell him, because he was fond of collecting obsolete words and sprinkling his conversation with them, to the confusion of his listeners.

From this central vantage point, Alvin could look clear across the park, above the screening trees, and out to the city itself. The nearest buildings were almost two miles away, and formed a low belt completely surrounding the park. Beyond them, rank after rank in ascending height, were the towers and terraces that made up the main bulk of the city. They stretched for mile upon mile, slowly climbing up the sky, becoming ever more complex and monumentally impressive. Diaspar had been planned as an entity; it was a single mighty machine. Yet though its outward appearance was almost overwhelming in its complexity, it merely hinted at the hidden marvels of technology without which all these great buildings would be lifeless sepulchers.

Alvin stared out toward the limits of his world. Ten—twenty miles away, their details lost in distance, were the outer ramparts of the city, upon which seemed to rest the roof of the sky. There was nothing beyond them—nothing at all except the aching emptiness of the desert in which a man would soon go mad.

Then why did that emptiness call to him, as it called to no one else whom he had ever met? Alvin did not know. He stared out across the colored spires and battlements that now enclosed the whole dominion of mankind, as if seeking an answer to his question.

He did not find it. But at that moment, as his heart yearned for the unattainable, he made his decision.

He knew now what he was going to do with life.

FOUR

Jeserac was not very helpful, though he was not as unco-operative as Alvin had half expected. He had been asked such questions before in his long career as mentor, and did not believe that even a Unique like Alvin could produce many surprises or set him problems which he could not solve.

It was true that Alvin was beginning to show certain minor eccentricities of behavior, which might eventually need correction. He did not join as fully as he should in the incredibly elaborate social life of the city or in the fantasy worlds of his companions. He showed no great interest in the higher realms of thought, though at his age that was hardly surprising. More remarkable was his erratic love life; he could not be expected to form any relatively stable partnerships for at least a century, yet the brevity of his affairs was already famous. They were intense while they lasted—but not one of them had lasted for more than a few weeks. Alvin, it seemed, could interest himself thoroughly only in one thing at a time. There were times when he would join wholeheartedly in the erotic games of his companions, or disappear with the partner of his choice for several days. But once the mood had passed, there would be long spells when he seemed totally uninterested in what should have been a major occupation at his age. This was probably bad for him, and it was certainly bad for his discarded lovers, who wandered despondently around the city and took an unusually long time to find consolation elsewhere. Alystra, Jeserac had noticed, had now arrived at this unhappy stage.

It was not that Alvin was heartless or inconsiderate. In love, as in everything else, it seemed that he was searching for a goal that Diaspar could not provide.

None of these characteristics worried Jeserac. A Unique might be expected to behave in such a manner, and in due course Alvin would conform to the general pattern of the city. No single individual, however eccentric or brilliant, could affect the enormous inertia of a society that had remained virtually unchanged for over a billion years. Jeserac did not merely believe in stability; he could conceive of nothing else.

"The problem that worries you is a very old one," he told Alvin, "but you will be surprised how many people take the world so much for granted that it never bothers them or even crosses their mind. It is true that the human race once occupied an infinitely greater space than this city. You have seen something of what Earth was like before the deserts came and the oceans vanished. Those records you are so fond of projecting are the earliest we possess; they are the only ones that show Earth as it was before the Invaders came. I do not imagine that many people have ever seen them; those limitless, open spaces are something we cannot bear to contemplate.

"And even Earth, of course, was only a grain of sand in the Galactic Empire. What the gulfs between the stars must have been like is a nightmare no sane man would try to imagine. Our ancestors crossed them at the dawn of history when they went out to build the Empire. They crossed them again for the last time when the Invaders drove them back to Earth.

"The legend is—and it is only a legend—that we made a pact with the Invaders. They could have the Universe if they needed it so badly, and we would be content with the world on which we were born.

"We have kept that pact and forgotten the vain dreams of our childhood, as you too will forget them, Alvin. The men who built this city, and designed the society that went with it, were lords of mind as well as matter. They put everything that the human race would ever need inside these walls—and then made sure that we would never leave them.

"Oh, the physical barriers are the least important ones. Perhaps there are routes that lead out of the city, but I do not think you would go along them for very far, even if you found them. And if you succeeded in the attempt, what good would it do? Your body would not last long in the desert, when the city could no longer protect or nourish it."

"If there is a route out of the city," said Alvin slowly, "then what is there to stop me from leaving?"

"That is a foolish question," answered Jeserac. "I think you already know the answer."

Jeserac was right, but not in the way he imagined. Alvin knew—or, rather, he had guessed. His companions had given him the answer, both in their waking life and in the dream adventures he had shared with them. They would never be able to leave Diaspar; what Jeserac did not know was that the compulsion which ruled their lives had no power over Alvin. Whether his uniqueness was due to accident or to an ancient design, he did not know, but this was one of its results. He wondered how many others he had yet to discover.

No one ever hurried in Diaspar, and this was a rule which even Alvin seldom broke. He considered the problem carefully for several weeks, and spent much time searching the earliest of the city's historical memories. For hours on end he would lie, supported by the impalpable arms of an antigravity field, while the hypnone projector opened his mind to the past. When the record was finished, the machine would blur and vanish—but still Alvin would lie staring into nothingness before he came back through the ages to meet reality again. He would see again the endless leagues of blue water, vaster than the land itself, rolling their waves against golden shores. His ears would ring with the boom of breakers stilled these billion years. He would remember the forests and the prairies, and the strange beasts that had once shared the world with Man.

Very few of these ancient records existed; it was generally accepted, though none knew the reason why, that somewhere between the coming of the Invaders and the building of Diaspar all memories of primitive times had been lost. So complete had been the obliteration that it was hard to believe it could have happened by accident alone. Mankind had lost its past, save for a few chronicles that might be wholly legendary. Before Diaspar there was simply the Dawn Ages. In that limbo were merged inextricably together the first men to tame fire and the first to release atomic energy—the first men to build a log canoe and the first to reach the stars. On the far side of this desert of time, they were all neighbors.

Alvin had intended to make this trip alone once more, but solitude was not always something that could be arranged in Diaspar. He had barely left his room when he encountered Alystra, who made no attempt to pretend that her presence was accidental.

It had never occurred to Alvin that Alystra was beautiful, for he had never seen human ugliness. When beauty is universal, it loses its power to move the heart, and only its absence can produce any emotional effect.

For a moment Alvin was annoyed by the meeting, with its reminder of passions that no longer moved him. He was still too young and self-reliant to feel the need for any lasting relationships, and when the time came he might find it hard to make them. Even in his most intimate moments, the barrier of his uniqueness came between him and his lovers. For all his fully formed body, he was still a child and would remain so for decades yet, while his companions one by one recalled the memories of their past lives and left him far behind. He had seen it happen before, and it made him wary of giving himself unreservedly to any other person. Even Alystra, who seemed so naïve and artless now, would soon become a complex of memories and talents beyond his imagination.

His mild annoyance vanished almost at once. There was no reason why Alystra should not come with him if she desired. He was not selfish and did not wish to clutch this new experience to his bosom like a miser. Indeed, he might be able to learn much from her reactions.

She asked no questions, which was unusual, as the express channel swept them out of the crowded heart of the city. Together they worked their way to the central high-speed section, never bothering to glance at the miracle beneath their feet. An engineer of the ancient world would have gone slowly mad trying to understand how an apparently solid roadway could be fixed at the sides while toward the center it moved at a steadily increasing velocity. But to Alvin and Alystra, it seemed perfectly natural that types of matter should exist that had the properties of solids in one direction and of liquids in another.

Around them the buildings rose higher and higher as if the city was strengthening its bulwarks against the outer world. How strange it would be, thought Alvin, if these towering walls became as transparent as glass, and one could watch the life within. Scattered throughout the space around him were friends he knew, friends he would one day know, and strangers he would never meet—though there could be very few of these, since in the course of his lifetime he would meet almost all the people in Diaspar. Most of them would be sitting in their separate rooms, but they would not be alone. They had only to form the wish and they could be, in all but physical fact, in the presence of any other person they chose. They were not bored, for they had access to everything that had happened in the realms of imagination or reality since the days when the city was built. To men whose minds were thus constituted, it was a completely satisfying existence. That it was also a wholly futile one, even Alvin did not yet comprehend.

As Alvin and Alystra moved outward from the city's heart, the number of people they saw in the streets slowly decreased, and there was no one in sight when they were brought to a smooth halt against a long platform of brightly colored marble. They stepped across the frozen whirlpool of matter where the substance of the moving way flowed back to its origin, and faced a wall pierced with brightly lighted tunnels. Alvin selected one without hesitation and stepped into it, with Alystra close behind. The peristaltic field seized them at once and propelled them forward as they lay back luxuriously, watching their surroundings.

It no longer seemed possible that they were in a tunnel far underground. The art that had used all of Diaspar for its canvas had been busy here, and above them the skies seemed open to the winds of heaven. All around were the spires of the city, gleaming in the sunlight. It was not the city that Alvin knew, but the Diaspar of a much earlier age. Although most of the great buildings were familiar, there were subtle differences that added to the interest of the scene. Alvin wished he could linger, but he had never found any way of retarding his progress through the tunnel.

All too soon they were set gently down in a large elliptical chamber, completely surrounded by windows. Through these they could catch tantalizing glimpses of gardens ablaze with brilliant flowers. There were gardens still in Diaspar, but these had existed only in the mind of the artist who conceived them. Certainly there were no such flowers as these in the world today.

Alystra was enchanted by their beauty, and was obviously under the impression that this was what Alvin had brought her to see. He watched her for a while as she ran gaily from scene to scene, enjoying her delight in each new discovery. There were hundreds of such places in the half-deserted buildings around the periphery of Diaspar, kept in perfect order by the hidden powers which watched over them. One day the tide of life might flow this way once more, but until then this ancient garden was a secret which they alone shared.

"We've further to go," said Alvin at last. "This is only the beginning." He stepped through one of the windows and the illusion was shattered.

There was no garden behind the glass, but a circular passageway curving steeply upward. He could still see Alystra a few feet away, though he knew that she could not see him. But she did not hesitate, and a moment later was standing beside him in the passage.

Beneath their feet the floor began to creep slowly forward, as if eager to lead them to their goal. They walked along it for a few paces, until their speed was so great that further effort would be wasted.

The corridor still inclined upward, and in a hundred feet had curved through a complete right angle. But only logic knew this; to all the senses it was as if one was now being hurried along an absolutely level corridor. The fact that they were in reality moving straight up a vertical shaft thousands of feet deep gave them no sense of insecurity, for a failure of the polarizing field was unthinkable.

Presently the corridor began to slope "downward" again until once more it had turned through a right angle. The movement of the floor slowed imperceptibly until it came to rest at the end of a long hall lined with mirrors, and Alvin knew that there was no hope of hurrying Alystra here. It was not merely that some feminine characteristics had survived unchanged since Eve; no one could have resisted the fascination of this place. There was nothing like it, as far as Alvin knew, in the rest of Diaspar. Through some whim of the artist, only a few of the mirrors reflected the scene as it really was—and even those, Alvin was convinced, were constantly changing their position. The rest certainly reflected *something*, but it was faintly disconcerting to see oneself walking amid ever-changing and quite imaginary surroundings.

Sometimes there were people going to and fro in the world behind the mirror, and more than once Alvin had seen faces that he recognized. He realized well enough that he had not been looking at any friends he knew in this existence. Through the mind of the unknown artist he had been seeing into the past, watching the previous incarnations of people who walked the world today. It saddened him, by reminding him of his own uniqueness, to think that however long he waited before these changing scenes he would never meet any ancient echo of himself.

"Do you know where we are?" Alvin asked Alystra when they had completed the tour of the mirrors. Alystra shook her head. "Somewhere near the edge of the city, I suppose," she answered carelessly. "We seem to have gone a long way, but I've no idea how far."

"We're in the Tower of Loranne," replied Alvin. "This is one of the highest points in Diaspar. Come—I'll show you." He caught Alystra's hand and led her out of the hall. There were no exits visible to the eye, but at various points the pattern on the floor indicated side corridors. As one approached the mirrors at these points, the reflections seemed to fuse into an archway of light and one could step through into another passage. Alystra lost all conscious track of their twistings and turnings, and at last they emerged into a long, perfectly straight tunnel through which blew a cold and steady wind. It stretched horizontally for hundreds of feet in either direction, and its far ends were tiny circles of light.

"I don't like this place," Alystra complained. "It's cold." She had probably never before experienced real coldness in her life, and Alvin felt somewhat guilty. He should have warned her to bring a cloak—and a good one, for all clothes in Diaspar were purely ornamental and quite useless as a protection.

Since her discomfort was entirely his fault, he handed over his cloak without a word. There was no trace of gallantry in this; the equality of the sexes had been complete for far too long for such conventions to survive. Had matters been the other way around, Alystra would have given Alvin her cloak and he would have as automatically accepted.

It was not unpleasant walking with the wind behind them, and they soon reached the end of the tunnel. A wide-meshed filigree of stone prevented them from going any further, which was just as well, for they stood on the brink of nothingness. The great air duct opened on the sheer face of the tower, and below them was a vertical drop of at least a thousand feet. They were high upon the outer ramparts of the city, and Diaspar lay spread beneath them as few in their world could ever have seen it.

The view was the obverse of the one that Alvin had obtained from the center of the park. He could look down upon the concentric waves of stone and metal as they descended in mile-long sweeps toward the heart of the city. Far away, partly hidden by the intervening towers, he could glimpse the distant fields and trees and the eternally circling river. Further still, the remoter bastions of Diaspar climbed once more toward the sky.

Beside him, Alystra was sharing the view with pleasure but with no surprise. She had seen the city countless times before from other, almost equally well-placed vantage points—and in considerably more comfort.

"That's our world—all of it," said Alvin. "Now I want to show you something else." He turned away from the grating and began to walk toward the distant circle of light at the far end of the tunnel. The wind was cold against his lightly clad body, but he scarcely noticed the discomfort as he walked forward into the air stream.

He had gone only a little way when he realized that Alystra was making no attempt to follow. She stood watching, her borrowed cloak streaming down the wind, one hand half raised to her face. Alvin saw her lips move, but the words did not reach him. He looked back at her first with astonishment, then with an impatience that was not totally devoid of pity. What Jeserac had said was true. She could not follow him. She had realized the meaning of that remote circle of light from which the wind blew forever into Diaspar. Behind Alystra was the known world, full of wonder yet empty of surprise, drifting like a brilliant but tightly closed bubble down the river of time. Ahead, separated from her by no more than the span of a few footsteps, was the empty wilderness—the world of the desert—the world of the Invaders.

Alvin walked back to join her and was surprised to find that she was trembling. "Why are you frightened?" he asked. "We're still safely here in Diaspar. You've looked out of that window behind us—surely you can look out of this one as well!"

Alystra was staring at him as if he was some strange monster. By her standards, indeed, he was.

"I couldn't do it," she said at last. "Even thinking about it makes me feel colder than this wind. Don't go any farther, Alvin!"

"But there's no logic in it!" Alvin persisted remorselessly. "What possible harm would it do you to walk to the end of this corridor and look out? It's strange and lonely out there, but it isn't horrible. In fact, the longer I look the more beautiful I think—"

Alystra did not stay to hear him finish. She turned on her heels and fled back down the long ramp that had brought them up through the floor of this tunnel. Alvin made no attempt to stop her, since that would have involved the bad manners of imposing one's will upon another. Persuasion, he could see, would have been utterly useless. He knew that Alystra would not pause until she had returned to her companions. There was no danger that she would lose herself in the labyrinths of the city, for she would have no difficulty in retracing her footsteps. An instinctive ability to extricate himself from even the most complex of mazes had been merely one of the many accomplishments Man had learned since he started to live in cities. The long-extinct rat had been forced to acquire similar skills when he left the fields and threw in his lot with humanity.

Alvin waited for a moment, as if half-expecting Alystra to return. He was not surprised at her reaction—only at its violence and irrationality. Though he was sincerely sorry that she had gone, he could not help wishing that she had remembered to leave the cloak.

It was not only cold, but it was also hard work moving against the wind which sighed through the lungs of the city. Alvin was fighting both the air current and whatever force it was that kept it moving. Not until he had reached the stone grille, and could lock his arms around its bars, could he afford to relax. There was just sufficient room for him to force his head through the opening, and even so his view was slightly restricted, as the entrance to the duct was partly recessed into the city's wall.

Yet he could see enough. Thousands of feet below, the sunlight was taking leave of the desert. The almost horizontal rays struck through the grating and threw a weird pattern of gold and shadow far down the tunnel. Alvin shaded his eyes against the glare and peered down at the land upon which no man had walked for unknown ages.

He might have been looking at an eternally frozen sea. For mile after mile, the sand dunes undulated into the west, their contours grossly exaggerated by the slanting light. Here and there some caprice of the wind had carved curious whirlpools and gullies in the sand, so that it was sometimes hard to realize that none of this sculpture was the work of intelligence. At a very great distance, so far away indeed that he had no way of judging their remoteness, was a range of softly rounded hills. They had been a disappointment to Alvin; he would have given much to have seen in reality the soaring mountains of the ancient records and of his own dreams.

The sun lay upon the rim of the hills, its light tamed and reddened by the hundreds of miles of atmosphere it was traversing. There were two great black spots upon its disc; Alvin had learned from his studies that such things existed, but he was surprised that he could see them so easily. They seemed almost like a pair of eyes peering back at him as he crouched in his lonely spy hole with the wind whistling ceaselessly past his ears.

There was no twilight. With the going of the sun, the pools of shadow lying among the sand dunes flowed swiftly together into one vast lake of darkness. Color ebbed from the sky; the warm reds and golds drained away leaving an antarctic blue that deepened and deepened into night. Alvin waited for that breathless moment that he alone of all mankind had known—the moment when the first star shivers into life.

It had been many weeks since he had last come to this place, and he knew that the pattern of the night sky must have changed meanwhile. Even so, he was not prepared for his first glimpse of the Seven Suns.

They could have no other name; the phrase leaped unbidden to his lips. They formed a tiny, very compact and astonishingly symmetrical group against the afterglow of sunset. Six of them were arranged in a slightly flattened ellipse, which, Alvin was sure, was in reality a perfect circle, slightly tilted toward the line of vision. Each star was a different color; he could pick out red, blue, gold, and green, but the other tints eluded his eye. At the precise center of the formation was a single white giant—the brightest star in all the visible sky. The whole group looked exactly like a piece of jewelry; it seemed incredible, and beyond all stretching of the laws of chance, that Nature could ever have contrived so perfect a pattern.

As his eyes grew slowly accustomed to the darkness, Alvin could make out the great misty veil that had once been called the Milky Way. It stretched from the zenith down to the horizon, and the Seven Suns were entangled in its folds. The other stars had now emerged to challenge them, and their random groupings only emphasized the enigma of that perfect symmetry. It was almost as if some power had deliberately opposed the disorder of the natural Universe by setting its sign upon the stars.

Ten times, no more, the Galaxy had turned upon its axis since Man first walked on Earth. By its own standards, that was but a moment. Yet in that short period it had changed completely—changed far more than it had any right to do in the natural course of events. The great suns that had once burned so fiercely in the pride of youth were now guttering to their doom. But Alvin had never seen the heavens in their ancient glory, and so was unaware of all that had been lost.

The cold, seeping through into his bones, drove him back to the city. He extricated himself from the grating and rubbed the circulation back into his limbs. Ahead of him, down the tunnel, the light streaming out from Diaspar was so brilliant that for a moment he had to avert his eyes. Outside the city there were such things as day and night, but within it there was only eternal day. As the sun descended the sky above Diaspar would fill with light and no one would notice when the natural illumination vanished. Even before men had lost the need for sleep, they had driven darkness from their cities. The only night that ever came to Diaspar was a rare and unpredictable obscuration that sometimes visited the park and transformed it into a place of mystery.

Alvin came slowly back through the hall of mirrors, his mind still filled with night and stars. He felt inspired and yet depressed. There seemed no way in which he could ever escape out into that enormous emptiness—and no rational purpose in doing so. Jeserac had said that a man would soon die out in the desert, and Alvin could well believe him. Perhaps he might one day discover some way of leaving Diaspar, but if he did, he knew that he must soon return. To reach the desert would be an amusing game, no more. It was a game he could share with no one, and it would lead him nowhere. But at least it would be worth doing if it helped to quench the longing in his soul.

As if unwilling to return to the familiar world, Alvin lingered among the reflections from the past. He stood before one of the great mirrors and watched the scenes that came and went within its depths. Whatever mechanism produced these images was controlled by his presence, and to some extent by his thoughts. The mirrors were always blank when he first came into the room, but filled with action as soon as he moved among them.

He seemed to be standing in a large open courtyard which he had never seen in reality, but which probably still existed somewhere in Diaspar. It was unusually crowded, and some kind of public meeting seemed to be in progress. Two men were arguing politely on a raised platform while their supporters stood around and made interjections from time to time. The complete silence added to the charm of the scene, for imagination immediately went to work supplying the missing sounds. What were they debating? Alvin wondered. Perhaps it was not a real scene from the past, but a purely created episode. The careful balance of figures, the slightly formal movements, all made it seem a little too neat for life.

He studied the faces in the crowd, seeking for anyone he could recognize. There was no one here that he knew, but he might be looking at friends he would not meet for centuries to come. How many possible patterns of human physiognomy were there? The number was enormous, but it was still finite, especially when all the unesthetic variations had been eliminated.

The people in the mirror world continued their long-forgotten argument, ignoring the image of Alvin which stood motionless among them. Sometimes it was very hard to believe that he was not part of the scene himself, for the illusion was so flawless. When one of the phantoms in the mirror appeared to move behind Alvin, it vanished just as a real object would have done; and when one moved in front of him, he was the one who was eclipsed.

He was preparing to leave when he noticed an oddly dressed man standing a little apart from the main group. His movements, his clothes, everything about him, seemed slightly out of place in this assembly. He spoiled the pattern; like Alvin, he was an anachronism.

He was a good deal more than that. He was real, and he was looking at Alvin with a slightly quizzical smile.

FIVE

In his short lifetime, Alvin had met less than one-thousandth of the inhabitants of Diaspar. He was not surprised, therefore, that the man confronting him was a stranger. What did surprise him was to meet anyone at all here in this deserted tower, so near the frontier of the unknown.

He turned his back on the mirror world and faced the intruder. Before he could speak, the other had addressed him.

"You are Alvin, I believe. When I discovered that someone was coming here, I should have guessed it was you."

The remark was obviously not intended to give offense; it was a simple statement of fact, and Alvin accepted it as such. He was not surprised to be recognized; whether he liked it or not, the fact of his uniqueness, and its unrevealed potentialities, had made him known to everyone in the city.

"I am Khedron," continued the stranger, as if that explained everything. "They call me the Jester."

Alvin looked blank, and Khedron shrugged his shoulders in mock resignation.

"Ah, such is fame! Still, you are young and there have been no jests in your lifetime. Your ignorance is excused."

There was something refreshingly unusual about Khedron. Alvin searched his mind for the meaning of the strange word "Jester"; it evoked the faintest of memories, but he could not identify it. There were many such titles in the complex social structure of the city, and it took a lifetime to learn them all.

"Do you often come here?" Alvin asked, a little jealously. He had grown to regard the Tower of Loranne as his personal property and felt slightly annoyed that its marvels were known to anyone else. But had Khedron, he wondered, ever looked out across the desert or seen the stars sinking down into the west?

"No," said Khedron, almost as if answering his unspoken thoughts. "I have never been here before. But it is my pleasure to learn of unusual happenings in the city, and it is a very long time since anyone went to the Tower of Loranne."

Alvin wondered fleetingly how Khedron knew of his earlier visits, but quickly dismissed the matter from his mind. Diaspar was full of eyes and ears and other more subtle sense organs which kept the city aware of all that was happening within it. Anyone who was sufficiently interested could no doubt find a way of tapping these channels.

"Even if it is unusual for anyone to come here," said Alvin, still fencing verbally, "why should you be interested?"

"Because in Diaspar," replied Khedron, "the unusual is my prerogative. I had marked you down a long time ago; I knew we should meet some day. After my fashion, I too am unique. Oh, not in the way that you are: this is not my first life. I have walked a thousand times out of the Hall of Creation. But somewhere back at the beginning I was chosen to be Jester, and there is only one Jester at a time in Diaspar. Most people think that is one too many."

There was an irony about Khedron's speech that left Alvin still floundering. It was not the best of manners to ask direct personal questions, but after all Khedron had raised the subject.

"I'm sorry about my ignorance," said Alvin. "But what is a Jester, and what does he do?"

"You ask 'what,'" replied Khedron, "so I'll start by telling you 'why.' It's a long story, but I think you will be interested."

"I am interested in everything," said Alvin, truthfully enough.

"Very well. The men—if they were men, which I sometimes doubt—who designed Diaspar had to solve an incredibly complex problem. Diaspar is not merely a machine, you know—it is a living organism, and an immortal one. We are so accustomed to our society that we can't appreciate how strange it would have seemed to our first ancestors. Here we have a tiny, closed world which never changes except in its minor details, and yet which is perfectly stable, age after age. It has probably lasted longer than the rest of human history—yet in *that* history there were, so it is believed, countless thousands of separate cultures and civilizations which endured for a little while and then perished. How did Diaspar achieve its extraordinary stability?"

Alvin was surprised that anyone should ask so elementary a question, and his hopes of learning something new began to wane.

"Through the Memory Banks, of course," he replied. "Diaspar is always composed of the same people, though their actual groupings change as their bodies are created or destroyed."

Khedron shook his head.

"That is only a very small part of the answer. With exactly the same people, you could build many different patterns of society. I can't prove that, and I've no direct evidence of it, but I believe it's true. The designers of the city did not merely fix its population; they fixed the laws governing its behavior. We're scarcely aware that those laws exist, but we obey them. Diaspar is a frozen culture, which cannot change outside of narrow limits. The Memory Banks store many other things outside the patterns of our bodies and personalities. They store the image of the city itself, holding its every atom rigid against all the changes that time can bring. Look at this pavement—it was laid down millions of years ago, and countless feet have walked upon it. Can you see any sign of wear? Unprotected matter, however adamant, would have been ground to dust ages ago. But as long as there is power to operate the Memory Banks, and as long as the matrices they contain can still control the patterns of the city, the physical structure of Diaspar will never change."

"But there have been *some* changes," protested Alvin. "Many buildings have been torn down since the city was built, and new ones erected."

"Of course—but only by discharging the information stored in the Memory Banks and then setting up new patterns. In any case, I was merely mentioning that as an example of the way the city preserves itself physically. The point I want to make is that in the same way there are machines in Diaspar that preserve our social structure. They watch for any changes, and correct them before they become too great. How do they do it? I don't know—perhaps by selecting those who emerge from the Hall of Creation. Perhaps by tampering with our personality patterns; we may think we have free will, but can we be certain of that?

"In any event, the problem was solved. Diaspar has survived and come safely down the ages, like a great ship carrying as its cargo all that is left of the human race. It is a tremendous achievement in social engineering, though whether it is worth doing is quite another matter.

"Stability, however, is not enough. It leads too easily to stagnation, and thence to decadence. The designers of the city took elaborate steps to avoid this, though these deserted buildings suggest that they did not entirely succeed. I, Khedron the Jester, am part of that plan. A very small part, perhaps. I like to think otherwise, but I can never be sure."

"And just what is that part?" asked Alvin, still very much in the dark, and becoming a little exasperated.

"Let us say that I introduce calculated amounts of disorder into the city. To explain my operations would be to destroy their effectiveness. Judge me by my deeds, though they are few, rather than my words, though they are many."

Alvin had never before met anyone quite like Khedron. The Jester was a real personality—a character who stood head and shoulders above the general level of uniformity which was typical of Diaspar. Though there seemed no hope of discovering precisely what his duties were and how he carried them out, that was of minor importance. All that mattered, Alvin sensed, was that here was someone to whom he could talk—when there was a gap in the monologue—and who might give him answers to many of the problems that had puzzled him for so long.

They went back together down through the corridors of the Tower of Loranne, and emerged beside the deserted moving way. Not until they were once more in the streets did it occur to Alvin that Khedron had never asked him what he had been doing out here at the edge of the unknown. He suspected that Khedron knew, and was interested but not surprised. Something told him that it would be very difficult to surprise Khedron.

They exchanged index numbers, so that they could call each other whenever they wished. Alvin was anxious to see more of the Jester, though he fancied that his company might prove exhausting if it was too prolonged. Before they met again, however, he wanted to find what his friends, and particularly Jeserac, could tell him about Khedron.

"Until our next meeting," said Khedron, and promptly vanished. Alvin was somewhat annoyed. If you met anyone when you were merely projecting yourself, and were not present in the flesh, it was good manners to make that clear from the beginning. It could sometimes put the party who was ignorant of the facts at a considerable disadvantage. Probably Khedron had been quietly at home all the time—wherever his home might be. The number that he had given Alvin would insure that any messages would reach him, but did not reveal where he lived. That at least was according to normal custom. You might be free enough with index numbers, but your actual address was something you disclosed only to your intimate friends.

As he made his way back into the city, Alvin pondered over all that Khedron had told him about Diaspar and its social organization. It was strange that he had met no one else who had ever seemed dissatisfied with their mode of life. Diaspar and its inhabitants had been designed as part of one master plan; they formed a perfect symbiosis. Throughout their long lives, the people of the city were never bored. Though their world might be a tiny one by the standard of earlier ages, its complexity was overwhelming, its wealth of wonder and treasure beyond calculation. Here Man had gathered all the fruits of his genius, everything that had been saved from the ruin of the past. All the cities that had ever been, so it was said, had given something to Diaspar; before the coming of the Invaders, its name had been known on all the worlds that Man had lost. Into the building of Diaspar had gone all the skill, all the artistry of the Empire. When the great days were coming to an end, men of genius had remolded the city and given it the machines that made it immortal. Whatever might be forgotten, Diaspar would live and bear the descendants of Man safely down the stream of time.

They had achieved nothing except survival, and were content with that. There were a million things to occupy their lives between the hour when they came, almost full-grown, from the Hall of Creation and the hour when, their bodies scarcely older, they returned to the Memory Banks of the city. In a world where all men and women possess an intelligence that would once have been the mark of genius, there can be no danger of boredom. The delights of conversation and argument, the intricate formalities of social intercourse—these alone were enough to occupy a goodly portion of a lifetime. Beyond those were the great formal debates, when the whole city would listen entranced while its keenest minds met in combat or strove to scale those mountain peaks of philosophy which are never conquered yet whose challenge never palls.

No man or woman was without some absorbing intellectual interest.

Eriston, for example, spent much of his time in prolonged soliloquies with the Central Computer, which virtually ran the city, yet which had leisure for scores of simultaneous discussions with anyone who cared to match his wits against it. For three hundred years, Eriston had been trying to construct logical paradoxes which the machine could not resolve. He did not expect to make serious progress before he had used up several lifetimes.

Etania's interests were of a more esthetic nature. She designed and constructed, with the aid of the matter organizers, three-dimensional interlacing patterns of such beautiful complexity that they were really extremely advanced problems in topology. Her work could be seen all over Diaspar, and some of her patterns had been incorporated in the floors of the great halls of choreography, where they were used as the basis for evolving new ballet creations and dance motifs.

Such occupations might have seemed arid to those who did not possess the intellect to appreciate their subtleties. Yet there was no one in Diaspar who could not understand something of what Eriston and Etania were trying to do and did not have some equally consuming interest of his own.

Athletics and various sports, including many only rendered possible by the control of gravity, made pleasant the first few centuries of youth. For adventure and the exercise of the imagination, the sagas provided all that anyone could desire. They were the inevitable end product of that striving for realism which began when men started to reproduce moving images and to record sounds, and then to use these techniques to enact scenes from real or imaginary life. In the sagas, the illusion was perfect because all the sense impressions involved were fed directly into the mind and any conflicting sensations were diverted. The entranced spectator was cut off from reality as long as the adventure lasted; it was as if he lived a dream yet believed he was awake.

In a world of order and stability, which in its broad outlines had not changed for a billion years, it was perhaps not surprising to find an absorbing interest in games of chance. Humanity had always been fascinated by the mystery of the falling dice, the turn of a card, the spin of the pointer. At its lowest level, this interest was based on mere cupidity—and that was an emotion that could have no place in a world where everyone possessed all that they could reasonably need. Even when this motive was ruled out, however, the purely intellectual fascination of chance remained to seduce the most sophisticated minds. Machines that behaved in a purely random way—events whose outcome could never be predicted, no matter how much information one had—from these philosopher and gambler could derive equal enjoyment.

And there still remained, for all men to share, the linked worlds of love and art. Linked, because love without art is merely the slaking of desire, and art cannot be enjoyed unless it is approached with love.

Men had sought beauty in many forms—in sequences of sound, in lines upon paper, in surfaces of stone, in the movements of the human body, in colors ranged through space. All these media still survived in Diaspar, and down the ages others had been added to them. No one was yet certain if all the possibilities of art had been discovered; or if it had any meaning outside the mind of man.

And the same was true of love.

SIX

Jeserac sat motionless within a whirlpool of numbers. The first thousand primes, expressed in the binary scale that had been used for all arithmetical operations since electronic computers were invented, marched in order before him. Endless ranks of 1's and 0's paraded past, bringing before Jeserac's eyes the complete sequence of all those numbers that possessed no factors except themselves and unity. There was a mystery about the primes that had always fascinated Man, and they held his imagination still.

Jeserac was no mathematician, though sometimes he liked to believe he was. All he could do was to search among the infinite array of primes for special relationships and rules which more talented men might incorporate in general laws. He could find how numbers behaved, but he could not explain why. It was his pleasure to hack his way through the arithmetical jungle, and sometimes he discovered wonders that more skillful explorers had missed.

He set up the matrix of all possible integers, and started his computer stringing the primes across its surface as beads might be arranged at the intersections of a mesh. Jeserac had done this a hundred times before, and it had never taught him anything. But he was fascinated by the way in which the numbers he was studying were scattered, apparently according to no laws, across the spectrum of the integers. He knew the laws of distribution that had already been discovered, but always hoped to discover more.

He could scarcely complain about the interruption. If he had wished to remain undisturbed, he should have set his annunciator accordingly. As the gentle chime sounded in his ear, the wall of numbers shivered, the digits blurred together, and Jeserac returned to the world of mere reality.

He recognized Khedron at once, and was none too pleased. Jeserac did not care to be disturbed from his ordered way of life, and Khedron represented the unpredictable. However, he greeted his visitor politely enough and concealed all trace of his mild concern.

When two people met for the first time in Diaspar—or even for the hundredth—it was customary to spend an hour or so in an exchange of courtesies before getting down to business, if any. Khedron somewhat offended Jeserac by racing through these formalities in a mere fifteen minutes and then saying abruptly: "I'd like to talk to you about Alvin. You're his tutor, I believe."

"That is true," replied Jeserac. "I still see him several times a week—as often as he wishes."

"And would you say that he was an apt pupil?"

Jeserac thought that over; it was a difficult question to answer. The pupil-tutor relationship was extremely important and was, indeed, one of the foundations of life in Diaspar. On the average, ten thousand new minds came into the city every year. Their previous memories were still latent, and for the first twenty years of their existence everything around them was fresh and strange. They had to be taught to use the myriad machines and devices that were the background of everyday life, and they had to learn their way through the most complex society Man had ever built.

Part of this instruction came from the couples chosen to be the parents of the new citizens. The selection was by lot, and the duties were not onerous. Eriston and Etania had devoted no more than a third of their time to Alvin's upbringing, and they had done all that was expected of them.

Jeserac's duties were confined to the more formal aspects of Alvin's education; it was assumed that his parents would teach him how to behave in society and introduce him to an ever-widening circle of friends. They were responsible for Alvin's character, Jeserac for his mind.

"I find it rather hard to answer your question," Jeserac replied. "Certainly there is nothing wrong with Alvin's intelligence, but many of the things that should concern him seem to be a matter of complete indifference. On the other hand, he shows a morbid curiosity regarding subjects which we do not generally discuss."

"The world outside Diaspar, for example?"

"Yes—but how did you know?"

Khedron hesitated for a moment, wondering how far he should take Jeserac into his confidence. He knew that Jeserac was kindly and well-intentioned, but he knew also that he must be bound by the same taboos that controlled everyone in Diaspar—everyone except Alvin.

"I guessed it," he said at last.

Jeserac settled down more comfortably in the depths of the chair he had just materialized. This was an interesting situation, and he wanted to analyze it as fully as possible. There was not much he could learn, however, unless Khedron was willing to co-operate.

He should have anticipated that Alvin would one day meet the Jester, with unpredictable consequences. Khedron was the only other person in the city who could be called eccentric—and even his eccentricity had been planned by the designers of Diaspar. Long ago it had been discovered that without some crime or disorder, Utopia soon became unbearably dull. Crime, however, from the nature of things, could not be guaranteed to remain at the optimum level which the social equations demanded. If it was licensed and regulated, it ceased to be crime.

The office of Jester was the solution—at first sight naïve, yet actually profoundly subtle—which the city's designers had evolved. In all the history of Diaspar there were less than two hundred persons whose mental inheritance fitted them for this peculiar role. They had certain privileges that protected them from the consequences of their actions, though there had been Jesters who had overstepped the mark and paid the only penalty that Diaspar could impose—that of being banished into the future before their current incarnation had ended.

On rare and unforeseeable occasions, the Jester would turn the city upside-down by some prank which might be no more than an elaborate practical joke, or which might be a calculated assault on some currently cherished belief or way of life. All things considered, the name "Jester" was a highly appropriate one. There had once been men with very similar duties, operating with the same license, in the days when there were courts and kings.

"It will help," said Jeserac, "if we are frank with one another. We both know that Alvin is a Unique—that he has never experienced any earlier life in Diaspar. Perhaps you can guess, better than I can, the implications of that. I doubt if anything that happens in the city is totally unplanned, so there must be a purpose in his creation. Whether he will achieve that purpose—whatever it is—I do not know. Nor do I know whether it is good or bad. I cannot guess what it is."

"Suppose it concerns something external to the city?"

Jeserac smiled patiently; the Jester was having his little joke, as was only to be expected.

"I have told him what lies there; he knows that there is nothing outside Diaspar except the desert. Take him there if you can; perhaps *you* know a way. When he sees the reality, it may cure the strangeness in his mind."

"I think he has already seen it," said Khedron softly. But he said it to himself, and not to Jeserac.

"I do not believe that Alvin is happy," Jeserac continued. "He has formed no real attachments, and it is hard to see how he can while he still suffers from this obsession. But after all, he is very young. He may grow out of this phase, and become part of the pattern of the city."

Jeserac was talking to reassure himself; Khedron wondered if he really believed what he was saying.

"Tell me, Jeserac," asked Khedron abruptly, "does Alvin know that he is not the first Unique?"

Jeserac looked startled, then a little defiant.

"I might have guessed," he said ruefully, "that *you* would know that. How many Uniques have there been in the whole history of Diaspar? As many as ten?"

"Fourteen," answered Khedron without hesitation. "Not counting Alvin."

"You have better information than I can command," said Jeserac wryly. "Perhaps you can tell me what happened to those Uniques?"

"They disappeared."

"Thank you: I knew that already. That is why I have told Alvin as little as possible about his predecessors: it would hardly help him in his present mood. Can I rely on your co-operation?"

"For the moment—yes. I want to study him myself; mysteries have always intrigued me, and there are too few in Diaspar. Besides, I think that Fate may be arranging a jest beside which all my efforts will look very modest indeed. In that case, I want to make sure that I am present at its climax."

"You are rather too fond of talking in riddles," complained Jeserac. "Exactly what are you anticipating?"

"I doubt if my guesses will be any better than yours. But I believe this—neither you nor I nor anyone in Diaspar will be able to stop Alvin when he has decided what he wants to do. We have a very interesting few centuries ahead of us."

Jeserac sat motionless for a long time, his mathematics forgotten, after the image of Khedron had faded from sight. A sense of foreboding, the like of which he had never known before, hung heavily upon him. For a fleeting moment he wondered if he should request an audience with the Council—but would that not be making a ridiculous fuss about nothing? Perhaps the whole affair was some complicated and obscure jest of Khedron's, though he could not imagine why he had been chosen to be its butt.

He thought the matter over carefully, examining the problem from every angle. After little more than an hour, he made a characteristic decision.

He would wait and see.

Alvin wasted no time learning all that he could about Khedron. Jeserac, as usual, was his main source of information. The old tutor gave a carefully factual account of his meeting with the Jester, and added what little he knew about the other's mode of life. Insofar as such a thing was possible in Diaspar, Khedron was a recluse: no one knew where he lived or anything about his way of life. The last jest he had contrived had been a rather childish prank involving a general paralysis of the moving ways. That had been fifty years ago; a century earlier he had let loose a particularly revolting dragon which had wandered around the city eating every existing specimen of the works of the currently most popular sculptor. The artist himself, justifiably alarmed when the beast's single-minded diet became obvious, had gone into hiding and not emerged until the monster had vanished as mysteriously as it had appeared.

One thing was obvious from these accounts. Khedron must have a profound understanding of the machines and powers that ruled the city, and could make them obey his will in ways which no one else could do. Presumably there must be some overriding control which prevented any too-ambitious Jester from causing permanent and irreparable damage to the complex structure of Diaspar.

Alvin filed all this information away, but made no move to contact Khedron. Though he had many questions to ask the Jester, his stubborn streak of independence—perhaps the most truly unique of all his qualities—made him determined to discover all he could by his own unaided efforts. He had embarked on a project that might keep him busy for years, but as long as he felt that he was moving toward his goal he was happy.

Like some traveler of old mapping out an unknown land, he had begun the systematic exploration of Diaspar. He spent his weeks and days prowling through the lonely towers at the margin of the city, in the hope that somewhere he might discover a way out into the world beyond. During the course of his search he found a dozen of the great air vents opening high above the desert, but they were all barred—and even if the bars had not been there, the sheer drop of almost a mile was sufficient obstacle.

He found no other exits, though he explored a thousand corridors and ten thousand empty chambers. All these buildings were in that perfect and spotless condition which the people of Diaspar took for granted as part of the normal order of things. Sometimes Alvin would meet a wandering robot, obviously on a tour of inspection, and he never failed to question the machine. He learned nothing, because the machines he encountered were not keyed to respond to human speech or thoughts. Though they were aware of his presence, for they floated politely aside to let him pass, they refused to engage in conversation.

There were times when Alvin did not see another human being for days. When he felt hungry, he would go into one of the living apartments and order a meal. Miraculous machines of whose existence he seldom gave a thought would wake to life after aeons of slumber. The patterns they had stored in their memories would flicker on the edge of reality, organizing and directing the matter they controlled. And so a meal prepared by a master chef a hundred million years before would be called again into existence to delight the palate or merely to satisfy the appetite.

The loneliness of this deserted world—the empty shell surrounding the living heart of the city—did not depress Alvin. He was used to loneliness, even when he was among those he called his friends. This ardent exploration, absorbing all his energy and interest, made him forget for the moment the mystery of his heritage and the anomaly that cut him off from all his fellows.

He had explored less than one-hundredth of the city's rim when he decided that he was wasting his time. His decision was not the result of impatience, but of sheer common sense. If needs be, he was prepared to come back and finish the task, even if it took him the remainder of his life. He had seen enough, however, to convince him that if a way out of Diaspar did exist, it would not be found as easily as this. He might waste centuries in fruitless search unless he called upon the assistance of wiser men.

Jeserac had told him flatly that he knew no road out of Diaspar, and doubted if one existed. The information machines, when Alvin had questioned them, had searched their almost infinite memories in vain. They could tell him every detail of the city's history back to the beginning of recorded times—back to the barrier beyond which the Dawn Ages lay forever hidden. But they could not answer Alvin's simple question, or else some higher power had forbidden them to do so.

He would have to see Khedron again.

SEVEN

"You took your time," said Khedron, "but I knew you would call sooner or later."

This confidence annoyed Alvin; he did not like to think that his behavior could be predicted so accurately. He wondered if the Jester had watched all his fruitless searching and knew exactly what he had been doing.

"I am trying to find a way out of the city," he said bluntly. "There *must* be one, and I think you could help me find it."

Khedron was silent for a moment. There was still time, if he wished, to turn back from the road that stretched before him, and which led into a future beyond all his powers of prophecy. No one else would have hesitated; no other man in the city, even if he had the power, would have dared to disturb the ghosts of an age that had been dead for millions of centuries. Perhaps there was no danger, perhaps nothing could alter the perpetual changelessness of Diaspar. But if there was any risk of something strange and new coming into the world, this might be the last chance to ward it off.

Khedron was content with the order of things as it was. True, he might upset that order from time to time—but only by a little. He was a critic, not a revolutionary. On the placidly flowing river of time, he wished only to make a few ripples: he shrank from diverting its course. The desire for adventure, other than that of the mind, had been eliminated from him as carefully and thoroughly as from all the other citizens of Diaspar.

Yet he still possessed, though it was almost extinguished, that spark of curiosity that was once Man's greatest gift. He was still prepared to take a risk.

He looked at Alvin and tried to remember his own youth, his own dreams of half a thousand years before. Any moment of his past that he cared to choose was still clear and sharp when he turned his memory upon it. Like beads upon a string, this life and all the ones before it stretched back through the ages; he could seize and re-examine any one he wished. Most of those older Khedrons were strangers to him now; the basic patterns might be the same, but the weight of experience separated him from them forever. If he wished, he could wash his mind clear of all his earlier incarnations, when next he walked back into the Hall of Creation to sleep until the city called him forth again. But that would be a kind of death, and he was not ready for that yet. He was still prepared to go on collecting all that life could offer, like a chambered nautilus patiently adding new cells to its slowly expanding spiral.

In his youth, he had been no different from his companions. It was not until he came of age and the latent memories of his earlier lives came flooding back that he had taken up the role for which he had been destined long ago. Sometimes he felt resentment that the intelligences which had contrived Diaspar with such infinite skill could even now, after all these ages, make him move like a puppet across their stage. Here, perhaps, was a chance of obtaining a long-delayed revenge. A new actor had appeared who might ring down the curtain for the last time on a play that already had seen far too many acts.

Sympathy, for one whose loneliness must be even greater than his own; an ennui produced by ages of repetition; and an impish sense of fun—these were the discordant factors that prompted Khedron to act.

"I may be able to help you," he told Alvin, "or I may not. I don't wish to raise any false hopes. Meet me in half an hour at the intersection of Radius 3 and Ring 2. If I cannot do anything else, at least I can promise you an interesting journey."

Alvin was at the rendezvous ten minutes ahead of time, though it was on the other side of the city. He waited impatiently as the moving ways swept eternally past him, bearing the placid and contented people of the city about their unimportant business. At last he saw the tall figure of Khedron appear in the distance, and a moment later he was for the first time in the physical presence of the Jester. This was no projected image; when they touched palms in the ancient greeting, Khedron was real enough.

The Jester sat down on one of the marble balustrades and regarded Alvin with a curious intentness.

"I wonder," he said, "if you know what you are asking. And I wonder what you would do if you obtained it. Do you *really* imagine that you could leave the city, even if you found a way?"

"I am sure of it," replied Alvin, bravely enough, though Khedron could sense the uncertainty in his voice.

"Then let me tell you something which you may not know. You see those towers there?" Khedron pointed to the twin peaks of Power Central and Council Hall, staring at each other across a canyon a mile deep. "Suppose I were to lay a perfectly firm plank between those two towers—a plank only six inches wide. Could you walk across it?"

Alvin hesitated.

"I don't know," he answered. "I wouldn't like to try."

"I'm quite sure you could never do it. You'd get giddy and fall off before you'd gone a dozen paces. Yet if that same plank was supported just clear of the ground, you'd be able to walk along it without difficulty."

"And what does that prove?"

"A simple point I'm trying to make. In the two experiments I've described, the plank would be exactly the same in both cases. One of those wheeled robots you sometimes meet could cross it just as easily if it was bridging those towers as if it was laid along the ground. *We* couldn't, because we have a fear of heights. It may be irrational, but it's too powerful to be ignored. It is built into us; we are born with it.

"In the same way, we have a fear of space. Show any man in Diaspar a road out of the city—a road that might be just like this road in front of us now—and he could not go far along it. He would have to turn back, as you would turn back if you started to cross a plank between those towers."

"But why?" asked Alvin. "There must have been a time—"

"I know, I know," said Khedron. "Men once went out over the whole world, and to the stars themselves. Something changed them and gave them this fear with which they are now born. You alone imagine that you do not possess it. Well, we shall see. I'm taking you to Council Hall."

The Hall was one of the largest buildings in the city, and was almost entirely given over to the machines that were the real administrators of Diaspar. Not far from its summit was the chamber where the Council met on those infrequent occasions when it had any business to discuss.

The wide entrance swallowed them up, and Khedron strode forward into the golden gloom. Alvin had never entered Council Hall before; there was no rule against it—there were few rules against anything in Diaspar—but like everyone else he had a certain half-religious awe of the place. In a world that had no gods, Council Hall was the nearest thing to a temple.

Khedron never hesitated as he led Alvin along corridors and down ramps that were obviously made for wheeled machines, not human traffic. Some of these ramps zigzagged down into the depths at such steep angles that it would have been impossible to keep a footing on them had not gravity been twisted to compensate for the slope.

They came at last to a closed door, which slid silently open as they approached, then barred their retreat. Ahead was another door, which did not open as they came up to it. Khedron made no move to touch the door, but stood motionless in front of it. After a short pause, a quiet voice said: "Please state your names."

"I am Khedron the Jester. My companion is Alvin."

"And your business?"

"Sheer curiosity."

Rather to Alvin's surprise, the door opened at once. In his experience, if one gave facetious replies to machines it always led to confusion and one had to go back to the beginning. The machine that had interrogated Khedron must have been a very sophisticated one—far up in the hierarchy of the Central Computer.

They met no more barriers, but Alvin suspected that they had passed many tests of which he had no knowledge. A short corridor brought them out abruptly into a huge circular chamber with a sunken floor, and set in that floor was something so astonishing that for a moment Alvin was overwhelmed with wonder. He was looking down upon the entire city of Diaspar, spread out before him with its tallest buildings barely reaching to his shoulder.

He spent so long picking out familiar places and observing unexpected vistas that it was some time before he paid any notice to the rest of the chamber. Its walls were covered with a microscopically detailed pattern of black and white squares; the pattern itself was completely irregular, and when he moved his eyes quickly he got the impression that it was flickering swiftly, though it never changed. At frequent intervals around the chamber were manually controlled machines of some type, each complete with a vision screen and a seat for the operator.

Khedron let Alvin look his fill. Then he pointed to the diminutive city and said: "Do you know what that is?"

Alvin was tempted to answer, "A model, I suppose," but that answer was so obvious that he was sure it must be wrong. So he shook his head and waited for Khedron to answer his own question.

"You remember," said the Jester, "that I once told you how the city was maintained—how the Memory Banks hold its pattern frozen forever. Those Banks are all around us, with all their immeasurable store of information, completely defining the city as it is today. Every atom of Diaspar is somehow keyed, by forces we have forgotten, to the matrices buried in these walls."

He waved toward the perfect, infinitely detailed simulacrum of Diaspar that lay below them.

"That is no model; it does not really exist. It is merely the projected image of the pattern held in the Memory Banks, and therefore it is absolutely identical with the city itself. These viewing machines here enable one to magnify any desired portion, to look at it life size or larger. They are used when it is necessary to make alterations in the design, though it is a very long time since that was done. If you want to know what Diaspar is like, this is the place to come. You can learn more here in a few days than you would in a lifetime of actual exploring."

"It's wonderful," said Alvin. "How many people know that it exists?"

"Oh, a good many, but it seldom concerns them. The Council comes down here from time to time; no alterations to the city can be made unless they are all here. And not even then, if the Central Computer doesn't approve of the proposed change. I doubt if this room is visited more than two or three times a year."

Alvin wanted to know how Khedron had access to it, and then remembered that many of his more elaborate jests must have involved a knowledge of the city's inner mechanisms that could have come only from very profound study. It must be one of the Jester's privileges to go anywhere and learn anything; he could have no better guide to the secrets of Diaspar.

"What you are looking for may not exist," said Khedron, "but if it does, this is where you will find it. Let me show you how to operate the monitors."

For the next hour Alvin sat before one of the vision screens, learning to use the controls. He could select at will any point in the city, and examine it with any degree of magnification. Streets and towers and walls and moving ways flashed across the screen as he changed the co-ordinates; it was as though he was an all-seeing, disembodied spirit that could move effortlessly over the whole of Diaspar, unhindered by any physical obstructions.

Yet it was not, in reality, Diaspar that he was examining. He was moving through the memory cells, looking at the dream image of the city—the dream that had had the power to hold the real Diaspar untouched by time for a billion years. He could see only that part of the city which was permanent; the people who walked its streets were no part of this frozen image. For his purpose, that did not matter. His concern now was purely with the creation of stone and metal in which he was imprisoned and not those who shared—however willingly—his confinement.

He searched for and presently found the Tower of Loranne, and moved swiftly through the corridors and passageways which he had already explored in reality. As the image of the stone grille expanded before his eyes, he could almost feel the cold wind that had blown ceaselessly through it for perhaps half the entire history of mankind, and that was blowing now. He came up to the grille, looked out—and saw nothing. For a moment the shock was so great that he almost doubted his own memory; had his vision of the desert been nothing more than a dream?

Then he remembered the truth. The desert was no part of Diaspar, and therefore no image of it existed in the phantom world he was exploring. Anything might lie beyond that grille in reality; this monitor screen could never show it.

Yet it could show him something that no living man had ever seen. Alvin advanced his viewpoint through the grille, out into the nothingness beyond the city. He turned the control which altered the direction of vision, so that he looked backward along the way that he had come. And there behind him lay Diaspar—seen from the outside.

To the computers, the memory circuits, and all the multitudinous mechanisms that created the image at which Alvin was looking, it was merely a simple problem of perspective. They "knew" the form of the city; therefore they could show it as it would appear from the outside. Yet even though he could appreciate how the trick was done, the effect on Alvin was overwhelming. In spirit, if not in reality, he had escaped from the city. He appeared to be hanging in space, a few feet away from the sheer wall of the Tower of Loranne. For a moment he stared at the smooth gray surface before his eyes; then he touched the control and let his viewpoint drop toward the ground.

Now that he knew the possibilities of this wonderful instrument, his plan of action was clear. There was no need to spend months and years exploring Diaspar from the inside, room by room and corridor by corridor. From this new vantage point he could wing his way along the outside of the city, and could see at once any openings that might lead to the desert and the world beyond.

The sense of victory, of achievement, made him feel lightheaded and anxious to share his joy. He turned to Khedron, wishing to thank the Jester for having made this possible. But Khedron was gone, and it took only a moment's thought to realize why.

Alvin was perhaps the only man in Diaspar who could look unaffected upon the images that were now drifting across the screen. Khedron could help him in his search, but even the Jester shared the strange terror of the Universe which had pinned mankind for so long inside its little world. He had left Alvin to continue his quest alone.

The sense of loneliness, which for a little while had lifted from Alvin's soul, pressed down upon him once more. But this was no time for melancholy; there was too much to do. He turned back to the monitor screen, set the image of the city wall drifting slowly across it, and began his search.

Diaspar saw little of Alvin for the next few weeks, though only a few people noticed his absence. Jeserac, when he discovered that his erstwhile pupil was spending all his time at Council Hall instead of prowling around the frontier of the city, felt slightly relieved, imagining that Alvin could come to no trouble there. Eriston and Etania called his room once or twice, found that he was out and thought nothing of it. Alystra was a little more persistent.

For her own peace of mind, it was a pity that she had become infatuated with Alvin, when there were so many more suitable choices. Alystra had never had any difficulty in finding partners, but by comparison with Alvin all the other men she knew were nonentities, cast from the same featureless mold. She would not lose him without a struggle: his aloofness and indifference set a challenge which she could not resist.

Yet perhaps her motives were not entirely selfish, and were maternal rather than sexual. Though birth had been forgotten, the feminine instincts of protection and sympathy still remained. Alvin might appear to be stubborn and self-reliant and determined to have his own way, yet Alystra could sense his inner loneliness.

When she found that Alvin had disappeared, she promptly asked Jeserac what had happened to him. Jeserac, with only a momentary hesitation, told her. If Alvin did not want company, the answer was in his own hands. His tutor neither approved nor disapproved of this relationship. On the whole, he rather liked Alystra and hoped that her influence would help Alvin to adjust himself to life in Diaspar.

The fact that Alvin was spending his time at Council Hall could only mean that he was engaged on some research project, and this knowledge at least served to quell any suspicions Alystra might have concerning possible rivals. But though her jealousy was not aroused, her curiosity was. She sometimes reproached herself for abandoning Alvin in the Tower of Loranne, though she knew that if the circumstances were repeated she would do exactly the same thing again. There was no way of understanding Alvin's mind, she told herself, unless she could discover what he was trying to do.

She walked purposefully into the main hall, impressed but not overawed by the hush that fell as soon as she passed through the entrance. The information machines were ranged side by side against the far wall, and she chose one at random.

As soon as the recognition signal lighted up, she said, "I am looking for Alvin; he is somewhere in this building. Where can I find him?"

Even after a lifetime, one never grew wholly accustomed to the complete absence of time lag when an information machine replied to an ordinary question. There were people who knew—or claimed to know—how it was done, and talked learnedly of "access time" and "storage space," but that made the final result none the less marvelous. Any question of a purely factual nature, within the city's truly enormous range of available information, could be answered immediately. Only if complex calculations were involved before a reply could be given would there be any appreciable delay.

"He is with the monitors," came the reply. It was not very helpful, since the name conveyed nothing to Alystra. No machine ever volunteered more information than it was asked for, and learning to frame questions properly was an art which often took a long time to acquire.

"How do I reach him?" asked Alystra. She would find what the monitors were when she got to them.

"I cannot tell you unless you have the permission of the Council."

This was a most unexpected, even a disconcerting, development. There were very few places in Diaspar that could not be visited by anyone who pleased. Alystra was quite certain that Alvin had *not* obtained Council permission, and this could only mean that a higher authority was helping him.

The Council ruled Diaspar, but the Council itself could be overridden by a superior power—the all-but-infinite intellect of the Central Computer. It was difficult not to think of the Central Computer as a living entity, localized in a single spot, though actually it was the sum total of all the machines in Diaspar. Even if it was not alive in the biological sense, it certainly possessed at least as much awareness and self-consciousness as a human being. It must know what Alvin was doing, and, therefore, it must approve, otherwise it would have stopped him or referred him to the Council, as the information machine had done to Alystra.

There was no point in staying here. Alystra knew that any attempt to find Alvin—even if she knew exactly where he was in this enormous building—would be doomed to failure. Doors would fail to open; slideways would reverse when she stood on them, carrying her backward instead of forward; elevator fields would be mysteriously inert, refusing to lift her from one floor to another. If she persisted, she would be gently conveyed out into the street by a polite but firm robot, or else shuttled round and round Council Hall until she grew fed up and left under her own volition.

She was in a bad temper as she walked out into the street. She was also more than a little puzzled, and for the first time felt that there was some mystery here which made her personal desires and interests seem very trivial indeed. That did not mean that they would be any the less important to her. She had no idea what she was going to do next, but she was sure of one thing. Alvin was not the only person in Diaspar who could be stubborn and persistent.

EIGHT

The image on the monitor screen faded as Alvin raised his hands from the control panel and cleared the circuits. For a moment he sat quite motionless, looking into the blank rectangle that had occupied all his conscious mind for so many weeks. He had circumnavigated his world; across that screen had passed every square foot of the outer wall of Diaspar. He knew the city better than any living man save perhaps Khedron; and he knew now that there was no way through the walls.

The feeling that possessed him was not mere despondency; he had never really expected that it would be as easy as this, that he would find what he sought at the first attempt. What was important was that he had eliminated one possibility. Now he must deal with the others.

He rose to his feet and walked over to the image of the city which almost filled the chamber. It was hard not to think of it as an actual model, though he knew that in reality it was no more than an optical projection of the pattern in the memory cells he had been exploring. When he altered the monitor controls and set his viewpoint moving through Diaspar, a spot of light would travel over the surface of this replica, so that he could see exactly where he was going. It had been a useful guide in the early days, but he soon had grown so skillful at setting the co-ordinates that he had not needed this aid.

The city lay spread out beneath him; he looked down upon it like a god. Yet he scarcely saw it as he considered, one by one, the steps he should now take.

If all else failed, there was one solution to the problem. Diaspar might be held in a perpetual stasis by its eternity circuits, frozen forever according to the pattern in the memory cells, but that pattern could itself be altered, and the city would then change with it. It would be possible to redesign a section of the outer wall so that it contained a doorway, feed this pattern into the monitors, and let the city reshape itself to the new conception.

Alvin suspected that the large areas of the monitor control board whose purpose Khedron had not explained to him were concerned with such alterations. It would be useless to experiment with them; controls that could alter the very structure of the city were firmly locked and could be operated only with the authority of the Council and the approval of the Central Computer. There was very little chance that the Council would grant him what he asked, even if he was prepared for decades or even centuries of patient pleading. That was not a prospect that appealed to him in the least.

He turned his thoughts toward the sky. Sometimes he had imagined, in fantasies which he was half-ashamed to recall, that he had regained the freedom of the air which man had renounced so long ago. Once, he knew, the skies of Earth had been filled with strange shapes. Out of space the great ships had come, bearing unknown treasures, to berth at the legendary Port of Diaspar. But the Port had been beyond the limits of the city; aeons ago it had been buried by the drifting sand. He could dream that somewhere in the mazes of Diaspar a flying machine might still be hidden, but he did not really believe it. Even in the days when small, personal flyers had been in common use, it was most unlikely that they had ever been allowed to operate inside the limits of the city.

For a moment he lost himself in the old, familiar dream. He imagined that he was master of the sky, that the world lay spread out beneath him, inviting him to travel where he willed. It was not the world of his own time that he saw, but the lost world of the dawn—a rich and living panorama of hills and lakes and forests. He felt a bitter envy of his unknown ancestors, who had flown with such freedom over all the earth and who had let its beauty die.

This mind-drugging reverie was useless; he tore himself back to the present and to the problem at hand. If the sky was unattainable and the way by land was barred, what remained?

Once again he had come to the point when he needed help, when he could make no further progress by his own efforts. He disliked admitting the fact, but was honest enough not to deny it. Inevitably, his thoughts turned to Khedron.

Alvin had never been able to decide whether he liked the Jester. He was very glad that they had met, and was grateful to Khedron for the assistance and implicit sympathy he had given him on his quest. There was no one else in Diaspar with whom he had so much in common, yet there was some element in the other's personality that jarred upon him. Perhaps it was Khedron's air of ironic detachment, which sometimes gave Alvin the impression that he was laughing secretly at all his efforts, even while he seemed to be doing his best to help. Because of this, as well as his own natural stubbornness and independence, Alvin hesitated to approach the Jester except as a last resort.

They arranged to meet in a small, circular court not far from Council Hall. There were many such secluded spots in the city, perhaps only a few yards from some busy thoroughfare, yet completely cut off from it. Usually they could be reached only on foot after a rather roundabout walk; sometimes, indeed, they were at the center of skillfully contrived mazes which enhanced their isolation. It was rather typical of Khedron that he should have chosen such a place for a rendezvous.

The court was little more than fifty paces across, and was in reality located deep within the interior of some great building. Yet it appeared to have no definite physical limits, being bounded by a translucent blue-green material which glowed with a faint internal light. However, though there were no visible limits, the court had been so laid out that there was no danger of feeling lost in infinite space. Low walls, less than waist high and broken at intervals so that one could pass through them, managed to give the impression of safe confinement without which no one in Diaspar could ever feel entirely happy.

Khedron was examining one of these walls when Alvin arrived. It was covered with an intricate mosaic of colored tiles, so fantastically involved that Alvin did not even attempt to unravel it.

"Look at this mosaic, Alvin," said the Jester. "Do you notice anything strange about it?"

"No," confessed Alvin after a brief examination. "I don't care for it—but there's nothing strange about *that.*"

Khedron ran his fingers over the colored tiles. "You are not very observant," he said. "Look at these edges here—see how they have become rounded and softened. This is something that one very seldom sees in Diaspar, Alvin. It is wear—the crumbling away of matter under the assault of time. I can remember when this pattern was new, only eighty thousand years ago, in my last lifetime. If I come back to this spot a dozen lives from now, these tiles will have been worn completely away."

"I don't see anything very surprising about that," answered Alvin. "There are other works of art in the city not good enough to be preserved in the memory circuits, but not bad enough to be destroyed outright. One day, I suppose, some other artist will come along and do a better job. And his work won't be allowed to wear out."

"I knew the man who designed this wall," said Khedron, his fingers still exploring the cracks in the mosaic. "Strange that I can remember that fact, when I don't recall the man himself. I could not have liked him, so I must have erased him from my mind." He gave a short laugh. "Perhaps I designed it myself, during one of my artistic phases, and was so annoyed when the city refused to make it eternal that I decided to forget the whole affair. There—I knew that piece was coming loose!"

He had managed to pull out a single flake of golden tile, and looked very pleased at this minor sabotage. He threw the fragment on the ground, adding, "Now the maintenance robots will have to do something about it!"

There was a lesson for him here, Alvin knew. That strange instinct known as intuition, which seemed to follow short cuts not accessible to mere logic, told him that. He looked at the golden shard lying at his feet, trying to link it somehow to the problem that now dominated his mind.

It was not hard to find the answer, once he realized that it existed.

"I see what you are trying to tell me," he said to Khedron. "There are objects in Diaspar that aren't preserved in the memory circuits, so I could never find them through the monitors at Council Hall. If I was to go there and focus on this court, there would be no sign of the wall we're sitting on."

"I think you might find the wall. But there would be no mosaic on it."

"Yes, I can see that," said Alvin, too impatient now to bother about such hairsplitting. "And in the same way, parts of the city might exist that had never been preserved in the eternity circuits, but which hadn't yet worn away. Still, I don't really see how that helps me. I *know* that the outer wall exists—and that it has no openings in it."

"Perhaps there is no way out," answered Khedron. "I can promise you nothing. But I think there is still a great deal that the monitors can teach us—if the Central Computer will let them. And it seems to have taken rather a liking to you."

Alvin pondered over this remark on their way to Council Hall. Until now, he had assumed that it was entirely through Khedron's influence that he had been able to gain access to the monitors. It had not occurred to him that it might be through some intrinsic quality of his own. Being a Unique had many disadvantages; it was only right that it should have some compensations.

The unchanging image of the city still dominated the chamber in which Alvin had spent so many hours. He looked at it now with a new understanding; all that he saw here existed—but all of Diaspar might not be mirrored here. Yet, surely, any discordancies must be trivial, and, as far as he could see, undetectable.

"I attempted to do this many years ago," said Khedron, as he sat down at the monitor desk, "but the controls were locked against me. Perhaps they will obey me now."

Slowly, and then with mounting confidence as he regained access to long-forgotten skills, Khedron's fingertips moved over the control desk, resting for a moment at the nodal points in the sensitive grid buried in the panel before him.

"I think that's correct," he said at last. "Anyway we'll soon see."

The screen glowed into life, but instead of the picture that Alvin had expected, there appeared a somewhat baffling message:

REGRESSION WILL COMMENCE AS SOON AS YOU HAVE SET RATE CONTROL

"Foolish of me," muttered Khedron. "I got everything else right and forgot the most important thing of all." His fingers now moved with a confident assurance over the board, and as the message faded from the screen he swung around in his seat so that he could look at the replica of the city.

"Watch this, Alvin," he said. "I think we are both going to learn something new about Diaspar."

Alvin waited patiently, but nothing happened. The image of the city floated there before his eyes in all its familiar wonder and beauty—though he was conscious of neither now. He was about to ask Khedron what he should look for when a sudden movement caught his attention, and he turned his head quickly to follow it. It had been no more than a half-glimpsed flash or flicker, and he was too late to see what had made it. Nothing had altered; Diaspar was just as he had always known it. Then he saw that Khedron was watching him with a sardonic smile, so he looked again at the city. This time, the thing happened before his eyes.

One of the buildings at the edge of the park suddenly vanished, and was replaced instantly by another of quite different design. The transformation was so abrupt that had Alvin been blinking he would have missed it. He stared in amazement at the subtly altered city, but even during the first shock of astonishment his mind was seeking for the answer. He remembered the words that had appeared on the monitor screen—REGRESSION WILL COMMENCE—and he knew at once what was happening.

"That's the city as it was thousands of years ago," he said to Khedron. "We're going back in time."

"A picturesque but hardly accurate way of putting it," replied the Jester. "What is actually happening is that the monitor is remembering the earlier versions of the city. When any modifications were made, the memory circuits were not simply emptied; the information in them was taken to subsidiary storage units, so that it could be recalled whenever needed. I have set the monitor to regress through those units at the rate of a thousand years a second. Already, we're looking at the Diaspar of half a million years ago. We'll have to go much further back than that to see any real changes—I'll increase the rate."

He turned back to the control board, and even as he did so, not one building but a whole block whipped out of existence and was replaced by a large oval amphitheater.

"Ah, the Arena!" said Khedron. "I can remember the fuss when we decided to get rid of that. It was hardly ever used, but a great many people felt sentimental about it."

The monitor was now recalling its memories at a far higher rate; the image of Diaspar was receding into the past at millions of years a minute, and changes were occurring so rapidly that the eye could not keep up with them. Alvin noticed that the alterations to the city appeared to come in cycles; there would be a long period of stasis, then a whole rash of rebuilding would break out, followed by another pause. It was almost as if Diaspar were a living organism, which had to regain its strength after each explosion of growth.

Through all these changes, the basic design of the city had not altered. Buildings came and went, but the pattern of streets seemed eternal, and the park remained as the green heart of Diaspar. Alvin wondered how far back the monitor could go. Could it return to the founding of the city, and pass through the veil that sundered known history from the myths and legends of the Dawn?

Already they had gone five hundred million years into the past. Outside the walls of Diaspar, beyond the knowledge of the monitors, it would be a different Earth. Perhaps there might still be oceans and forests, even other cities which Man had not yet deserted in the long retreat to his final home.

The minutes drifted past, each minute an aeon in the little universe of the monitors. Soon, thought Alvin, the earliest of all these stored memories must be reached and the regression would end. But fascinating though this lesson was, he did not see how it could help him to escape from the city as it was here and now.

With a sudden, soundless implosion, Diaspar contracted to a fraction of its former size. The park vanished; the boundary wall of linked, titanic towers instantly evaporated. This city was open to the world, for the radial roads stretched out to the limits of the monitor image without obstruction. Here was Diaspar as it had been before the great change came upon mankind.

"We can go no further," said Khedron, pointing to the monitor screen. On it had appeared the words: REGRESSION CONCLUDED. "This must be the earliest version of the city that has been preserved in the memory cells. Before that, I doubt if the eternity circuits were used, and the buildings were allowed to wear out naturally."

For a long time, Alvin stared at this model of the ancient city. He thought of the traffic those roads had borne, as men came and went freely to all the corners of the world—and to other worlds as well. Those men were his ancestors; he felt a closer kinship to them than to the people who now shared his life. He wished that he could see them and share their thoughts, as they moved through the streets of that billion-year-remote Diaspar. Yet those thoughts could not have been happy ones, for they must have been living then beneath the shadow of the Invaders. In a few more centuries, they were to turn their faces from the glory they had won and build a wall against the Universe.

Khedron ran the monitor backward and forward a dozen times through the brief period of history that had wrought the transformation. The change from a small open city to a much larger closed one had taken little more than a thousand years. In that time, the machines that had served Diaspar so faithfully must have been designed and built, and the knowledge that would enable them to carry out their tasks had been fed into their memory circuits. Into the memory circuits, also, must have gone the essential patterns of all the men who were now alive, so that when the right impulse called them forth again they could be clothed in matter and would emerge reborn from the Hall of Creation. In some sense, Alvin realized, he must have existed in that ancient world. It was possible, of course, that he was completely synthetic—that his entire personality had been designed by artist-technicians who had worked with tools of inconceivable complexity toward some clearly envisaged goal. Yet he thought it more likely that he was a composite of men who had once lived and walked on Earth.

Very little of the old Diaspar had remained when the new city was created; the park had obliterated it almost completely. Even before the transformation, there had been a small, grass-covered clearing at the center of Diaspar, surrounding the junction of all the radial streets. Afterward it had expanded tenfold, wiping out streets and buildings alike. The Tomb of Yarlan Zey had been brought into existence at this time, replacing a very large circular structure which had previously stood at the meeting point of all the streets. Alvin had never really believed the legends of the Tomb's antiquity, but now it seemed that they were true.

"I suppose," said Alvin, struck by a sudden thought, "that we can explore this image, just as we explored the image of today's Diaspar?"

Khedron's fingers flickered over the monitor control board, and the screen answered Alvin's question. The long-vanished city began to expand before his eyes as his viewpoint moved along the curiously narrow streets. This memory of the Diaspar that once had been was still as sharp and clear as the image of the city he lived in today. For a billion years, the information circuits had held it in ghostly pseudo-existence, waiting for the moment when someone should call it forth again. And it was not, thought Alvin, merely a memory he was seeing now. It was something more complex than that—it was the memory of a memory.

He did not know what he could learn from it, and whether it could help him in his quest. No matter; it was fascinating to look into the past and to see a world that had existed in the days when men still roamed among the stars. He pointed to the low, circular building that stood at the city's heart.

"Let's start there," he told Khedron. "That seems as good a place as any to begin."

Perhaps it was sheer luck; perhaps it was some ancient memory; perhaps it was elementary logic. It made no difference, since he would have arrived at this spot sooner or later—this spot upon which all the radial streets of the city converged.

It took him ten minutes to discover that they did not meet here for reasons of symmetry alone—ten minutes to know that his long search had met its reward.

NINE

Alystra had found it very easy to follow Alvin and Khedron without their knowledge. They seemed in a great hurry—something which in itself was most unusual—and never looked back. It had been an amusing game to pursue them along the moving ways, hiding in the crowds yet always keeping them in sight. Toward the end their goal had been obvious; when they left the pattern of streets and went into the park, they could only be heading for the Tomb of Yarlan Zey. The park contained no other buildings, and people in such eager haste as Alvin and Khedron would not be interested merely in enjoying the scenery.

Because there was no way of concealing herself on the last few hundred yards to the Tomb, Alystra waited until Khedron and Alvin had disappeared into the marbled gloom. Then, as soon as they were out of sight, she hurried up the grass-covered slope. She felt fairly sure that she could hide behind one of the great pillars long enough to discover what Alvin and Khedron were doing; it did not matter if they detected her after that.

The Tomb consisted of two concentric rings of columns, enclosing a circular courtyard. Except in one sector, the columns screened off the interior completely, and Alystra avoided approaching through this opening, but entered the Tomb from the side. She cautiously negotiated the first ring of columns, saw that there was no one in sight, and tiptoed across to the second. Through the gaps, she could see Yarlan Zey looking out through the entrance, across the park he had built, and beyond that to the city over which he had watched for so many ages.

And there was no one else in all this marble solitude. The Tomb was empty.

At that moment, Alvin and Khedron were a hundred feet underground, in a small, boxlike room whose walls seemed to be flowing steadily upward. That was the only indication of movement; there was no trace of vibration to show that they were sinking swiftly into the earth, descending toward a goal that even now neither of them fully understood.

It had been absurdly easy, for the way had been prepared for them. (By whom? wondered Alvin. By the Central Computer? Or by Yarlan Zey himself, when he transformed the city?) The monitor screen had shown them the long, vertical shaft plunging into the depths, but they had followed its course only a little way when the image had blanked out.

That meant, Alvin knew, that they were asking for information that the monitor did not possess, and perhaps never had possessed.

He had scarcely framed this thought when the screen came to life once more. On it appeared a brief message, printed in the simplified script that machines had used to communicate with men ever since they had achieved intellectual equality:

STAND WHERE THE STATUE GAZES—AND REMEMBER:
DIASPAR WAS NOT ALWAYS THUS

The last five words were in larger type, and the meaning of the entire message was obvious to Alvin at once. Mentally framed code messages had been used for ages to unlock doors or set machines in action. As for "Stand where the statue gazes"—that was really *too* simple.

"I wonder how many people have read this message?" said Alvin thoughtfully.

"Fourteen, to my knowledge," replied Khedron. "And there may have been others." He did not amplify this rather cryptic remark, and Alvin was in too great a hurry to reach the park to question him further.

They could not be certain that the mechanisms would still respond to the triggering impulse. When they reached the Tomb, it had taken them only a moment to locate the single slab, among all those paving the floor, upon which the gaze of Yarlan Zey was fixed. It was only at first sight that the statue seemed to be looking out across the city; if one stood directly in front of it, one could see that the eyes were downcast and that the elusive smile was directed toward a spot just inside the entrance to the Tomb. Once the secret was realized, there could be no doubt about it. Alvin moved to the next slab, and found that Yarlan Zey was no longer looking toward him.

He rejoined Khedron, and mentally echoed the words that the Jester spoke aloud: "Diaspar was not always thus." Instantly, as if the millions of years that had lapsed since their last operation had never existed, the waiting machines responded. The great slab of stone on which they were standing began to carry them smoothly into the depths.

Overhead, the patch of blue suddenly flickered out of existence. The shaft was no longer open; there was no danger that anyone should accidentally stumble into it. Alvin wondered fleetingly if another slab of stone had somehow been materialized to replace the one now supporting him and Khedron, then decided against it. The original slab probably still paved the Tomb; the one upon which they were standing might only exist for infinitesimal fractions of a second, being continuously re-created at greater and greater depths in the earth to give the illusion of steady downward movement.

Neither Alvin nor Khedron spoke as the walls flowed silently past them. Khedron was once again wrestling with his conscience, wondering if this time he had gone too far. He could not imagine where this route might lead, if indeed it led anywhere. For the first time in his life, he began to understand the real meaning of fear.

Alvin was not afraid; he was too excited. This was the sensation he had known in the Tower of Loranne, when he had looked out across the untrodden desert and seen the stars conquering the night sky. He had merely gazed at the unknown then; he was being carried toward it now.

The walls ceased to flow past them. A patch of light appeared at one side of their mysteriously moving room, grew brighter and brighter, and was suddenly a door. They stepped through it, took a few paces along the short corridor beyond—and then were standing in a great, circular cavern whose walls came together in a sweeping curve three hundred feet above their heads.

The column down whose interior they had descended seemed far too slim to support the millions of tons of rock above it; indeed, it did not seem to be an integral part of the chamber at all, but gave the impression of being an afterthought. Khedron, following Alvin's gaze, arrived at the same conclusion.

"This column," he said, speaking rather jerkily, as if anxious to find something to say, "was built simply to house the shaft down which we came. It could never have carried the traffic that must have passed through here when Diaspar was still open to the world. *That* came through those tunnels over there; I suppose you recognize what they are?"

Alvin looked toward the walls of the chamber, more than a hundred yards away. Piercing them at regular intervals were large tunnels, twelve of them, radiating in all directions exactly as the moving ways still did today. He could see that they sloped gently upward, and now he recognized the familiar gray surface of the moving ways. These were only the severed stumps of the great roads; the strange material that gave them life was now frozen into immobility. When the park had been built, the hub of the moving way system had been buried. But it had never been destroyed.

Alvin began to walk toward the nearest of the tunnels. He had gone only a few paces when he realized that something was happening to the ground beneath his feet. *It was becoming transparent*. A few more yards, and he seemed to be standing in midair without visible support. He stopped and stared down into the void beneath him.

"Khedron!" he called. "Come and look at this!"

The other joined him, and together they gazed at the marvel beneath their feet. Faintly visible, at an indefinite depth, lay an enormous map—a great network of lines converging toward a spot beneath the central shaft. They stared at it in silence for a moment; then Khedron said quietly: "You realize what this is?"

"I think so," replied Alvin. "It's a map of the entire transport system, and those little circles must be the other cities of Earth. I can just see names beside them, but they're too faint to read."

"There must have been some form of internal illumination once," said

Khedron absently. He was tracing the lines beneath his feet, following them with his eyes out toward the walls of the chamber.

"I thought so!" he exclaimed suddenly. "Do you see how all these radiating lines lead toward the small tunnels?"

Alvin had noticed that besides the great arches of the moving ways there were innumerable smaller tunnels leading out of the chamber—tunnels that sloped *downward* instead of up.

Khedron continued without waiting for a reply.

"It would be hard to think of a simpler system. People would come down the moving ways, select the place they wished to visit, and then follow the appropriate line on the map."

"And what happened to them after that?" asked Alvin. Khedron was silent, his eyes searching out the mystery of those descending tunnels. There were thirty or forty of them, all looking exactly the same. Only the names on the map would have enabled one to distinguish between them, and those names were indecipherable now.

Alvin had wandered away and was circumnavigating the central pillar. Presently his voice came to Khedron, slightly muffled and overlaid with echoes from the walls of the chamber.

"What is it?" called Khedron, not wishing to move, because he had nearly succeeded in reading one of the dimly visible groups of characters. But Alvin's voice was insistent, so he went to join him.

Far beneath was the other half of the great map, its faint webwork radiating to the points of the compass. This time, however, not all of it was too dim to be clearly seen, for one of the lines—and only one—was brilliantly illuminated. It seemed to have no connection with the rest of the system, and pointed like a gleaming arrow to one of the downward-sloping tunnels. Near its end the line transfixed a circle of golden light, and against that circle was the single word LYS. That was all.

For a long time Alvin and Khedron stood gazing down at that silent symbol. To Khedron it was a challenge he knew he could never accept—and which, indeed, he would rather did not exist. But to Alvin it hinted at the fulfillment of all his dreams; though the word Lys meant nothing to him, he let it roll around his mouth, tasting its sibilance like some exotic flavor. The blood was pounding in his veins, and his cheeks were flushed as by a fever. He stared around this great concourse, trying to imagine it as it had been in the ancient days, when air transport had come to an end but the cities of Earth still had contact with one another. He thought of the countless millions of years that had passed with the traffic steadily dwindling and the lights on the great map dying one by one, until at last only this single line remained. How long, he wondered, had it gleamed there among its darkened companions, waiting to guide the steps that never came, until Yarlan Zey had sealed the moving ways and closed Diaspar against the world?

And that had been a billion years ago. Even then, Lys must have lost touch with Diaspar. It seemed impossible that it could have survived; perhaps, after all, the map meant nothing now.

Khedron broke into his reverie at last. He seemed nervous and ill at ease, not at all like the confident and self-assured person that he had always been in the city above.

"I do not think that we should go any further now," he said. "It may not be safe until—until we are more prepared."

There was wisdom in this, but Alvin recognized the underlying note of fear in Khedron's voice. Had it not been for that, he might have been sensible, but a too-acute awareness of his own valor, combined with a contempt for Khedron's timidity, drove Alvin onward. It seemed foolish to have come so far, only to turn back when the goal might be in sight.

"I'm going down that tunnel," he said stubbornly, as if challenging Khedron to stop him. "I want to see where it leads." He set off resolutely, and after a moment's hesitation the Jester followed him along the arrow of light that burned beneath their feet.

As they stepped into the tunnel, they felt the familiar tug of the peristaltic field, and in a moment were being swept effortlessly into the depths. The journey lasted scarcely a minute; when the field released them they were standing at one end of a long narrow chamber in the form of a half-cylinder. At its distant end, two dimly lit tunnels stretched away toward infinity.

Men of almost every civilization that had existed since the Dawn would have found their surroundings completely familiar, yet to Alvin and Khedron this was a glimpse of another world. The purpose of the long, streamlined machine that lay aimed like a projectile at the far tunnel was obvious, but that made it none the less novel. Its upper portion was transparent, and looking through the walls Alvin could see rows of luxuriously appointed seats. There was no sign of any entrance, and the entire machine was floating about a foot above a single metal rod that stretched away into the distance, disappearing in one of the tunnels. A few yards away another rod led to the second tunnel, but no machine floated above it. Alvin knew, as surely as if he had been told, that somewhere beneath unknown, far-off Lys, that second machine was waiting in another such chamber as this.

Khedron began to talk, a little too swiftly.

"What a peculiar transport system! It could only handle a hundred people at a time, so they could not have expected much traffic. And why did they go to all this trouble to bury themselves in the Earth if the skies were still open? Perhaps the Invaders would not even permit them to fly, though I find that hard to believe. Or was this built during the transition period, while men still traveled but did not wish to be reminded of space? They could go from city to city, and never see the sky and the stars." He gave a nervous laugh. "I feel sure of one thing, Alvin. When Lys existed, it was much like Diaspar. All cities must be essentially the same. No wonder that they were all abandoned in the end, and merged into Diaspar. What was the point of having more than one?"

Alvin scarcely heard him. He was busy examining the long projectile, trying to find the entrance. If the machine was controlled by some mental or verbal code order, he might never be able to make it obey him, and it would remain a maddening enigma for the rest of his life.

The silently opening door took him completely unawares. There was no sound, no warning when a section of the wall simply faded from sight and the beautifully designed interior lay open before his eyes.

This was the moment of choice. Until this instant, he had always been able to turn back if he wished. But if he stepped inside that welcoming door, he knew what would happen, though not where it would lead. He would no longer be in control of his own destiny, but would have placed himself in the keeping of unknown forces.

He scarcely hesitated. He was afraid to hold back, being fearful that if he waited too long this moment might never come again—or that if it did, his courage might not match his desire for knowledge. Khedron opened his mouth in anxious protest, but before he could speak, Alvin had stepped through the entrance. He turned to face Khedron, who was standing framed in the barely visible rectangle of the doorway, and for a moment there was a strained silence while each waited for the other to speak.

The decision was made for them. There was a faint flicker of translucence, and the wall of the machine had closed again. Even as Alvin raised his hand in farewell, the long cylinder started to ease itself forward. Before it had entered the tunnel, it was already moving faster than a man could run.

There had been a time when, every day, millions of men made such journeys, in machines basically the same as this, as they shuttled between their homes and their humdrum jobs. Since that far-off day, Man had explored the Universe and returned again to Earth—had won an empire, and had it wrestled from his grasp. Now such a journey was being made again, in a machine wherein legions of forgotten and unadventurous men would have felt completely at home.

And it was to be the most momentous journey any human being had undertaken for a billion years.

Alystra had searched the Tomb a dozen times, though once was quite sufficient, for there was nowhere anyone could hide. After the first shock of surprise, she had wondered if what she had followed across the park had not been Alvin and Khedron at all, but only their projections. But that made no sense; projections were materialized at any spot one wished to visit, without the trouble of going there in person. No sane person would "walk" his projected image a couple of miles, taking half an hour to reach his destination, when he could be there instantly. No; it was the real Alvin and the real Khedron that she had followed into the Tomb.

Somewhere, then, there must be a secret entrance. She might as well look for it while she was waiting for them to come back.

As luck would have it, she missed Khedron's reappearance, for she was examining a column behind the statue when he emerged on the other side of it. She heard his footsteps, turned toward him, and saw at once that he was alone.

"Where is Alvin?" she cried.

It was some time before the Jester answered. He looked distraught and irresolute, and Alystra had to repeat her question before he took any notice of her. He did not seem in the least surprised to find her there. "I do not know where he is," he answered at last. "I can only tell you that he is on his way to Lys. Now you know as much as I do."

It was never wise to take Khedron's words at their face value. But Alystra needed no further assurance that the Jester was not playing his role today. He was telling her the truth—whatever it might mean.

TEN

When the door closed behind him, Alvin slumped into the nearest seat. All strength seemed suddenly to have been drained from his legs: at last he knew, as he had never known before, that fear of the unknown that haunted all his fellow men. He felt himself trembling in every limb, and his sight became misty and uncertain. Could he have escaped from this speeding machine he would willing have done so, even at the price of abandoning all his dreams.

It was not fear alone that overwhelmed him, but a sense of unutterable loneliness. All that he knew and loved was in Diaspar; even if he was going into no danger, he might never see his world again. He knew, as no man had known for ages, what it meant to leave one's home forever. In this moment of desolation, it seemed to him of no importance whether the path he was following led to peril or to safety; all that mattered to him now was that it led away from home.

The mood slowly passed; the dark shadows lifted from his mind. He began to pay attention to his surroundings, and to see what he could learn from the unbelievably ancient vehicle in which he was traveling. It did not strike Alvin as particularly strange or marvelous that this buried transport system should still function perfectly after such aeons of time. It was not preserved in the eternity circuits of the city's own monitors, but there must be similar circuits elsewhere guarding it from change or decay.

For the first time he noticed the indicator board that formed part of the forward wall. It carried a brief but reassuring message:

LYS
35 MINUTES

Even as he watched, the number changed to "34." That at least was useful information, though since he had no idea of the machine's speed it told him nothing about the length of the journey. The walls of the tunnel were one continual blur of gray, and the only sensation of movement was a very slight vibration he would never have noticed had he not looked for it.

Diaspar must be many miles away by now, and above him would be the desert with its shifting sand dunes. Perhaps at this very moment he was racing below the broken hills he had watched so often from the Tower of Loranne.

His imagination sped onward to Lys, as if impatient to arrive ahead of his body. What sort of a city would it be? No matter how hard he tried, he could only picture another and smaller version of Diaspar. He wondered if it still existed, then assured himself that not otherwise would this machine be carrying him swiftly through the Earth.

Suddenly there was a distinct change in the vibration underfoot. The vehicle was slowing down—there was no question of that. The time must have passed more swiftly than he had thought; somewhat surprised, Alvin glanced at the indicator.

LYS
23 MINUTES

Feeling puzzled, and a little worried, he pressed his face against the side of the machine. His speed was still blurring the walls of the tunnel into a featureless gray, yet now from time to time he could catch a glimpse of markings that disappeared almost as quickly as they came. And at each disappearance, they seemed to remain in his field of vision for a little longer.

Then, without any warning, the walls of the tunnel were snatched away on either side. The machine was passing, still at a very great speed, through an enormous empty space, far larger even than the chamber of the moving ways.

Peering in wonder through the transparent walls, Alvin could glimpse beneath him an intricate network of guiding rods, rods that crossed and crisscrossed to disappear into a maze of tunnels on either side. A flood of bluish light poured down from the arched dome of the ceiling, and silhouetted against the glare he could just make out the frameworks of great machines. The light was so brilliant that it pained the eyes, and Alvin knew that this place had not been intended for man. A moment later, his vehicle flashed past row after row of cylinders, lying motionless above their guide rails. They were much larger than the one in which he was traveling, and Alvin guessed that they must have been used for transporting freight. Around them were grouped incomprehensible, many-jointed mechanisms, all silent and stilled.

Almost as quickly as it had appeared, the vast and lonely chamber vanished behind him. Its passing left a feeling of awe in Alvin's mind; for the first time he really understood the meaning of that great, darkened map below Diaspar. The world was more full of wonder than he had ever dreamed.

Alvin glanced again at the indicator. It had not changed; he had taken less than a minute to flash through the great cavern. The machine was accelerating again; though there was little sense of motion, the tunnel walls were flowing past on either side at a speed he could not even guess.

It seemed an age before that indefinable change of vibration occurred again. Now the indicator was reading:

LYS
1 MINUTE

That minute was the longest that Alvin had ever known. More and more slowly moved the machine; this was no mere slackening of its speed. It was coming at last to rest.

Smoothly and silently the long cylinder slid out of the tunnel into a cavern that might have been the twin of the one below Diaspar. For a moment Alvin was too excited to see anything clearly; the door had been open for a considerable time before he realized that he could leave the vehicle. As he hurried out of the machine, he caught a last glimpse of the indicator. Its wording had now changed and its message was infinitely reassuring:

DIASPAR
35 MINUTES

As he began to search for a way out of the chamber, Alvin found the first hint that he might be in a civilization different from his own. The way to the surface clearly lay through a low, wide tunnel at one end of the cavern—and leading up through the tunnel was a flight of steps. Such a thing was extremely rare in Diaspar; the architects of the city had built ramps or sloping corridors whenever there was a change of level. This was a survival from the days when most robots had moved on wheels, and so found steps an impassible barrier.

The stairway was very short, and ended against doors that opened automatically at Alvin's approach. He walked into a small room like that which had carried him down the shaft under the Tomb of Yarlan Zey, and was not surprised when a few minutes later the doors opened again to reveal a vaulted corridor rising slowly to an archway that framed a semicircle of sky. There had been no sensation of movement, but Alvin knew that he must have risen many hundreds of feet. He hurried forward up the slope to the sunlit opening, all fear forgotten in his eagerness to see what lay before him.

He was standing at the brow of a low hill, and for an instant it seemed as if he were once again in the central park of Diaspar. Yet if this were indeed a park, it was too enormous for his mind to grasp. The city he had expected to see was nowhere visible. As far as the eye could reach there was nothing but forest and grass-covered plains.

Then Alvin lifted his eyes to the horizon, and there above the trees, sweeping from right to left in a great arc that encircled the world, was a line of stone which would have dwarfed the mightiest giants of Diaspar. It was so far away that its details were blurred by sheer distance, but there was something about its outlines that Alvin found puzzling. Then his eyes became at last accustomed to the scale of that colossal landscape, and he knew that those far-off walls had not been built by man.

Time had not conquered everything; Earth still possessed mountains of which she could be proud.

For a long time Alvin stood at the mouth of the tunnel, slowly growing accustomed to the strange world in which he had found himself. He was half stunned by the impact of sheer size and space; that ring of misty mountains could have enclosed a dozen cities as large as Diaspar. Search as he might, however, Alvin could see no trace of human life. Yet the road that led down the hillside seemed well-kept; he could do no better than accept its guidance.

At the foot of the hill, the road disappeared between great trees that almost hid the sun. As Alvin walked into their shadow, a strange medley of scents and sounds greeted him. The rustle of the wind among the leaves he had known before, but underlying that were a thousand vague noises that conveyed nothing to his mind. Unknown odors assailed him, smells that had been lost even to the memory of his race. The warmth, the profusion of scent and color, and the unseen presences of a million living things, smote him with almost physical violence.

He came upon the lake without any warning. The trees to the right suddenly ended, and before him was a great expanse of water, dotted with tiny islands. Never in his life had Alvin seen so much water; by comparison, the largest pools in Diaspar were scarcely more than puddles. He walked slowly down to the edge of the lake and cupped the warm water in his hands, letting it trickle through his fingers.

The great silver fish that suddenly forced its way through the underwater reeds was the first nonhuman creature that Alvin had ever seen. It should have been utterly strange to him, yet its shape teased his mind with a haunting familiarity. As it hung there in the pale green void, its fins a faint blur of motion, it seemed the very embodiment of power and speed. Here, incorporated in living flesh, were the graceful lines of the great ships that had once ruled the skies of Earth. Evolution and science had come to the same answers; and the work of Nature had lasted longer.

At last Alvin broke the lake's enchantment, and continued along the winding road. The forest closed around him once more, but only for a little while. Presently the road ended, in a great clearing half a mile wide and twice as long—and Alvin understood why he had seen no trace of man before.

The clearing was full of low, two-storied buildings, colored in soft shades that rested the eye even in the full glare of the sun. Most were of clean, straightforward design, but several were built in a complex architectural style involving the use of fluted columns and gracefully fretted stone. In these buildings, which seemed of great age, the immeasurably ancient device of the pointed arch was used.

As he walked slowly toward the village, Alvin was still struggling to grasp his new surroundings. Nothing was familiar; even the air had changed, with its hint of throbbing, unknown life. And the tall, golden-haired people going among the buildings with such unconscious grace were obviously of a different stock from the men of Diaspar.

They took no notice of Alvin, and that was strange, for his clothing was totally different from theirs. Since the temperature never changed in Diaspar, dress there was purely ornamental and often extremely elaborate. Here it seemed mainly functional, designed for use rather than display, and frequently consisted of a single sheet draped around the body.

It was not until Alvin was well inside the village that the people of Lys reacted to his presence, and then their response took a somewhat unexpected form. A group of five men emerged from one of the houses and began to walk purposefully toward him—almost as if, indeed, they had been expecting his arrival. Alvin felt a sudden, heady excitement, and the blood pounded in his veins. He thought of all the fateful meetings men must have had with other races on far-off worlds. Those he was meeting now were of his own species—but how far had they diverged in the aeons that had sundered them from Diaspar?

The delegation came to a halt a few feet away from Alvin. Its leader smiled, holding out his hand in the ancient gesture of friendship.

"We thought it best to meet you here," he said. "Our home is very different from Diaspar, and the walk from the terminus gives visitors a chance to become—acclimatized."

Alvin accepted the outstretched hand, but for a moment was too surprised to reply. Now he understood why all the other villagers had ignored him so completely.

"You knew I was coming?" he said at length.

"Of course. We always know when the carriers start to move. Tell me —how did you discover the way? It has been such a long time since the last visit that we feared the secret had been lost."

The speaker was interrupted by one of his companions.

"I think we'd better restrain our curiosity, Gerane. Seranis is waiting."

The name "Seranis" was preceded by a word unfamiliar to Alvin, and he assumed that it was a title of some kind. He had no difficulty in understanding the others, and it never occurred to him that there was anything surprising about this. Diaspar and Lys shared the same linguistic heritage, and the ancient invention of sound recording had long ago frozen speech in an unbreakable mold.

Gerane gave a shrug of mock resignation. "Very well," he smiled. "Seranis has few privileges—I should not rob her of this one."

As they walked deeper into the village, Alvin studied the men around him. They appeared kindly and intelligent, but these were virtues he had taken for granted all his life, and he was looking for ways in which they differed from a similar group in Diaspar. There were differences, but it was hard to define them. They were all somewhat taller than Alvin, and two of them showed the unmistakable marks of physical age. Their skins were very brown, and in all their movements they seemed to radiate a vigor and zest which Alvin found refreshing, though at the same time a little bewildering. He smiled as he remembered Khedron's prophecy that, if he ever reached Lys, he would find it exactly the same as Diaspar.

The people of the village now watched with frank curiosity as Alvin followed his guides; there was no longer any pretense that they took him for granted. Suddenly there were shrill, high-pitched shouts from the trees on the right, and a group of small, excited creatures burst out of the woods and crowded around Alvin. He stopped in utter amazement, unable to believe his eyes. Here was something that his world had lost so long ago that it lay in the realms of mythology. This was the way that life had once begun; these noisy, fascinating creatures were human children.

Alvin watched them with wondering disbelief—and with another sensation which tugged at his heart but which he could not yet identify. No other sight could have brought home to him so vividly his remoteness from the world he knew. Diaspar had paid, and paid in full, the price of immortality.

The party halted before the largest building Alvin had yet seen. It stood in the center of the village and from a flagpole on its small circular tower a green pennant floated along the breeze.

All but Gerane dropped behind as he entered the building. Inside it was quiet and cool; sunlight filtering through the translucent walls lit up everything with a soft, restful glow. The floor was smooth and resilient, inlaid with fine mosaics. On the walls, an artist of great ability and power had depicted a set of forest scenes. Mingled with these paintings were other murals which conveyed nothing to Alvin's mind, yet which were attractive and pleasant to look upon. Let into one wall was a rectangular screen filled with a shifting maze of colors—presumably a visiphone receiver, though a rather small one.

They walked together up a short circular stairway that led them out onto the flat roof of the building. From this point, the entire village was visible, and Alvin could see that it consisted of about a hundred buildings. In the distance the trees opened out to enclose wide meadows, where animals of several different types were grazing. Alvin could not imagine what these were; most of them were quadrupeds, but some seemed to have six or even eight legs.

Seranis was waiting for him in the shadow of the tower. Alvin wondered how old she was; her long, golden hair was touched with gray, which he guessed must be some indication of age. The presence of children, with all the consequences that implied, had left him very confused. Where there was birth, then surely there must also be death, and the life span here in Lys might be very different from that in Diaspar. He could not tell whether Seranis was fifty, five hundred, or five thousand years old, but looking into her eyes he could sense that wisdom and depth of experience he sometimes felt when he was with Jeserac.

She pointed to a small seat, but though her eyes smiled a welcome she said nothing until Alvin had made himself comfortable—or as comfortable as he could be under that intense though friendly scrutiny. Then she sighed, and addressed Alvin in a low, gentle voice.

"This is an occasion which does not often arise, so you will excuse me if I do not know the correct behavior. But there are certain rights due to a guest, even if an unexpected one. Before we talk, there is something about which I should warn you. I can read your mind."

She smiled at Alvin's obvious consternation, and added quickly: "There is no need to let that worry you. No right is respected more strongly than that of mental privacy. I will enter your mind only if you invite me to. But it would not be fair to hide this fact from you, and it will explain why we find speech somewhat slow and difficult. It is not often used here."

This revelation, though slightly alarming, did not surprise Alvin. Once both men and machines had possessed this power, and the unchanging machines could still read their masters' orders. But in Diaspar, man himself had lost the gift he had once shared with his slaves.

"I do not know what brought you from your world to ours," continued Seranis, "but if you are looking for life, your search has ended. Apart from Diaspar, there is only desert beyond our mountains."

It was strange that Alvin, who had questioned accepted beliefs so often before, did not doubt the words of Seranis. His only reaction was one of sadness that all his teaching had been so nearly true.

"Tell me about Lys," he begged. "Why have you been cut off from Diaspar for so long, when you seem to know so much about us?"

Seranis smiled at his eagerness.

"Presently," she said. "But first I would like to know something about you. Tell me how you found the way here, and why you came."

Haltingly at first, and then with growing confidence, Alvin told his story. He had never spoken with such freedom before; here at last was someone who would not laugh at his dreams, because they knew those dreams were true. Once or twice Seranis interrupted him with swift questions, when he mentioned some aspect of Diaspar that was unfamiliar to her. It was hard for Alvin to realize that things which were part of his everyday life would be meaningless to someone who had never lived in the city and knew nothing of its complex culture and social organization. Seranis listened with such understanding that he took her comprehension for granted; not until much later did he realize that many other minds besides hers were listening to his words.

When he had finished, there was silence for a while. Then Seranis looked at him and said quietly: "Why did you come to Lys?"

Alvin glanced at her in surprise.

"I've told you," he said. "I wanted to explore the world. Everyone told me that there was only desert beyond the city, but I had to see for myself."

"And was that the only reason?"

Alvin hesitated. When at last he answered, it was not the indomitable explorer who spoke, but the lost child who had been born into an alien world.

"No," he said slowly, "that wasn't the only reason—though I did not know it until now. I was lonely."

"Lonely? In Diaspar?" There was a smile on the lips of Seranis, but sympathy in her eyes, and Alvin knew that she expected no further answer.

Now that he had told his story, he waited for her to keep her share of the bargain. Presently Seranis rose to her feet and began to pace to and fro on the roof.

"I know the questions you wish to ask," she said. "Some of them I can answer, but it would be wearisome to do it in words. If you will open your mind to me, I will tell you what you need to know. You can trust me: I will take nothing from you without your permission."

"What do you want me to do?" said Alvin cautiously.

"Will yourself to accept my help—look at my eyes—and forget everything," commanded Seranis.

Alvin was never sure what happened then. There was a total eclipse of all his senses, and though he could never remember acquiring it, when he looked into his mind the knowledge was there.

He saw back into the past, not clearly, but as a man on some high mountain might look out across a misty plain. He understood that Man had not always been a city dweller, and that since the machines gave him freedom from toil there had always been a rivalry between two different types of civilization. In the Dawn Ages there had been thousands of cities, but a large part of mankind had preferred to live in relatively small communities. Universal transport and instantaneous communication had given them all the contact they required with the rest of the world, and they felt no need to live huddled together with millions of their fellows.

Lys had been little different, in the early days, from hundreds of other communities. But gradually, over the ages, it developed an independent culture which was one of the highest that mankind had ever known. It was a culture based largely upon the direct use of mental power, and this set it apart from the rest of human society, which came to rely more and more upon machines.

Through the aeons, as they advanced along their different roads, the gulf between Lys and the cities widened. It was bridged only in times of great crisis; when the Moon was falling, its destruction was carried out by the scientists of Lys. So also was the defense of Earth against the Invaders, who were held at bay in the final Battle of Shalmirane.

That great ordeal exhausted mankind; one by one the cities died and the desert rolled over them. As the population fell, humanity began the migration that was to make Diaspar the last and greatest of all cities.

Most of these changes did not affect Lys, but it had its own battle to fight—the battle against the desert. The natural barrier of the mountains was not enough, and many ages passed before the great oasis was made secure. The picture was blurred here, perhaps deliberately. Alvin could not see what had been done to give Lys the virtual eternity that Diaspar had achieved.

The voice of Seranis seemed to come to him from a great distance—yet it was not her voice alone, for it was merged into a symphony of words, as though many other tongues were chanting in unison with hers.

"That, very briefly, is our history. You will see that even in the Dawn Ages we had little to do with the cities, though their people often came into our land. We never hindered them, for many of our greatest men came from outside, but when the cities were dying we did not wish to be involved in their downfall. With the ending of air transport there was only one way into Lys—the carrier system from Diaspar. It was closed at your end, when the park was built—and you forgot us, though we have never forgotten you.

"Diaspar has surprised us. We expected it to go the way of all other cities, but instead it has achieved a stable culture that may last as long as Earth. It is not a culture that we admire, yet we are glad that those who wish to escape have been able to do so. More than you might think have made the journey, and they have almost always been outstanding men who brought something of value with them when they came to Lys."

The voice faded; the paralysis of Alvin's senses ebbed away and he was himself again. He saw with astonishment that the sun had fallen far below the trees and that the eastern sky already held a hint of night. Somewhere a great bell vibrated with a throbbing boom that pulsed slowly into silence, leaving the air tense with mystery and premonition. Alvin found himself trembling slightly, not with the first touch of the evening's chill, but through sheer awe and wonder at all that he had learned. It was very late, and he was far from home. He had a sudden need to see his friends again, and to be among the familiar sights and scenes of Diaspar.

"I must return," he said. "Khedron—my parents—they will be expecting me."

That was not wholly true; Khedron would certainly be wondering what had happened to him, but as far as Alvin was aware no one else knew that he had left Diaspar. He could not have explained the reason for this mild deceit, and was slightly ashamed of himself as soon as he had uttered the words.

Seranis looked at him thoughtfully.

"I am afraid it is not as easy as that," she said.

"What do you mean?" asked Alvin. "Won't the carrier that brought me here take me back again?" He still refused to face the fact that he might be held in Lys against his will, though the idea had briefly crossed his mind.

For the first time, Seranis seemed slightly ill at ease.

"We have been talking about you," she said—not explaining who the "we" might be, nor exactly how they had consulted together. "If you return to Diaspar, the whole city will know about us. Even if you promised to say nothing, you would find it impossible to keep our secret."

"Why should you wish it kept?" asked Alvin. "Surely it would be a good thing for both our peoples if they could meet again."

Seranis looked displeased.

"We do not think so," she said. "If the gates were opened, our land would be flooded with the idly curious and the sensation seekers. As it is now, only the best of your people have ever reached us."

This reply radiated so much unconscious superiority, yet was based on such false assumptions, that Alvin felt his annoyance quite eclipse his alarm.

"That isn't true," he said flatly. "I do not believe you would find another person in Diaspar who could leave the city, even if he wanted to—even if he knew that there was somewhere to go. If you let me return, it would make no difference to Lys."

"It is not my decision," explained Seranis, "and you underestimate the powers of the mind if you think that the barriers that keep your people inside their city can never be broken. However, we do not wish to hold you here against your will, but if you return to Diaspar we must erase all memories of Lys from your mind." She hesitated for a moment. "This has never risen before; all your predecessors came here to stay."

Here was a choice that Alvin refused to accept. He wanted to explore Lys, to learn all its secrets, to discover the ways in which it differed from his own home, but equally he was determined to return to Diaspar, so that he could prove to his friends that he had been no idle dreamer. He could not understand the reasons prompting this desire for secrecy; even if he had, it would not have made any difference in his behavior.

He realized that he must play for time or else convince Seranis that what she asked him was impossible.

"Khedron knows where I am," he said. "You cannot erase *his* memories."

Seranis smiled. It was a pleasant smile, and one that in any other circumstances would have been friendly enough. But behind it Alvin glimpsed, for the first time, the presence of overwhelming and implacable power.

"You underestimate us, Alvin," she replied. "That would be very easy. I can reach Diaspar more quickly than I can cross Lys. Other men have come here before, and some of them told their friends where they were going. Yet those friends forgot them, and they vanished from the history of Diaspar."

Alvin had been foolish to ignore this possibility, though it was obvious, now that Seranis had pointed it out. He wondered how many times, in the millions of years since the two cultures were separated, men from Lys had gone into Diaspar in order to preserve their jealously guarded secret. And he wondered just how extensive were the mental powers which these strange people possessed and did not hesitate to use.

Was it safe to make any plans at all? Seranis had promised that she would not read his mind without his consent, but he wondered if there might be circumstances in which that promise would not be kept.

"Surely," he said, "you don't expect me to make the decision at once. Cannot I see something of your country before I make my choice?"

"Of course," replied Seranis. "You can stay here as long as you wish, and still return to Diaspar eventually if you change your mind. But if you can decide within the next few days, it will be very much easier. You do not want your friends to be worried, and the longer you are missing the harder it will be for us to make the necessary adjustments."

Alvin could appreciate that; he would like to know just what those "adjustments" were. Presumably someone from Lys would contact Khedron—without the Jester ever being aware of it—and tamper with his mind. The fact of Alvin's disappearance could not be concealed, but the information that he and Khedron had discovered could be obliterated. As the ages passed, Alvin's name would join those of the other Uniques who had mysteriously vanished without trace and had then been forgotten.

There were many mysteries here, and he seemed no closer to solving any of them. Was there any purpose behind the curious, one-sided relationship between Lys and Diaspar, or was it merely a historical accident? Who and what were the Uniques, and if the people from Lys could enter Diaspar, why had they not canceled the memory circuits that held the clue to their existence? Perhaps that was the only question to which Alvin could give a plausible answer. The Central Computer might be too stubborn an opponent to tackle, and would hardly be affected by even the most advanced of mental techniques.

He put these problems aside; one day, when he had learned a great deal more, he might have some chance of answering them. It was idle to speculate, to build pyramids of surmise on a foundation of ignorance.

"Very well," he said, though not too graciously, for he was still annoyed that this unexpected obstacle had been placed in his path. "I'll give you my answer as soon as I can, if you will show me what your land is like."

"Good," said Seranis, and this time her smile held no hidden threat. "We are proud of Lys, and it will be a pleasure to show you how men can live without the aid of cities. Meanwhile, there is no need for you to worry—your friends will not be alarmed by your absence. We shall see to that, if only for our own protection."

It was the first time Seranis had ever made a promise that she could not keep.

ELEVEN

Try as she would, Alystra could extract no further information from Khedron. The Jester had recovered quickly from his initial shock, and from the panic that had sent him flying back to the surface when he found himself alone in the depths beneath the Tomb. He also felt ashamed of his cowardly behavior, and wondered if he would ever have the courage to return to the chamber of the moving ways and the network of world-ranging tunnels that radiated from it. Although he felt that Alvin had been impatient, if not indeed foolhardy, he did not really believe that he would run into any danger. He would return in his own good time, Khedron was certain of that. Well, almost certain; there was just enough doubt to make him feel the need for caution. It would be wise, he decided, to say as little as possible for the time being, and to pass the whole thing off as another joke.

Unfortunately for this plan, he had not been able to mask his emotions when Alystra encountered him on his return to the surface. She had seen the fear written so unmistakably in his eyes, and had at once interpreted it as meaning that Alvin was in danger. All Khedron's reassurances were in vain, and she became more and more angry with him as they walked together back through the park. At first Alystra had wanted to remain at the Tomb, waiting for Alvin to return in whatever mysterious manner he had vanished. Khedron had managed to convince her that this would be a waste of time, and was relieved when she followed him back to the city. There was a chance that Alvin might return almost at once, and he did not wish anyone else to discover the secret of Yarlan Zey.

By the time they had reached the city, it was obvious to Khedron that his evasive tactics had failed completely and that the situation was seriously out of hand. It was the first time in his life that he had ever been at a loss and had not felt himself capable of dealing with any problem that arose. His immediate and irrational fear was being slowly replaced by a profounder and more firmly based alarm. Until now, Khedron had given little thought to the consequences of his actions. His own interests, and a mild but genuine sympathy toward Alvin, had been sufficient motive for all that he had done. Though he had given encouragement and assistance to Alvin, he had never believed that anything like this could ever really happen.

Despite the gulf of years and experience between them, Alvin's will had always been more powerful than his own. It was too late to do anything about it now; Khedron felt that events were sweeping him along toward a climax utterly beyond his control.

In view of this, it was a little unfair that Alystra obviously regarded him as Alvin's evil genius and showed an inclination to blame him for all that had happened. Alystra was not really vindictive, but she was annoyed, and part of her annoyance focused on Khedron. If any action of hers caused him trouble, she would be the last person to be sorry.

They parted in stony silence when they had reached the great circular way that surrounded the park. Khedron watched Alystra disappear into the distance and wondered wearily what plans were brewing in her mind.

There was only one thing of which he could be certain now. Boredom would not be a serious problem for a considerable time to come.

Alystra acted swiftly and with intelligence. She did not bother to contact Eriston and Etania; Alvin's parents were pleasant nonentities for whom she felt some affection but no respect. They would only waste time in futile arguments and would then do exactly as Alystra was doing now.

Jeserac listened to her story without apparent emotion. If he was alarmed or surprised, he concealed it well—so well that Alystra was somewhat disappointed. It seemed to her that nothing so extraordinary and important as this had ever happened before, and Jeserac's matter-of-fact behavior made her feel deflated. When she had finished, he questioned her at some length, and hinted, without actually saying so, that she might have made a mistake. What reason was there for supposing that Alvin had really left the city? Perhaps it had all been a trick at her expense; the fact that Khedron was involved made this seem highly probable. Alvin might be laughing at her, concealed somewhere in Diaspar, at this very moment.

The only positive reaction she got out of Jeserac was a promise to make inquiries and to contact her again within a day. In the meantime she was not to worry, and it would also be best if she said nothing to anyone else about the whole affair. There was no need to spread alarm over an incident that would probably be cleared up in a few hours.

Alystra left Jeserac in a mood of mild frustration. She would have been more satisfied could she have seen his behavior immediately after she had left.

Jeserac had friends on the Council; he had been a member himself in his long life, and might be again if he was unlucky. He called three of his most influential colleagues and cautiously aroused their interest. As Alvin's tutor, he was well aware of his own delicate position and was anxious to safeguard himself. For the present, the fewer who knew what had happened, the better.

It was immediately agreed that the first thing to do was to contact Khedron and ask him for an explanation. There was only one defect in this excellent plan. Khedron had anticipated it and was nowhere to be found.

If there was any ambiguity about Alvin's position, his hosts were very careful not to remind him of it. He was free to go anywhere he wished in Airlee, the little village over which Seranis ruled—though that was too strong a word to describe her position. Sometimes it seemed to Alvin that she was a benevolent dictator, but at others it appeared that she had no powers at all. So far he had failed completely to understand the social system of Lys, either because it was too simple or else so complex that its ramifications eluded him. All he had discovered for certain was that Lys was divided into innumerable villages, of which Airlee was a quite typical example. Yet in a sense there were no typical examples, for Alvin had been assured that every village tried to be as unlike its neighbors as possible. It was all extremely confusing.

Though it was very small, and contained less than a thousand people, Airlee was full of surprises. There was hardly a single aspect of life that did not differ from its counterpart in Diaspar. The differences extended even to such fundamentals as speech. Only the children used their voices for normal communication; the adults scarcely ever spoke, and after a while Alvin decided that they did so only out of politeness to him. It was a curiously frustrating experience to feel oneself enmeshed in a great net of soundless and undetectable words, but after a while Alvin grew accustomed to it. It seemed surprising that vocal speech had survived at all since there was no longer any use for it, but Alvin later discovered that the people of Lys were very fond of singing, and indeed of all forms of music. Without this incentive, it was very likely that they would long ago have become completely mute.

They were always busy, engaged on tasks or problems which were usually incomprehensible to Alvin. When he could understand what they were doing, much of their work seemed quite unnecessary. A considerable part of their food, for example, was actually grown, and not synthesized in accordance with patterns worked out ages ago. When Alvin commented on this, it was patiently explained to him that the people of Lys liked to watch things grow, to carry out complicated genetic experiments and to evolve ever more subtle tastes and flavors. Airlee was famous for its fruit, but when Alvin ate some choice samples they seemed to him no better than those he could have conjured up in Diaspar by no more effort than raising a finger.

At first he wondered if the people of Lys had forgotten, or had never possessed, the powers and machines that he took for granted and upon which all life in Diaspar was based. He soon found that this was not the case. The tools and the knowledge were there, but they were used only when it was essential. The most striking example of this was provided by the transport system, if it could be dignified by such a name. For short distances, people walked, and seemed to enjoy it. If they were in a hurry, or had small loads to move, they used animals which had obviously been developed for the purpose. The freight-carrying species was a low, six-legged beast, very docile and strong but of poor intelligence. The racing animals were of a different breed altogether, normally walking on four legs but using only their heavily muscled hind limbs when they really got up speed. They could cross the entire width of Lys in a few hours, and the passenger rode in a pivoted seat strapped on the creature's back. Nothing in the world would have induced Alvin to risk such a ride, though it was a very popular sport among the younger men. Their finely bred steeds were the aristocrats of the animal world, and were well aware of it. They had fairly large vocabularies, and Alvin often overheard them talking boastfully among themselves about past and future victories. When he tried to be friendly and attempted to join in the conversation, they pretended that they could not understand him, and if he persisted would go bounding off in outraged dignity.

These two varieties of animal sufficed for all ordinary needs, and gave their owners a great deal of pleasure which no mechanical contrivances could have done. But when extreme speed was required or vast loads had to be moved, the machines were there, and were used without hesitation.

Though the animal life of Lys presented Alvin with a whole world of new interests and surprises, it was the two extremes of the human population range that fascinated him most of all. The very young and the very old—both were equally strange to him and equally amazing. Airlee's most senior inhabitant had barely attained his second century, and had only a few more years of life before him. When *he* had reached that age, Alvin reminded himself, his body would scarcely have altered, whereas this old man, who had no chain of future existences to look forward to as compensation, had almost exhausted his physical powers. His hair was completely white, and his face an unbelievably intricate mass of wrinkles. He seemed to spend most of his time sitting in the sun or walking slowly around the village exchanging soundless greetings with everyone he met. As far as Alvin could tell he was completely contented, asking no more of life, and was not distressed by its approaching end.

Here was a philosophy so much at variance with that of Diaspar as to be completely beyond Alvin's comprehension. Why should anyone accept death when it was so unnecessary, when you had the choice of living for a thousand years and then leaping forward through the millenniums to make a new start in a world that you had helped to shape? This was one mystery he was determined to solve as soon as he had the chance of discussing it frankly. It was very hard for him to believe that Lys had made this choice of its own free will, if it knew the alternative that existed.

He found part of his answer among the children, those little creatures who were as strange to him as any of the animals of Lys. He spent much of his time among them, watching them at their play and eventually being accepted by them as a friend. Sometimes it seemed to him that they were not human at all, their motives, their logic, and even their language were so alien. He would look unbelievingly at the adults and ask himself how it was possible that they could have evolved from these extraordinary creatures who seemed to spend most of their lives in a private world of their own.

And yet, even while they baffled him, they aroused within his heart a feeling he had never known before. When—which was not often, but sometimes happened—they burst into tears of utter frustration or despair, their tiny disappointments seemed to him more tragic than Man's long retreat after the loss of his Galactic Empire. That was something too huge and remote for comprehension, but the weeping of a child could pierce one to the heart.

Alvin had met love in Diaspar, but now he was learning something equally precious, and without which love itself could never reach its highest fulfillment but must remain forever incomplete. He was learning tenderness.

If Alvin was studying Lys, Lys was also studying him, and was not dissatisfied with what it had found. He had been in Airlee for three days when Seranis suggested that he might like to go further afield and see something more of her country. It was a proposal he accepted at once—on condition that he was not expected to ride one of the village's prize racing beasts.

"I can assure you," said Seranis, with a rare flash of humor, "that no one here would dream of risking one of their precious animals. Since this is an exceptional case, I will arrange transport in which you will feel more at home. Hilvar will act as your guide, but of course you can go wherever you please."

Alvin wondered if that was strictly true. He imagined that there would be some objection if he tried to return to the little hill from whose summit he had first emerged into Lys. However, that did not worry him for the moment since he was in no hurry to go back to Diaspar, and indeed had given little thought to the problem after his initial meeting with Seranis. Life here was still so interesting and so novel that he was still quite content to live in the present.

He appreciated Seranis's gesture in offering her son as his guide, though doubtless Hilvar had been given careful instructions to see that he did not get into mischief. It had taken Alvin some time to get accustomed to Hilvar, for a reason which he could not very well explain to him without hurting his feelings. Physical perfection was so universal in Diaspar that personal beauty had been completely devalued; men noticed it no more than the air they breathed. This was not the case in Lys, and the most flattering adjective that could be applied to Hilvar was "homely." By Alvin's standards, he was downright ugly, and for a while he had deliberately avoided him. If Hilvar was aware of this, he showed no sign of it, and it was not long before his good-natured friendliness had broken through the barrier between them. The time was to come when Alvin would be so accustomed to Hilvar's broad, twisted smile, his strength, and his gentleness that he could scarcely believe he had ever found him unattractive, and would not have had him changed for any consideration in the world.

They left Airlee soon after dawn in a small vehicle which Hilvar called a ground-car, and which apparently worked on the same principle as the machine that had brought Alvin from Diaspar. It floated in the air a few inches above the turf, and although there was no sign of any guide rail, Hilvar told him that the cars could run only on predetermined routes. All the centers of population were linked together in this fashion, but during his entire stay in Lys Alvin never saw another ground-car in use.

Hilvar had put a great deal of effort into organizing this expedition, and was obviously looking forward to it quite as much as Alvin. He had planned the route with his own interests in mind, for natural history was his consuming passion and he hoped to find new types of insect life in the relatively uninhabited regions of Lys which they would be visiting. He intended to travel as far south as the machine could take them, and the rest of the way they would have to go on foot. Not realizing the full implications of this, Alvin made no objections.

They had a companion with them on the journey—Krif, the most spectacular of Hilvar's many pets. When Krif was resting, his six gauzy wings lay folded along his body, which glittered through them like a jeweled scepter. If something disturbed him, he would rise into the air with a flicker of iridescence and a faint whirring of invisible wings. Though the great insect would come when called and would—sometimes—obey simple orders, it was almost wholly mindless. Yet it had a definite personality of its own, and for some reason was suspicious of Alvin, whose sporadic attempts to gain its confidence always ended in failure.

To Alvin, the journey across Lys had a dreamlike unreality. Silent as a ghost, the machine slid across rolling plains and wound its way through forests, never deviating from its invisible track. It traveled perhaps ten times as fast as a man could comfortably walk; seldom indeed was any inhabitant of Lys in a greater hurry than that.

They passed through many villages, some larger than Airlee but most of them built along very similar lines. Alvin was interested to notice the subtle but significant differences in clothing and even physical appearance that occurred as they moved from one community to the next. The civilization of Lys was composed of hundreds of distinct cultures, each contributing some special talent toward the whole. The ground-car was well stocked with Airlee's most famous product, a small, yellow peach which was gratefully received whenever Hilvar gave away some samples. He often stopped to talk to friends and to introduce Alvin, who never ceased to be impressed by the simple courtesy with which everyone used vocal speech as soon as they knew who he was. It must often have been very tedious to them, but as far as he could judge they always resisted the temptation to lapse into telepathy and he never felt excluded from their conversation.

They made their longest pause at a tiny village almost hidden in a sea of tall golden grass, which soared high above their heads and which undulated in the gentle wind as if it was endowed with life. As they moved through it, they were continually overtaken by rolling waves as the countless blades bowed in unison above them. At first it was faintly disturbing, for Alvin had a foolish fancy that the grass was bending down to look at him, but after a while he found the continual motion quite restful.

Alvin soon discovered why they had made this stop. Among the little crowd that had already gathered before the car came gliding into the village was a shy, dark girl whom Hilvar introduced as Nyara. They were obviously very pleased to see one another again, and Alvin felt envious of their patent happiness at this brief reunion. Hilvar was clearly torn between his duties as a guide and his desire to have no other company but Nyara, and Alvin soon rescued him from his quandary by setting off on a tour of exploration by himself. There was not much to see in the little village, but he took his time.

When they started on their way again, there were many questions he was anxious to ask Hilvar. He could not imagine what love must be like in a telepathic society, and after a discreet interval he broached the subject. Hilvar was willing enough to explain, even though Alvin suspected that he had made his friend interrupt a prolonged and tender mental leave-taking.

In Lys, it seemed, all love began with mental contact, and it might be months or years before a couple actually met. In this way, Hilvar explained, there could be no false impressions, no deceptions on either side. Two people whose minds were open to one another could hide no secrets. If either attempted it, the other partner would know at once that something was being concealed.

Only very mature and well-balanced minds could afford such honesty; only love based upon absolute unselfishness could survive it. Alvin could well understand that such a love would be deeper and richer than anything his people could know; it could be so perfect, in fact, that he found it hard to believe that it could ever occur at all.

Yet Hilvar assured him that it did, and became starry-eyed and lost in his own reveries when Alvin pressed him to be more explicit. There were some things that could not be communicated; one either knew them or one did not. Alvin decided sadly that he could never attain the kind of mutual understanding which these fortunate people had made the very basis of their lives.

When the ground-car emerged from the savanna, which ended abruptly as though a frontier had been drawn beyond which the grass was not permitted to grow, there was a range of low, heavily wooded hills ahead of them. This was an outpost, Hilvar explained, of the main rampart guarding Lys. The real mountains lay beyond, but to Alvin even these small hills were an impressive and awe-inspiring sight.

The car came to a halt in a narrow, sheltered valley which was still flooded by the warmth and light of the descending sun. Hilvar looked at Alvin with a kind of wide-eyed candor which, one could have sworn, was totally innocent of any guile.

"This is where we start to walk," he said cheerfully, beginning to throw equipment out of the vehicle. "We can't ride any farther."

Alvin looked at the hills surrounding them, then at the comfortable seat in which he had been riding.

"Isn't there a way around?" he asked, not very hopefully.

"Of course," replied Hilvar. "But we're not going around. We're going to the top, which is much more interesting. I'll put the car on automatic so that it will be waiting for us when we get down the other side."

Determined not to give in without a struggle, Alvin made one last effort.

"It will soon be dark," he protested. "We'll never be able to go all that way before sunset."

"Exactly," said Hilvar, sorting packages and equipment with incredible speed. "We'll spend the night on the summit, and finish the journey in the morning."

For once, Alvin knew when he was beaten.

The gear that they were carrying looked very formidable, but though it was bulky it weighed practically nothing. It was all packed in gravity-polarizing containers that neutralized its weight, leaving only inertia to be contended with. As long as Alvin moved in a straight line, he was not conscious that he was carrying any load. Dealing with these containers required a little practice, for if he attempted to make a sudden change of direction his pack seemed to develop a stubborn personality and did its best to keep him on his original course, until he had overcome its momentum.

When Hilvar had adjusted all the straps and satisfied himself that everything was in order, they began to walk slowly up the valley. Alvin looked back wistfully as the ground-car retraced its track and disappeared from sight; he wondered how many hours would elapse before he could again relax in its comfort.

Nevertheless, it was very pleasant climbing upward with the mild sun beating on their backs, and seeing ever-new vistas unfold around them. There was a partly obliterated path which disappeared from time to time but which Hilvar seemed able to follow even when Alvin could see no trace of it. He asked Hilvar what had made the path, and was told that there were many small animals in these hills—some solitary, and some living in primitive communities which echoed many of the features of human civilization. A few had even discovered, or been taught, the use of tools and fire. It never occurred to Alvin that such creatures might be other than friendly; both he and Hilvar took this for granted, for it had been so many ages since anything on Earth had challenged the supremacy of Man.

They had been climbing for half an hour when Alvin first noticed the faint, reverberating murmur in the air around him. He could not detect its source, for it seemed to come from no particular direction. It never ceased, and it grew steadily louder as the landscape widened around them. He would have asked Hilvar what it was, but it had become necessary to save his breath for more essential purposes.

Alvin was in perfect health; indeed, he had never had an hour's illness in his life. But physical well-being, however important and necessary it might be, was not sufficient for the task he was facing now. He had the body, but he did not possess the skill. Hilvar's easy strides, the effortless surge of power which took him up every slope, filled Alvin with envy—and a determination not to give in while he could still place one foot in front of the other. He knew perfectly well that Hilvar was testing him, and did not resent the fact. It was a good-natured game, and he entered into the spirit of it even while the fatigue spread slowly through his legs.

Hilvar took pity on him when they had completed two-thirds of the ascent, and they rested for a while propped up against a westward-facing bank, letting the mellow sunlight drench their bodies. The throbbing thunder was very strong now, and although Alvin questioned him Hilvar refused to explain it. It would, he said, spoil the surprise if Alvin knew what to expect at the end of the climb.

They were now racing against the sun, but fortunately the final ascent was smooth and gentle. The trees that had covered the lower part of the hill had now thinned out, as if they too were tired of the fight against gravity, and for the last few hundred yards the ground was carpeted with short, wiry grass on which it was very pleasant to walk. As the summit came in sight, Hilvar put forth a sudden burst of energy and went racing up the slope. Alvin decided to ignore the challenge; indeed, he had no choice. He was quite content to plod steadily onward, and when he had caught up with Hilvar to collapse in contented exhaustion by his side.

Not until he had regained his breath was he able to appreciate the view spread out beneath him, and to see the origin of the endless thunder which now filled the air. The ground ahead fell away steeply from the crest of the hill—so steeply, indeed, that it soon became an almost vertical cliff. And leaping far out from the face of the cliff was a mighty ribbon of water, which curved out through space to crash into the rocks a thousand feet below. There it was lost in a shimmering mist of spray, while up from the depths rose that ceaseless, drumming thunder that reverberated in hollow echoes from the hills on either side.

Most of the waterfall was now in shadow, but the sunlight streaming past the mountain still illuminated the land beneath, adding the final touch of magic to the scene. For quivering in evanescent beauty above the base of the fall was the last rainbow left on Earth.

Hilvar waved his arm in a sweep which embraced the whole horizon. "From here," he said, raising his voice so that it could be heard above the thunder of the waterfall, "you can see right across Lys."

Alvin could well believe him. To the north lay mile upon mile of forest, broken here and there by clearings and fields and the wandering threads of a hundred rivers. Hidden somewhere in that vast panorama was the village of Airlee, but it was hopeless to try to find it. Alvin fancied that he could catch a glimpse of the lake past which the path led to the entrance into Lys, but decided that his eyes had tricked him. Still further north, trees and clearings alike were lost in a mottled carpet of green, rucked here and there by lines of hills. And beyond that, at the very edge of vision, the mountains that hemmed Lys from the desert lay like a bank of distant clouds.

East and west the view was little different, but to the south the mountains seemed only a few miles away. Alvin could see them very clearly, and he realized that they were far higher than the little peak on which he was standing. They were separated from him by country that was much wilder than the land through which he had just passed. In some indefinable way it seemed deserted and empty, as if Man had not lived here for many, many years.

Hilvar answered Alvin's unspoken question.

"Once that part of Lys was inhabited," he said. "I don't know why it was abandoned, and perhaps one day we shall move into it again. Only the animals live there now."

Indeed, there was nowhere any sign of human life—none of the clearings or well-disciplined rivers that spoke of Man's presence. Only in one spot was there any indication that he had ever lived here, for many miles away a solitary white ruin jutted above the forest roof like a broken fang. Elsewhere, the jungle had returned to its own.

The sun was sinking below the western walls of Lys. For a breathless moment, the distant mountains seemed to burn with golden flames; then the land they guarded was swiftly drowned with shadow and the night had come.

"We should have done this before," said Hilvar, practical as ever, as he started to unload their equipment. "It'll be pitch dark in five minutes—and cold, too."

Curious pieces of apparatus began to cover the grass. A slim tripod extended a vertical rod carrying a pear-shaped bulge at its upper end. Hilvar raised this until the pear was just clear of their heads, and gave some mental signal which Alvin could not intercept. At once their little encampment was flooded with light, and the darkness retreated. The pear gave not only light but also heat, for Alvin could feel a gentle, caressing glow that seemed to sink into his very bones.

Carrying the tripod in one hand and his pack in the other, Hilvar walked down the slope while Alvin hurried behind, doing his best to keep in the circle of light. He finally pitched camp in a small depression a few hundred yards below the crest of the hill, and started to put the rest of his equipment into operation.

First came a large hemisphere of some rigid and almost invisible material which englobed them completely and protected them from the cool breeze which had now begun to blow up the face of the hill. The dome appeared to be generated by a small rectangular box which Hilvar placed on the ground and then ignored completely, even to the extent of burying it beneath the rest of his paraphernalia. Perhaps this also projected the comfortable, semitransparent couches on which Alvin was so glad to relax.

It was the first time he had seen furniture materialized in Lys, where it seemed to him that the houses were terribly cluttered up with permanent artifacts which would be much better kept safely out of the way in Memory Banks.

The meal which Hilvar produced from yet another of his receptacles was also the first purely synthetic one that Alvin had eaten since reaching Lys. There was a steady blast of air, sucked through some orifice in the dome overhead, as the matter-converter seized its raw material and performed its everyday miracle. On the whole, Alvin was much happier with purely synthetic food. The way in which the other kind was prepared struck him as being appallingly unhygienic, and at least with the matter-converters you knew exactly what you were eating.

They settled down for their evening meal as the night deepened around them and the stars came out. When they had finished, it was completely dark beyond their circle of light, and at the edge of that circle Alvin could see dim shapes moving as the creatures of the forest crept out of their hiding places. From time to time he caught the glint of reflected light as pale eyes stared back at him, but whatever beasts were watching out there would come no closer, so he could see nothing more of them.

It was very peaceful, and Alvin felt utterly content. For a while they lay on their couches and talked about the things that they had seen, the mystery that enmeshed them both, and the many ways in which their two cultures differed. Hilvar was fascinated by the miracle of the Eternity Circuits which had put Diaspar beyond the reach of time, and Alvin found some of his questions very hard to answer.

"What I don't understand," said Hilvar, "is how the designers of Diaspar made certain that nothing would ever go wrong with the memory circuits. You tell me that the information defining the city, and all the people who live in it, is stored as patterns of electric charge inside crystals. Well, crystals will last forever—but what about all the circuits associated with them? Aren't there ever any failures of *any* kind?"

"I asked Khedron that same question, and he told me that the Memory Banks are virtually triplicated. Any one of the three banks can maintain the city, and if anything goes wrong with one of them, the other two automatically correct it. Only if the same failure occurred simultaneously in two of the banks would any permanent damage be done—and the chances of that are infinitesimal."

"And how is the relation maintained between the pattern stored in the memory units and the actual structure of the city? Between the plan, as it were, and the thing it describes?"

Alvin was now completely out of his depth. He knew that the answer involved technologies that relied on the manipulation of space itself—but how one could lock an atom rigidly in the position defined by data stored elsewhere was something he could not begin to explain.

On a sudden inspiration, he pointed to the invisible dome protecting them from the night.

"Tell me how this roof above our heads is created by that box you're sitting on," he answered, "and then I'll explain how the Eternity Circuits work."

Hilvar laughed.

"I suppose it's a fair comparison. You'd have to ask one of our field theory experts if you wanted to know that. I certainly couldn't tell you."

This reply made Alvin very thoughtful. So there were still men in Lys who understood how their machines worked; that was more than could be said of Diaspar.

Thus they talked and argued, until presently Hilvar said: "I'm tired. What about you—are you going to sleep?"

Alvin rubbed his still-weary limbs.

"I'd like to," he confessed, "but I'm not sure I can. It still seems a strange custom to me."

"It is a good deal more than a custom," smiled Hilvar. "I have been told that it was once a necessity to every human being. We still like to sleep at least once a day, even if only for a few hours. During that time the body refreshes itself, and the mind as well. Does no one in Diaspar *ever* sleep?"

"Only on very rare occasions," said Alvin. "Jeserac, my tutor, has done it once or twice, after he had made some exceptional mental effort. A well-designed body should have no need for such rest periods; we did away with them millions of years ago."

Even as he spoke these rather boastful words, his actions belied them. He felt a weariness such as he had never before known; it seemed to spread from his calves and thighs until it flowed through all his body. There was nothing unpleasant about the sensation—rather the reverse. Hilvar was watching him with an amused smile, and Alvin had enough faculties left to wonder if his companion was exercising any of his mental powers upon him. If so, he did not object in the least.

The light flooding down from the metal pear overhead sank to a faint glow, but the warmth it was radiating continued unabated. By the last flicker of light, Alvin's drowsy mind registered a curious fact which he would have to inquire about in the morning.

Hilvar had stripped off his clothes, and for the first time Alvin saw how much the two branches of the human race had diverged. Some of the changes were merely ones of emphasis or proportion, but others, such as the external genitals and the presence of teeth, nails, and definite body hair, were more fundamental. What puzzled him most of all, however, was the curious small hollow in the pit of Hilvar's stomach.

When, some days later, he suddenly remembered the subject, it took a good deal of explaining. By the time that Hilvar had made the functions of the navel quite clear, he had uttered many thousands of words and drawn half a dozen diagrams.

And both he and Alvin had made a great step forward in understanding the basis of each other's cultures.

TWELVE

The night was at its deepest when Alvin woke. Something had disturbed him, some whisper of sound that had crept into his mind despite the endless thunder of the falls. He sat up in the darkness, straining his eyes across the hidden land, while with indrawn breath he listened to the drumming roar of the water and the softer, more fugitive sounds of the creatures of the night.

Nothing was visible. The starlight was too dim to reveal the miles of country that lay hundreds of feet below; only a jagged line of darker night eclipsing the stars told of the mountains on the southern horizon. In the darkness beside him Alvin heard his companion roll over and sit up.

"What is it?" came a whispered voice.

"I thought I heard a noise."

"What sort of noise?"

"I don't know: perhaps it was just imagination."

There was a silence while two pairs of eyes peered out into the mystery of the night. Then, suddenly, Hilvar caught Alvin's arm.

"Look!" he whispered.

Far to the south glowed a solitary point of light, too low in the heavens to be a star. It was a brilliant white, tinged with violet, and even as they watched it began to climb the spectrum of intensity, until the eye could no longer bear to look upon it. Then it exploded—and it seemed as if lightning had struck below the rim of the world. For a brief instant the mountains, and the land they encircled, were etched with fire against the darkness of the night. Ages later came the ghost of a far-off explosion, and in the woods below a sudden wind stirred among the trees. It died away swiftly, and one by one the routed stars crept back into the sky.

For the second time in his life, Alvin knew fear. It was not as personal and imminent as it had been in the chamber of the moving ways, when he had made the decision that took him to Lys. Perhaps it was awe rather than fear; he was looking into the face of the unknown, and it was as if he had already sensed that out there beyond the mountains was something he must go to meet.

"What was that?" he whispered at length.

There was a pause so long that he repeated the question.

"I am trying to find out," said Hilvar, and was silent again. Alvin guessed what he was doing and did not interrupt his friend's silent quest.

Presently Hilvar gave a little sigh of disappointment. "Everyone is asleep," he said. "There was no one who could tell me. We must wait until morning, unless I wake one of my friends. And I would not like to do that unless it is really important."

Alvin wondered what Hilvar would consider a matter of real importance. He was just going to suggest, a little sarcastically, that this might well merit interrupting someone's sleep. Before he could make the proposal, Hilvar spoke again.

"I've just remembered," he said, rather apologetically, "it's a long time since I came here, and I'm not quite certain about my bearings. But that must be Shalmirane."

"Shalmirane! Does it still exist?"

"Yes; I'd almost forgotten. Seranis once told me that the fortress lies in those mountains. Of course, it's been in ruins for ages, but perhaps someone still lives there."

Shalmirane! To these children of two races, so widely differing in culture and history, this was indeed a name of magic. In all the long story of Earth, there had been no greater epic than the defense of Shalmirane against an invader who had conquered all the Universe. Though the true facts were utterly lost in the mists which had gathered so thickly around the Dawn Ages, the legends had never been forgotten and would last as long as man endured.

Presently Hilvar's voice came again out of the darkness.

"The people of the south could tell us more. I have some friends there; I will call them in the morning."

Alvin scarcely heard him; he was deep in his own thoughts, trying to remember all that he had ever heard of Shalmirane. It was little enough; after this immense lapse of time, no one could tell the truth from the legend. All that was certain was that the Battle of Shalmirane marked the end of Man's conquests and the beginning of his long decline.

Among those mountains, thought Alvin, might lie the answers to all the problems that had tormented him for so many years.

"How long," he said to Hilvar, "would it take us to reach the fortress?"

"I've never been there, but it's much farther than I intended to go. I doubt if we could do it in a day."

"Can't we use the ground-car?"

"No; the way lies through the mountains and no cars can go there."

Alvin thought it over. He was tired, his feet were sore, and the muscles of his thighs were still aching from the unaccustomed effort. It was very tempting to leave it for another time. Yet there might be no other time.

Beneath the dim light of the failing stars, not a few of which had died since Shalmirane was built, Alvin wrestled with his thoughts and presently made his decision. Nothing had changed; the mountains resumed their watch over the sleeping land. But a turning point in history had come and gone, and the human race was moving toward a strange new future.

Alvin and Hilvar slept no more that night, but broke camp with the first glow of dawn. The hill was drenched with dew, and Alvin marveled at the sparkling jewelry which weighed down each blade and leaf. The "swish" of the wet grass fascinated him as he plowed through it, and looking back up the hill he could see his path stretching behind him like a dark band across the shining ground.

The sun had just lifted above the eastern wall of Lys when they reached the outskirts of the forest. Here, Nature had returned to her own. Even Hilvar seemed somewhat lost among the gigantic trees that blocked the sunlight and cast pools of shadow on the jungle floor. Fortunately the river from the fall flowed south in a line too straight to be altogether natural, and by keeping to its edge they could avoid the denser undergrowth. A good deal of Hilvar's time was spent in controlling Krif, who disappeared occasionally into the jungle or went skimming wildly across the water. Even Alvin, to whom everything was still so new, could feel that the forest had a fascination not possessed by the smaller, more cultivated woods of northern Lys. Few trees were alike; most of them were in various stages of devolution and some had reverted through the ages almost to their original, natural forms. Many were obviously not of Earth at all—probably not even of the Solar System. Watching like sentinels over the lesser trees were giant sequoias, three or four hundred feet high. Once they had been called the oldest things on Earth; they were still a little older than Man.

The river was widening now; ever and again it opened into small lakes, upon which tiny islands lay at anchor. There were insects here, brilliantly colored creatures swinging to and fro over the surface of the water. Once, despite Hilvar's commands, Krif darted away to join his distant cousins. He disappeared instantly in a cloud of glittering wings, and the sound of angry buzzing floated toward them. A moment later the cloud erupted and Krif came back across the water, almost too quickly for the eye to follow. Thereafter he kept very close to Hilvar and did not stray again.

Toward evening they caught occasional glimpses of the mountains ahead. The river that had been so faithful a guide was flowing sluggishly now, as if it too were nearing the end of its journey. But it was clear that they could not reach the mountains by nightfall; well before sunset the forest had become so dark that further progress was impossible. The great trees lay in pools of shadow, and a cold wind was sweeping through the leaves. Alvin and Hilvar settled down for the night beside a giant redwood whose topmost branches were still ablaze with sunlight.

When at last the hidden sun went down, the light still lingered on the dancing waters. The two explorers—for such they now considered themselves, and such indeed they were—lay in the gathering gloom, watching the river and thinking of all that they had seen. Presently Alvin felt once again steal over him that sense of delicious drowsiness he had known for the first time on the previous night, and he gladly resigned himself to sleep. It might not be needed in the effortless life of Diaspar, but he welcomed it here. In the final moment before unconsciousness overcame him, he found himself wondering who last had come this way, and how long since.

The sun was high when they left the forest and stood at last before the mountain walls of Lys. Ahead of them the ground rose steeply to the sky in waves of barren rock. Here the river came to an end as spectacular as its beginning, for the ground opened in its path and it sank roaring from sight. Alvin wondered what happened to it, and through what subterranean caves it traveled before it emerged again into the light of day. Perhaps the lost oceans of Earth still existed, far down in the eternal darkness, and this ancient river still felt the call that drew it to the sea.

For a moment Hilvar stood looking at the whirlpool and the broken land beyond. Then he pointed to a gap in the hills.

"Shalmirane lies in that direction," he said confidently. Alvin did not ask how he knew; he assumed that Hilvar's mind had made brief contact with that of a friend many miles away, and the information he needed had been silently passed to him.

It did not take long to reach the gap, and when they had passed through it they found themselves facing a curious plateau with gently sloping sides. Alvin felt no tiredness now, and no fear—only a taut expectancy and a sense of approaching adventure. What he would discover, he had no conception. That he would discover something he did not doubt at all.

As they approached the summit, the nature of the ground altered abruptly. The lower slopes had consisted of porous, volcanic stone, piled here and there in great mounds of slag. Now the surface turned suddenly to hard, glassy sheets, smooth and treacherous, as if the rock had once run in molten rivers down the mountain.

The rim of the plateau was almost at their feet. Hilvar reached it first, and a few seconds later Alvin overtook him and stood speechless at his side. For they stood on the edge, not of the plateau they had expected, but of a giant bowl half a mile deep and three miles in diameter. Ahead of them the ground plunged steeply downward, slowly leveling out at the bottom of the valley and rising again, more and more steeply, to the opposite rim. The lowest part of the bowl was occupied by a circular lake, the surface of which trembled continually, as if agitated by incessant waves.

Although it lay in the full glare of the sun, the whole of that great depression was ebon black. What material formed the crater, Alvin and Hilvar could not even guess, but it was black as the rock of a world that had never known a sun. Nor was that all, for lying beneath their feet and ringing the entire crater was a seamless band of metal, some hundred feet wide, tarnished by immeasurable age but still showing no slightest sign of corrosion.

As their eyes grew accustomed to the unearthly scene, Alvin and Hilvar realized that the blackness of the bowl was not as absolute as they had thought. Here and there, so fugitive that they could only see them indirectly, tiny explosions of light were flickering in the ebon walls. They came at random, vanishing as soon as they were born, like the reflections of stars on a broken sea.

"It's wonderful!" gasped Alvin. "But what *is* it?"

"It looks like a reflector of some kind."

"But it's so black!"

"Only to our eyes, remember. We do not know what radiations they used."

"But surely there must be more than this! Where *is* the fortress?"

Hilvar pointed to the lake.

"Look carefully," he said.

Alvin stared through the quivering roof of the lake, trying to plumb the secrets it concealed within its depths. At first he could see nothing; then, in the shallows near its edge, he made out a faint reticulation of light and shade. He was able to trace the pattern out toward the center of the lake until the deepening water hid all further details.

The dark lake had engulfed the fortress. Down there lay the ruins of once mighty buildings, overthrown by time. Yet not all of them had been submerged, for on the far side of the crater Alvin now noticed piles of jumbled stones, and great blocks that must once have formed part of massive walls. The waters lapped around them, but had not yet risen far enough to complete their victory.

"We'll go around the lake," said Hilvar, speaking softly as if the majestic desolation had struck awe into his soul. "Perhaps we may find something in those ruins over there."

For the first few hundred yards the crater walls were so steep and smooth that it was difficult to stand upright, but after a while they reached the gentler slopes and could walk without difficulty. Near the border of the lake the smooth ebony of the surface was concealed by a thin layer of soil, which the winds of Lys must have brought here through the ages.

A quarter of a mile away, titanic blocks of stone were piled one upon the other, like the discarded toys of an infant giant. Here, a section of a massive wall was still recognizable; there, two carven obelisks marked what had once been a mighty entrance. Everywhere grew mosses and creeping plants, and tiny stunted trees. Even the wind was hushed.

So Alvin and Hilvar came to the ruins of Shalmirane. Against those walls, and against the energies they had housed, forces that could shatter a world to dust had flamed and thundered and been utterly defeated. Once these peaceful skies had blazed with fires torn from the hearts of suns, and the mountains of Lys must have quailed like living things beneath the fury of their masters.

No one had ever captured Shalmirane. But now the fortress, the impregnable fortress, had fallen at last—captured and destroyed by the patient tendrils of the ivy, the generations of blindly burrowing worms, and the slowly rising waters of the lake.

Overawed by its majesty, Alvin and Hilvar walked in silence toward the colossal wreck. They passed into the shadow of a broken wall, and entered a canyon where the mountains of stone had split asunder. Before them lay the lake, and presently they stood with the dark water lapping at their feet. Tiny waves, no more than a few inches high, broke endlessly upon the narrow shore.

Hilvar was the first to speak, and his voice held a hint of uncertainty which made Alvin glance at him in sudden surprise.

"There's something here I don't understand," he said slowly. "There's no wind, so what causes these ripples? The water should be perfectly still."

Before Alvin could think of any reply, Hilvar dropped to the ground, turned his head on one side, and immersed his right ear in the water. Alvin wondered what he hoped to discover in such a ludicrous position; then he realized that he was listening. With some repugnance—for the rayless waters looked singularly uninviting—he followed Hilvar's example.

The first shock of coldness lasted only for a second; when it passed he could hear, faint but distinct, a steady, rhythmic throbbing. It was as if he could hear, from far down in the depths of the lake, the beating of a giant heart.

They shook the water from their hair and stared at each other with silent surmise. Neither liked to say what he thought—that the lake was alive.

"It would be best," said Hilvar presently, "if we searched among these ruins and kept away from the lake."

"Do you think there's something down there?" asked Alvin, pointing to the enigmatic ripples that were still breaking against his feet. "Could it be dangerous?"

"Nothing that possesses a mind is dangerous," Hilvar replied. (Is that true? thought Alvin. What of the Invaders?) "I can detect no thoughts of any kind here, but I do not believe we are alone. It is very strange."

They walked slowly back toward the ruins of the fortress, each carrying in his mind the sound of that steady, muffled pulsing. It seemed to Alvin that mystery was piling upon mystery, and that for all his efforts he was getting further and further from any understanding of the truths he sought.

It did not seem that the ruins could teach them anything, but they searched carefully among the piles of rubble and the great mounds of stone. Here, perhaps, lay the graves of buried machines—the machines that had done their work so long ago. They would be useless now, thought Alvin, if the Invaders returned. Why had they never come back? But that was yet another mystery: he had enough enigmas to deal with—there was no need to seek for any more.

A few yards from the lake they found a small clearing among the rubble. It had been covered with weeds, but they were now blackened and charred by tremendous heat, so that they crumbled to ashes as Alvin and Hilvar approached, smearing their legs with streaks of charcoal. At the center of the clearing stood a metal tripod, firmly anchored to the ground, and supporting a circular ring which was tilted on its axis so that it pointed to a spot halfway up the sky. At first sight it seemed that the ring enclosed nothing; then, as Alvin looked more carefully, he saw that it was filled with a faint haze that tormented the eye by lurking at the edge of the visible spectrum. It was the glow of power, and from this mechanism, he did not doubt, had come the explosion of light that had lured them to Shalmirane.

They did not venture any closer, but stood looking at the machine from a safe distance. They were on the right track, thought Alvin; now it only remained to discover who, or what, had set this apparatus here, and what their purpose might be. That tilted ring—it was clearly aimed out into space. Had the flash they had observed been some kind of signal? That was a thought which had breath-taking implications.

"Alvin," said Hilvar suddenly, his voice quiet but urgent, "we have visitors."

Alvin spun on his heels and found himself staring at a triangle of lidless eyes. That, at least, was his first impression; then behind the staring eyes he saw the outlines of a small but complex machine. It was hanging in the air a few feet above the ground, and it was like no robot he had ever before seen.

Once the initial surprise had worn off, he felt himself the complete master of the situation. All his life he had given orders to machines, and the fact that this one was unfamiliar was of no importance. For that matter, he had never seen more than a few per cent of the robots that provided his daily needs in Diaspar.

"Can you speak?" he asked.

There was silence.

"Is anyone controlling you?"

Still silence.

"Go away. Come here. Rise. Fall."

None of the conventional control thoughts produced any effect. The machine remained contemptuously inactive. That suggested two possibilities. It was either too unintelligent to understand him or it was very intelligent indeed, with its own powers of choice and volition. In that case, he must treat it as an equal. Even then he might underestimate it, but it would bear him no resentment, for conceit was not a vice from which robots often suffered.

Hilvar could not help laughing at Alvin's obvious discomfiture. He was just about to suggest that he should take over the task of communicating, when the words died on his lips. The stillness of Shalmirane was shattered by an ominous and utterly unmistakable sound—the gurgling splash of a very large body emerging from water.

It was the second time since he had left Diaspar that Alvin wished he were at home. Then he remembered that this was not the spirit in which to meet adventure, and he began to walk slowly but deliberately toward the lake.

The creature now emerging from the dark water seemed a monstrous parody, in living matter, of the robot that was still subjecting them to its silent scrutiny. That same equilateral arrangement of eyes could be no coincidence; even the pattern of tentacles and little jointed limbs had been roughly reproduced. Beyond that, however, the resemblance ceased. The robot did not possess—it obviously did not require—the fringe of delicate, feathery palps which beat the water with a steady rhythm, the stubby multiple legs on which the beast was humping itself ashore, or the ventilating inlets, if that was what they were, which now wheezed fitfully in the thin air.

Most of the creature's body remained in the water; only the first ten feet reared itself into what was clearly an alien element. The entire beast was about fifty feet long, and even anyone with no knowledge of biology would have realized that there was something altogether wrong about it. It had an extraordinary air of improvisation and careless design, as if its components had been manufactured without much forethought and thrown roughly together when the need arose.

Despite its size and their initial doubts, neither Alvin nor Hilvar felt the slightest nervousness once they had had a clear look at the dweller in the lake. There was an engaging clumsiness about the creature which made it quite impossible to regard it as a serious menace, even if there was any reason to suppose it might be dangerous. The human race had long ago overcome its childhood terror of the merely alien in appearance. That was a fear which could no longer survive after the first contact with friendly extraterrestrial races.

"Let me deal with this," said Hilvar quietly. "I'm used to handling animals."

"But this isn't an animal," whispered Alvin in return. "I'm sure it's intelligent, and owns that robot."

"The robot may own *it*. In any case, its mentality must be very strange. I can still detect no sign of thought. Hello—what's happening?"

The monster had not moved from its half-raised position at the water's edge, which it seemed to be maintaining with considerable effort. But a semitransparent membrane had begun to form at the center of the triangle of eyes—a membrane that pulsed and quivered and presently started to emit audible sounds. They were low-pitched, resonant boomings which created no intelligible words, though it was obvious that the creature was trying to speak to them.

It was painful to watch this desperate attempt at communication. For several minutes the creature struggled in vain; then, quite suddenly, it seemed to realize that it had made a mistake. The throbbing membrane contracted in size, and the sounds it emitted rose several octaves in frequency until they entered the spectrum of normal speech. Recognizable words began to form, though they were still interspersed with gibberish. It was as if the creature was remembering a vocabulary it had known long ago but had had no occasion to use for many years.

Hilvar tried to give what assistance he could.

"We can understand you now," he said, speaking slowly and distinctly. "Can we help you? We saw the light you made. It brought us here from Lys."

At the word "Lys" the creature seemed to droop as if it had suffered some bitter disappointment.

"Lys," it repeated; it could not manage the "s" very well, so that the word sounded like "Lyd." "Always from Lys. No one else ever comes. We call the Great Ones, but they do not hear."

"Who are the Great Ones?" asked Alvin, leaning forward eagerly. The delicate, ever-moving palps waved briefly toward the sky.

"The Great Ones," it said. "From the planets of eternal day. They will come. The Master promised us."

This did not seem to make matters any clearer. Before Alvin could continue his cross-examination, Hilvar intervened again. His questioning was so patient, so sympathetic, and yet so penetrating that Alvin knew better than to interrupt, despite his eagerness. He did not like to admit that Hilvar was his superior in intelligence, but there was no doubt that his flair for handling animals extended even to this fantastic being. What was more, it seemed to respond to him. Its speech became more distinct as the conversation proceeded, and where at first it had been brusque to the point of rudeness, it presently elaborated its answers and volunteered information on its own.

Alvin lost all consciousness of the passage of time as Hilvar pieced together the incredible story. They could not discover the whole truth; there was endless room for conjecture and debate. As the creature answered Hilvar's questions ever more and more willingly, its appearance began to change. It slumped back into the lake, and the stubby legs that had been supporting it seemed to dissolve into the rest of its body. Presently a still more extraordinary change occurred; the three huge eyes slowly closed, shrank to pinpoints, and vanished completely. It was as if the creature had seen all that it wished to for the moment, and therefore had no further use for eyes.

Other and more subtle alterations were continually taking place, and eventually almost all that remained above the surface of the water was the vibrating diaphragm through which the creature spoke. Doubtless this too would be dissolved back into the original amorphous mass of protoplasm when it was no longer required.

Alvin found it hard to believe that intelligence could reside in so unstable a form—and his biggest surprise was yet to come. Though it seemed obvious that the creature was not of terrestrial origin, it was some time before even Hilvar, despite his greater knowledge of biology, realized the type of organism they were dealing with. It was not a single entity; in all their conversations with it, it always referred to itself as "we." In fact, it was nothing less than a colony of independent creatures, organized and controlled by unknown forces.

Animals of a remotely similar type—the medusae, for example—had once flourished in the ancient oceans of Earth. Some of them had been of great size, trailing their translucent bodies and forests of stinging tentacles over fifty or a hundred feet of water. But none of them had attained even the faintest flicker of intelligence, beyond the power to react to simple stimuli.

There was certainly intelligence here, though it was a failing, degenerating intelligence. Never was Alvin to forget this unearthly meeting, as Hilvar slowly pieced together the story of the Master, while the protean polyp groped for unfamiliar words, the dark lake lapped at the ruins of Shalmirane, and the trioptic robot watched them with unwavering eyes.

THIRTEEN

The Master had come to Earth amid the chaos of the Transition Centuries, when the Galactic Empire was crumbling but the lines of communication among the stars had not yet completely broken. He had been of human origin, though his home was a planet circling one of the Seven Suns. While still a young man, he had been forced to leave his native world, and its memory had haunted him all his life. His expulsion he blamed on vindictive enemies, but the fact was that he suffered from an incurable malady which, it seemed, attacked only Homo sapiens among all the intelligent races of the Universe. That disease was religious mania.

Throughout the earlier part of its history, the human race had brought forth an endless succession of prophets, seers, messiahs, and evangelists who convinced themselves and their followers that to them alone were the secrets of the Universe revealed. Some of them succeeded in establishing religions that survived for many generations and influenced billions of men; others were forgotten even before their deaths.

The rise of science, which with monotonous regularity refuted the cosmologies of the prophets and produced miracles which they could never match, eventually destroyed all these faiths. It did not destroy the awe, nor the reverence and humility, which all intelligent beings felt as they contemplated the stupendous Universe in which they found themselves. What it did weaken, and finally obliterate, were the countless religions, each of which claimed, with unbelievable arrogance, that it was the sole repository of the truth and that its millions of rivals and predecessors were all mistaken.

Yet, though they never possessed any real power once humanity had reached a very elementary level of civilization, all down the ages isolated cults had continued to appear, and however fantastic their creeds they had always managed to attract some disciples. They thrived with particular strength during periods of confusion and disorder, and it was not surprising that the Transition Centuries had seen a great outburst of irrationality. When reality was depressing, men tried to console themselves with myths.

The Master, even if he was expelled from his own world, did not leave it unprovided. The Seven Suns had been the center of galactic power and science, and he must have possessed influential friends. He had made his hegira in a small but speedy ship, reputed to be one of the fastest ever built. With him into exile he had taken another of the ultimate products of galactic science—the robot that was looking at Alvin and Hilvar even now.

No one had ever known the full talents and functions of this machine. To some extent, indeed, it had become the Master's alter ego; without it, the religion of the Great Ones would probably have collapsed after the Master's death. Together they had roved among the star clouds on a zigzag trail which led at last, certainly not by accident, back to the world from which the Master's ancestors had sprung.

Entire libraries had been written about that saga, each work therein inspiring a host of commentaries until, by a kind of chain reaction, the original volumes were lost beneath mountains of exegesis and annotation. The Master had stopped at many worlds, and made disciples among many races. His personality must have been an immensely powerful one for it to have inspired humans and nonhumans alike, and there was no doubt that a religion of such wide appeal must have contained much that was fine and noble. Probably the Master was the most successful—as he was also the last—of all mankind's messiahs. None of his predecessors could have won so many converts or had their teachings carried across such gulfs of time and space.

What those teachings were neither Alvin nor Hilvar could ever discover with any accuracy. The great polyp did its desperate best to convey them, but many of the words it used were meaningless and it had a habit of repeating sentences or whole speeches with a kind of swift mechanical delivery that made them very hard to follow. After a while Hilvar did his best to steer the conversation away from these meaningless morasses of theology in order to concentrate on ascertainable facts.

The Master and a band of his most faithful followers had arrived on Earth in the days before the cities had passed away, and while the Port of Diaspar was still open to the stars. They must have come in ships of many kinds; the polyps, for example, in one filled with the waters of the sea which was their natural home. Whether the movement was well received on Earth was not certain; but at least it met no violent opposition, and after further wanderings it set up its final retreat among the forests and mountains of Lys.

At the close of his long life, the Master's thoughts had turned once more toward the home from which he had been exiled, and he had asked his friends to carry him out into the open so that he could watch the stars. He had waited, his strength waning, until the culmination of the Seven Suns, and toward the end he babbled many things which were to inspire yet more libraries of interpretation in future ages. Again and again he spoke of the "Great Ones" who had now left this universe of space and matter but who would surely one day return, and he charged his followers to remain to greet them when they came. Those were his last rational words. He was never again conscious of his surroundings, but just before the end he uttered one phrase that had come down the ages to haunt the minds of all who heard it: "*It is lovely to watch the colored shadows on the planets of eternal light.*" Then he died.

At the Master's death, many of his followers broke away, but others remained faithful to his teachings, which they slowly elaborated through the ages. At first they believed that the Great Ones, whoever they were, would soon return, but that hope faded with the passing centuries. The story here grew very confused, and it seemed that truth and legend were inextricably intertwined. Alvin had only a vague picture of generations of fanatics, waiting for some great event which they did not understand to take place at some unknown future date.

The Great Ones never returned. Slowly the power of the movement failed as death and disillusion robbed it of its disciples. The short-lived human followers were the first to go, and there was something supremely ironic in the fact that the very last adherent of a human prophet was a creature utterly unlike Man.

The great polyp had become the Master's last disciple for a very simple reason. It was immortal. The billions of individual cells from which its body was built would die, but before that happened they would have reproduced themselves. At long intervals the monster would disintegrate into its myriad separate cells, which would go their own way and multiply by fission if their environment was suitable. During this phase the polyp did not exist as a self-conscious, intelligent entity—and here Alvin was irresistibly reminded of the manner in which the inhabitants of Diaspar spent their quiescent millenniums in the city's Memory Banks.

In due time some mysterious biological force brought the scattered components together again, and the polyp began a new cycle of existence. It returned to awareness and recollected its earlier lives, though often imperfectly since accident sometimes damaged the cells that carried the delicate patterns of memory.

Perhaps no other form of life could have kept faith so long to a creed otherwise forgotten for a billion years. In a sense, the great polyp was a helpless victim of its biological nature. Because of its immortality, it could not change, but was forced to repeat eternally the same invariant pattern.

The religion of the Great Ones, in its later stages, had become identified with a veneration of the Seven Suns. When the Great Ones stubbornly refused to appear, attempts were made to signal their distant home. Long ago the signaling had become no more than a meaningless ritual, now maintained by an animal that had forgotten how to learn and a robot that had never known how to forget.

As the immeasurably ancient voice died away into the still air, Alvin found himself overwhelmed by a surge of pity. The misplaced devotion, the loyalty that had held to its futile course while suns and planets passed away—he could never have believed such a tale had he not seen the evidence before his eyes. More than ever before the extent of his ignorance saddened him. A tiny fragment of the past had been illuminated for a little while, but now the darkness had closed over it again.

The history of the Universe must be a mass of such disconnected threads, and no one could say which were important and which were trivial. This fantastic tale of the Master and the Great Ones seemed like another of the countless legends that had somehow survived from the civilizations of the Dawn. Yet the very existence of the huge polyp, and of the silently watching robot, made it impossible for Alvin to dismiss the whole story as a fable built of self-delusion upon a foundation of madness.

What was the relationship, he wondered, between these two entities, which though so different in every possible way had maintained their extraordinary partnership over such aeons of time? He was somehow certain that the robot was much the more important of the two. It had been the confidant of the Master and must still know all his secrets.

Alvin looked at the enigmatic machine that still regarded him so steadily. Why would it not speak? What thoughts were passing through its complicated and perhaps alien mind? Yet, surely, if it had been designed to serve the Master, its mind would not be altogether alien, and it should respond to human orders.

As he thought of all the secrets which that stubbornly mute machine must possess, Alvin felt a curiosity so great that it verged upon greed. It seemed unfair that such knowledge should be wasted and hidden from the world; here must lie wonders beyond even the ken of the Central Computer in Diaspar.

"Why won't your robot speak to us?" he asked the polyp, when Hilvar had momentarily run out of questions. The answer was one he had half expected.

"It was against the Master's wishes for it to speak with any voice but his, and his voice is silent now."

"But it will obey you?"

"Yes; the Master placed it in our charge. We can see through its eyes, wherever it goes. It watches over the machines that preserve this lake and keep its water pure. Yet it would be truer to call it our partner than our servant."

Alvin thought this over. An idea, still vague and half-formed, was beginning to take shape in his mind. Perhaps it was inspired by pure lust for knowledge and power; when he looked back on this moment he could never be certain just what his motives were. They might be largely selfish, but they also contained some element of compassion. If he could do so, he would like to break this futile sequence and release these creatures from their fantastic fate. He was not sure what could be done about the polyp, but it might be possible to cure the robot of its insanity and at the same time to release its priceless, pent-up memories.

"Are you certain," he said slowly, talking to the polyp but aiming his words at the robot, "that you are really carrying out the Master's wishes by remaining here? He desired the world to know of his teachings, but they have been lost while you hide here in Shalmirane. It was only by chance that we discovered you, and there may be many others who would like to hear the doctrine of the Great Ones."

Hilvar glanced at him sharply, obviously uncertain of his intentions. The polyp seemed agitated, and the steady beating of its respiratory equipment faltered for a few seconds. Then it replied, in a voice not altogether under control: "We have discussed this problem for many years. But we cannot leave Shalmirane, so the world must come to us, no matter how long it takes."

"I have a better idea," said Alvin eagerly. "It is true that *you* may have to stay here in the lake, but there is no reason why your companion should not come with us. He can return whenever he wishes or whenever you need him. Many things have changed since the Master died—things which you should know about, but which you can never understand if you stay here."

The robot never moved, but in its agony of indecision the polyp sank completely below the surface of the lake and remained there for several minutes. Perhaps it was having a soundless argument with its colleague; several times it began to re-emerge, thought better of it, and sank into the water again. Hilvar took this opportunity to exchange a few words with Alvin.

"I'd like to know what you are trying to do," he said softly, his voice half-bantering and half-serious. "Or don't you know yourself?"

"Surely," replied Alvin, "you feel sorry for these poor creatures? Don't you think it would be a kindness to rescue them?"

"I do, but I've learned enough about you to be fairly certain that altruism isn't one of your dominant emotions. You must have some other motive."

Alvin smiled ruefully. Even if Hilvar did not read his mind—and he had no reason to suppose that he did—he could undoubtedly read his character.

"Your people have remarkable mental powers," he replied, trying to divert the conversation from dangerous ground. "I think they might be able to do something for the robot, if not for this animal." He spoke very softly, lest he be overheard. The precaution might have been a useless one, but if the robot did intercept his remarks it gave no sign of it.

Fortunately, before Hilvar could press the inquiry any further, the polyp emerged once more from the lake. In the last few minutes it had become a good deal smaller and its movements were more disorganized. Even as Alvin watched, a segment of its complex, translucent body broke away from the main bulk and then disintegrated into multitudes of smaller sections, which swiftly dispersed. The creature was beginning to break up before their eyes.

Its voice, when it spoke again, was very erratic and hard to understand.

"Next cycle starting," it jerked out in a kind of fluctuating whisper. "Did not expect it so soon—only few minutes left—stimulation too great—cannot hold together much longer."

Alvin and Hilvar stared at the creature in horrified fascination. Even though the process they were watching was a natural one, it was not pleasant to watch an intelligent creature apparently in its death throes. They also felt an obscure sense of guilt; it was irrational to have the feeling, since it was of no great importance *when* the polyp began another cycle, but they realized that the unusual effort and excitement caused by their presence was responsible for this premature metamorphosis.

Alvin realized that he would have to act quickly or his opportunity would be gone—perhaps only for a few years, perhaps for centuries.

"What have you decided?" he said eagerly. "Is the robot coming with us?"

There was an agonizing pause while the polyp tried to force its dissolving body to obey its will. The speech diaphragm fluttered, but no audible sound came from it. Then, as if in a despairing gesture of farewell, it waved its delicate palps feebly and let them fall back into the water, where they promptly broke adrift and went floating out into the lake. In a matter of minutes, the transformation was over. Nothing of the creature larger than an inch across remained. The water was full of tiny, greenish specks, which seemed to have a life and mobility of their own and which rapidly disappeared into the vastness of the lake.

The ripples on the surface had now altogether died away, and Alvin knew that the steady pulse beat that had sounded in the depths would now be stilled. The lake was dead again—or so it seemed. But that was an illusion; one day the unknown forces that had never failed to do their duty in the past would exert themselves again, and the polyp would be reborn. It was a strange and wonderful phenomenon, yet was it so much stranger than the organization of the human body, itself a vast colony of separate, living cells?

Alvin wasted little effort on such speculations. He was oppressed by his sense of failure, even though he had never clearly conceived the goal he was aiming for. A dazzling opportunity had been missed and might never again return. He stared sadly out across the lake, and it was some time before his mind registered the message which Hilvar was speaking quietly in his ear.

"Alvin," his friend said softly. "I think you have won your point."

He spun swiftly on his heels. The robot, which until now had been floating aloofly in the distance, never approaching within twenty feet of them, had moved up in silence and was now poised a yard above his head. Its unmoving eyes, with their wide angles of vision, gave no indication of its direction of interest. Probably it saw the entire hemisphere in front of it with equal clarity, but Alvin had little doubt that its attention was now focused upon him.

It was waiting for his next move. To some extent, at least, it was now under his control. It might follow him to Lys, perhaps even to Diaspar—unless it changed its mind. Until then, he was its probationary master.

FOURTEEN

The journey back to Airlee lasted almost three days—partly because Alvin, for his own reasons, was in no hurry to return. The physical exploration of Lys had now taken second place to a more important and exciting project; he was slowly making contact with the strange, obsessed intelligence which had now become his companion.

He suspected that the robot was trying to use him for its own purposes, which would be no more than poetic justice. What its motives were he could never be quite certain, since it still stubbornly refused to speak to him. For some reason of his own—perhaps fear that it might reveal too many of his secrets—the Master must have placed very efficient blocks upon its speech circuits, and Alvin's attempts to clear them were completely unsuccessful. Even indirect questioning of the "If you say nothing I shall assume you mean 'Yes'" type failed; the robot was much too intelligent to be taken in by such simple tricks.

In other respects, however, it was more co-operative. It would obey any orders that did not require it to speak or reveal information. After a while Alvin found that he could control it, as he could direct the robots in Diaspar, by thought alone. This was a great step forward, and a little later the creature—it was hard to think of it as a mere machine—relaxed its guard still further and allowed him to see through its eyes. It did not object, it seemed, to such passive forms of communication, but it blocked all attempts at closer intimacy.

Hilvar's existence it ignored completely; it would obey none of his commands, and its mind was closed to all his probing. At first this was something of a disappointment to Alvin, who had hoped that Hilvar's greater mental powers would enable him to force open this treasure chest of hidden memories. It was not until later that he realized the advantage of possessing a servant who would obey no one else in all the world.

The member of the expedition who strongly objected to the robot was Krif. Perhaps he imagined that he now had a rival, or perhaps he disapproved, on general principles, of anything that flew without wings. When no one was looking, he had made several direct assaults on the robot, which had infuriated him still further by taking not the slightest notice of his attacks. Eventually Hilvar had been able to calm him down, and on the homeward journey in the ground-car he seemed to have resigned himself to the situation. Robot and insect escorted the vehicle as it glided silently through forest and field—each keeping to the side of its respective master and pretending that its rival was not there.

Seranis was already waiting for them as the car floated into Airlee. It was impossible, Alvin thought, to surprise these people. Their interlinked minds kept them in touch with everything that was happening in their land. He wondered how they had reacted to his adventures in Shalmirane, which presumably everyone in Lys now knew about.

Seranis seemed to be worried and more uncertain than he had ever seen her before, and Alvin remembered the choice that now lay before him. In the excitement of the last few days he had almost forgotten it; he did not like to spend energy worrying about problems that still lay in the future. But the future was now upon him; he must decide in which of these two worlds he wished to live.

The voice of Seranis was troubled when she began to speak, and Alvin had the sudden impression that something had gone awry with the plans that Lys had been making for him. What had been happening during his absence? Had emissaries gone into Diaspar to tamper with Khedron's mind—and had they failed in their duty?

"Alvin," began Seranis, "there are many things I did not tell you before, but which you must now learn if you are to understand our actions.

"You know one of the reasons for the isolation of our two races. The fear of the Invaders, that dark shadow in the depths of every human mind, turned your people against the world and made them lose themselves in their own dreams. Here in Lys that fear has never been so great, though we bore the burden of the final attack. We had a better reason for our actions, and what we did, we did with open eyes.

"Long ago, Alvin, men sought immortality and at last achieved it. They forgot that a world which had banished death must also banish life. The power to extend his life indefinitely might bring contentment to the individual, but brought stagnation to the race. Ages ago we sacrificed our immortality, but Diaspar still follows the false dream. That is why our ways parted—*and why they must never meet again.*"

Although the words had been more than half expected, the blow seemed none the less for its anticipation. Yet Alvin refused to admit the failure of all his plans—half-formed though they were—and only part of his brain was listening to Seranis now. He understood and noted all her words, but the conscious portion of his mind was retracing the road to Diaspar, trying to imagine every obstacle that could be placed in his way.

Seranis was clearly unhappy. Her voice was almost pleading as it spoke, and Alvin knew that she was talking not only to him but to her son. She must be aware of the understanding and affection that had grown up between them during the days they had spent together. Hilvar was watching his mother intently as she spoke, and it seemed to Alvin that his gaze held not merely concern but also more than a trace of censure.

"We do not wish to make you do anything against your will, but you must surely realize what it would mean if our people met again. Between our culture and yours is a gulf as great as any that ever separated Earth from its ancient colonies. Think of this one fact, Alvin. You and Hilvar are now of nearly the same age—*but both he and I will have been dead for centuries while you are still a youth.* And this is only your first in an infinite series of lives."

The room was very quiet, so quiet that Alvin could hear the strange, plaintive cries of unknown beasts in the fields beyond the village. Presently he said, almost in a whisper: "What do you want me to do?"

"We hoped that we could give you the choice of staying here or returning to Diaspar, but now that is impossible. Too much has happened for us to leave the decision in your hands. Even in the short time you have been here, your influence has been highly disturbing. No, I am not reproving you; I am sure you intended no harm. But it would have been best to leave the creatures you met in Shalmirane to their own destiny.

"And as for Diaspar—" Seranis gave a gesture of annoyance. "Too many people know where you have gone; we did not act in time. What is most serious, the man who helped you discover Lys has vanished; neither your Council nor our agents can discover him, so he remains a potential danger to our security. Perhaps you are surprised that I am telling you all this, but it is quite safe for me to do so. I am afraid we have only one choice before us; we must send you back to Diaspar with a false set of memories. Those memories have been constructed with great care, and when you return home you will know nothing of us. You will believe that you have had rather dull and dangerous adventures in gloomy underground caverns, where the roofs continually collapsed behind you and you kept alive only through eating unappetizing weeds and drinking from occasional springs. For the rest of your life you will believe this to be the truth, and everyone in Diaspar will accept your story. There will be no mystery, then, to lure any future explorers; they will think they know all there is to be known about Lys."

Seranis paused and looked at Alvin with anxious eyes. "We are very sorry that this is necessary and ask your forgiveness while you still remember us. You may not accept our verdict, but we know many facts that are hidden from you. At least you will have no regrets, for you will believe that you have discovered all that there is to be found."

Alvin wondered if that was true. He was not sure that he would ever settle down to the routine of life in Diaspar, even when he had convinced himself that nothing worthwhile existed beyond its walls. What was more, he had no intention of putting the matter to the test.

"When do you wish me to undergo this—treatment?" Alvin asked.

"Immediately. We are ready now. Open your mind to me, as you did before, and you will know nothing until you find yourself back in Diaspar."

Alvin was silent for a while. Then he said quietly: "I would like to say good-by to Hilvar."

Seranis nodded.

"I understand. I will leave you here for a while and return when you are ready." She walked over to the stairs that led down to the interior of the house, and left them alone on the roof.

It was some time before Alvin spoke to his friend; he felt a great sadness, yet also an unbroken determination not to permit the wreck of all his hopes. He looked once more down upon the village where he had found a measure of happiness and which he might never see again if those who were ranged behind Seranis had their way. The ground-car was still standing beneath one of the wide-branching trees, with the patient robot hanging in the air above it. A few children had gathered around to examine this strange newcomer, but none of the adults seemed in the least interested.

"Hilvar," said Alvin abruptly, "I'm very sorry about this."

"So am I," Hilvar answered, his voice unstable with emotion. "I had hoped that you could have remained here."

"Do you think that what Seranis wants to do is right?"

"Do not blame my mother. She is only doing as she is asked," replied Hilvar. Though he had not answered his question, Alvin had not the heart to ask it again. It was unfair to put such a strain on his friend's loyalty.

"Then tell me this," asked Alvin, "how could your people stop me if I tried to leave with my memories untouched?"

"It would be easy. If you tried to escape, we would take control of your mind and force you to come back."

Alvin had expected as much and was not discouraged. He wished that he could confide in Hilvar, who was obviously upset by their impending separation, but he dared not risk the failure of his plans. Very carefully, checking every detail, he traced out the only road that could lead him back to Diaspar on the terms he wished.

There was one risk which he had to face, and against which he could do nothing to protect himself. If Seranis broke her promise and dipped into his mind, all his careful preparations might be in vain.

He held out his hand to Hilvar, who grasped it firmly but seemed unable to speak.

"Let's go downstairs to meet Seranis," said Alvin. "I'd like to see some of the people in the village before I go."

Hilvar followed him silently into the peaceful coolness of the house and then out through the hallway and onto the ring of colored grass that surrounded the building. Seranis was waiting for them there, looking calm and resolute. She knew that Alvin was trying to hide something from her, and thought again of the precautions she had taken. As a man may flex his muscles before some great effort, she ran through the compulsion patterns she might have to use.

"Are you ready, Alvin?" she asked.

"Quite ready," replied Alvin, and there was a tone in his voice that made her look at him sharply.

"Then it will be best if you make your mind a blank, as you did before.

You will feel and know nothing after that, until you find yourself back in Diaspar."

Alvin turned to Hilvar and said in a quick whisper that Seranis could not hear: "Good-by, Hilvar. Don't worry–*I'll be back.*" Then he faced Seranis again.

"I don't resent what you are trying to do," he said. "No doubt you believe it is for the best, but I think you are wrong. Diaspar and Lys should not remain apart forever; one day they may need each other desperately. So I am going home with all that I have learned–*and I do not think that you can stop me.*"

He waited no longer, and it was just as well. Seranis never moved, but instantly he felt his body slipping from his control. The power that had brushed aside his own will was even greater than he had expected, and he realized that many hidden minds must be aiding Seranis. Helplessly he began to walk back into the house, and for an awful moment he thought his plan had failed.

Then there came a flash of steel and crystal, and metal arms closed swiftly around him. His body fought against them, as he had known that it must do, but his struggles were useless. The ground fell away beneath him and he caught a glimpse of Hilvar, frozen by surprise, with a foolish smile upon his face.

The robot was carrying him a dozen feet above the ground, much faster than a man could run. It took Seranis only a moment to understand his ruse, and his struggles died away as she relaxed her control. But she was not defeated yet, and presently there happened that which Alvin had feared and done his best to counteract.

There were now two separate entities fighting inside his mind, and one of them was pleading with the robot, begging it to set him down. The real Alvin waited, breathlessly, resisting only a little against forces he knew he could not hope to fight. He had gambled; there was no way of telling beforehand if his uncertain ally would obey orders as complex as those that he had given it. Under no circumstances, he had told the robot, must it obey any further commands of his until he was safely inside Diaspar. Those were the orders. If they were obeyed, Alvin had placed his fate beyond the reach of human interference.

Never hesitating, the machine raced on along the path he had so carefully mapped out for it. A part of him was still pleading angrily to be released, but he knew now that he was safe. And presently Seranis understood that too, for the forces inside his brain ceased to war with one another. Once more he was at peace, as ages ago an earlier wanderer had been when, lashed to the mast of his ship, he had heard the song of the Sirens die away across the wine-dark sea.

FIFTEEN

Alvin did not relax until the chamber of the moving ways was around him once more. There had still been the danger that the people of Lys might be able to stop, or even to reverse, the vehicle in which he was traveling, and bring him back helplessly to his starting point. But his return was an uneventful repetition of the outward trip; forty minutes after he had left Lys he was in the Tomb of Yarlan Zey.

The servants of the Council were waiting for him, dressed in the formal black robes which they had not worn for centuries. Alvin felt no surprise, and little alarm, at the presence of this reception committee. He had now overcome so many obstacles that one more made little difference. He had learned a great deal since leaving Diaspar, and with that knowledge had come a confidence verging upon arrogance. Moreover, he now had a powerful, if erratic, ally. The best minds of Lys had been unable to interfere with his plans; somehow, he believed that Diaspar could do no better.

There were rational grounds for this belief, but it was based partly upon something beyond reason—a faith in his destiny which had slowly been growing in Alvin's mind. The mystery of his origin, his success in doing what no earlier man had ever done, the way in which new vistas had opened up before him, and the manner in which obstacles had failed to halt him—all these things added to his self-confidence. Faith in one's own destiny was among the most valuable of the gifts which the gods could bestow upon a man, but Alvin did not know how many it had led to utter disaster.

"Alvin," said the leader of the city's proctors, "we have orders to accompany you wherever you go, until the Council has heard your case and rendered its verdict."

"With what offense am I charged?" asked Alvin. He was still exhilarated by the excitement and elation of his escape from Lys and could not yet take this new development very seriously. Presumably Khedron had talked; he felt a brief annoyance at the Jester for betraying his secret.

"No charge has been made," came the reply. "If necessary, one will be framed after you have been heard."

"And when will that be?"

"Very soon, I imagine." The proctor was obviously ill at ease and was not sure how to handle his unwelcome assignment. At one moment he would treat Alvin as a fellow citizen, and then he would remember his duties as a custodian and would adopt an attitude of exaggerated aloofness.

"This robot," he said abruptly, pointing to Alvin's companion, "where did it come from? Is it one of ours?"

"No," replied Alvin. "I found it in Lys, the country I have been to. I have brought it here to meet the Central Computer."

This calm statement produced a considerable commotion. The fact that there was something outside Diaspar was hard enough to accept, but that Alvin should have brought back one of its inhabitants and proposed to introduce it to the brain of the city was even worse. The proctors looked at each other with such helpless alarm that Alvin could hardly refrain from laughing at them.

As they walked back through the park, his escort keeping discreetly at the rear and talking among itself in agitated whispers, Alvin considered his next move. The first thing he must do was to discover exactly what had happened during his absence. Khedron, Seranis had told him, had vanished. There were countless places where a man could hide in Diaspar, and since the Jester's knowledge of the city was unsurpassed it was not likely that he would be found until he chose to reappear. Perhaps, thought Alvin, he could leave a message where Khedron would be bound to see it, and arrange a rendezvous. However, the presence of his guard might make that impossible.

He had to admit that the surveillance was very discreet. By the time he had reached his apartment, he had almost forgotten the existence of the proctors. He imagined that they would not interfere with his movements unless he attempted to leave Diaspar, and for the time being he had no intention of doing that. Indeed, he was fairly certain that it would be impossible to return to Lys by his original route. By this time, surely, the underground carrier system would have been put out of action by Seranis and her colleagues.

The proctors did not follow him into his room; they knew that there was only the one exit, and stationed themselves outside that. Having had no instructions regarding the robot, they let it accompany Alvin. It was not a machine which they had any desire to interfere with, since its alien construction was obvious. From its behavior they could not tell whether it was a passive servant of Alvin's or whether it was operating under its own volition. In view of this uncertainty, they were quite content to leave it severely alone.

Once the wall had sealed itself behind him, Alvin materialized his favorite divan and threw himself down upon it. Luxuriating in his familiar surroundings, he called out of the memory units his last efforts in painting and sculpture, and examined them with a critical eye. If they had failed to satisfy him before, they were doubly displeasing now, and he could take no further pride in them. The person who had created them no longer existed; into the few days he had been away from Diaspar, it seemed to Alvin that he had crowded the experience of a lifetime.

He canceled all these products of his adolescence, erasing them forever and not merely returning them to the Memory Banks. The room was empty again, apart from the couch on which he was reclining, and the robot that still watched with wide, unfathomable eyes. What did the robot think of Diaspar? wondered Alvin. Then he remembered that it was no stranger here, for it had known the city in the last days of its contact with the stars.

Not until he felt thoroughly at home once more did Alvin begin to call his friends. He began with Eriston and Etania, though out of a sense of duty rather than any real desire to see and speak to them again. He was not sorry when their communicators informed him that they were unavailable, but he left them both a brief message announcing his return. This was quite unnecessary, since by now the whole city would know that he was back. However, he hoped that they would appreciate his thoughtfulness; he was beginning to learn consideration, though he had not yet realized that, like most virtues, it had little merit unless it was spontaneous and unself-conscious.

Then, acting on a sudden impulse, he called the number that Khedron had given him so long ago in the Tower of Loranne. He did not, of course, expect an answer, but there was always the possibility that Khedron had left a message.

His guess was correct; but the message itself was shatteringly unexpected.

The wall dissolved, and Khedron was standing before him. The Jester looked tired and nervous, no longer the confident, slightly cynical person who had set Alvin on the path that led to Lys. There was a haunted look in his eyes, and he spoke as though he had very little time.

"Alvin," he began, "this is a recording. Only you can receive it, but you can make what use of it you wish. It will not matter to me.

"When I got back to the Tomb of Yarlan Zey, I found that Alystra had been following us. She must have told the Council that you had left Diaspar, and that I had helped you. Very soon the proctors were looking for me, and I decided to go into hiding. I am used to that—I have done it before when some of my jests failed to be appreciated." (There, thought Alvin, was a flash of the old Khedron.) "They could not have found me in a thousand years—but someone else nearly did. There are strangers in Diaspar, Alvin; they could only have come from Lys, and they are looking for me. I do not know what this means, and I do not like it. The fact that they nearly caught me, though they are in a city that must be strange to them, suggests that they possess telepathic powers. I could fight the Council, but this is an unknown peril which I do not care to face.

"I am therefore anticipating a step which I think the Council might well force upon me, since it has been threatened before. I am going where no one can follow, and where I shall escape whatever changes are now about to happen to Diaspar. Perhaps I am foolish to do this; that is something which only time can prove. I shall know the answer one day.

"By now you will have guessed that I have gone back into the Hall of Creation, into the safety of the Memory Banks. Whatever happens, I put my trust in the Central Computer and the forces it controls for the benefit of Diaspar. If anything tampers with the Central Computer, we are all lost. If not, I have nothing to fear.

"To me, only a moment will seem to pass before I walk forth into Diaspar again, fifty or a hundred thousand years from now. I wonder what sort of city I shall find? It will be strange if you are there; some day, I suppose, we will meet again. I cannot say whether I look forward to that meeting, or fear it.

"I have never understood you, Alvin, though there was a time when I was vain enough to think I did. Only the Central Computer knows the truth, as it knows the truth about those other Uniques who have appeared from time to time down the ages and then were seen no more. Have you discovered what happened to them?

"One reason, I suppose, why I am escaping into the future is because I am impatient. I want to see the results of what you have started, but I am anxious to miss the intermediate stages—which I suspect may be unpleasant. It will be interesting to see, in that world which will be around me in only a few minutes of apparent time from now, whether you are remembered as a creator or as a destroyer—or whether you are remembered at all.

"Good-by, Alvin. I had thought of giving you some advice, but I do not suppose you would take it. You will go your own way, as you always have, and your friends will be tools to use or discard as occasion suits.

"That is all. I can think of nothing more to say."

For a moment Khedron—the Khedron who no longer existed save as a pattern of electric charges in the memory cells of the city—looked at Alvin with resignation and, it seemed, with sadness. Then the screen was blank again.

Alvin remained motionless for a long time after the image of Khedron had faded. He was searching his soul as he had seldom done before in all his life, for he could not deny the truth of much that Khedron had said. When had he paused, in all his schemes and adventures, to consider the effect of what he was doing upon any of his friends? He had brought anxiety to them and might soon bring worse—all because of his insatiable curiosity and the urge to discover what should not be known.

He had never been fond of Khedron; the Jester's astringent personality prevented any close relationship, even if Alvin had desired it. Yet now, as he thought of Khedron's parting words, he was shaken with remorse. Because of his actions, the Jester had fled from this age into the unknown future.

But surely, thought Alvin, he had no need to blame himself for that. It proved only what he had already known—that Khedron was a coward. Perhaps he was no more of a coward than anyone else in Diaspar; he had the additional misfortune of possessing a powerful imagination. Alvin could accept some responsibility for his fate, but by no means all.

Who else in Diaspar had he harmed or distressed? He thought of Jeserac, his tutor, who had been patient with what must have been his most difficult pupil. He remembered all the little kindnesses that his parents had shown him over the years; now that he looked back upon them, there were more than he had imagined.

And he thought of Alystra. She had loved him, and he had taken that love or ignored it as he chose. Yet what else was he to have done? Would she have been any happier had he spurned her completely?

He understood now why he had never loved Alystra, or any of the women he had known in Diaspar. That was another lesson that Lys had taught him. Diaspar had forgotten many things, and among them was the true meaning of love. In Airlee he had watched the mothers dandling their children on their knees, and had himself felt that protective tenderness for all small and helpless creatures that is love's unselfish twin. Yet now there was no woman in Diaspar who knew or cared for what had once been the final aim of love.

There were no real emotions, no deep passions, in the immortal city. Perhaps such things only thrived because of their very transience, because they could not last forever and lay always under the shadow which Diaspar had banished.

That was the moment, if such a moment ever existed, when Alvin realized what his destiny must be. Until now he had been the unconscious agent of his own impulses. If he could have known so archaic an analogy, he might have compared himself to a rider on a runaway horse. It had taken him to many strange places, and might do so again, but in its wild galloping it had shown him its powers and taught him where he really wished to go.

Alvin's reverie was rudely interrupted by the chimes of the wall screen. The timbre of the sound told him at once that this was no incoming call, but that someone had arrived to see him. He gave the admission signal, and a moment later was facing Jeserac.

His tutor looked grave, but not unfriendly.

"I have been asked to take you to the Council, Alvin," he said. "It is waiting to hear you." Then Jeserac saw the robot and examined it curiously. "So this is the companion you have brought back from your travels. I think it had better come with us."

This suited Alvin very well. The robot had already extricated him from one dangerous situation, and he might have to call upon it again. He wondered what the machine had thought about the adventures and vicissitudes in which he had involved it, and wished for the thousandth time that he could understand what was going on inside its closely shuttered mind. Alvin had the impression that for the moment it had decided to watch, analyze, and draw its own conclusion, doing nothing of its own volition until it had judged the time was ripe. Then, perhaps quite suddenly, it might decide to act; and what it chose to do might not suit Alvin's plans. The only ally he possessed was bound to him by the most tenuous ties of self-interest and might desert him at any moment.

Alystra was waiting for them on the ramp that led out into the street. Even if Alvin had wished to blame her for whatever part she had played in revealing his secret, he did not have the heart to do so. Her distress was too obvious, and her eyes brimmed with tears as she ran up to greet him.

"Oh, Alvin!" she cried. "What are they going to do with you?"

Alvin took her hands in his with a tenderness that surprised them both.

"Don't worry, Alystra," he said. "Everything is going to be all right. After all, at the very worst the Council can only send me back to the Memory Banks—and somehow I don't think that will happen."

Her beauty and her unhappiness were so appealing that, even now, Alvin felt his body responding to her presence after its old fashion. But it was the lure of the body alone; he did not disdain it, but it was no longer enough. Gently he disengaged his hands and turned to follow Jeserac toward the Council Chamber.

Alystra's heart was lonely, but no longer bitter, as she watched him go. She knew now that she had not lost him, for he had never belonged to her. And with the acceptance of that knowledge, she had begun to put herself beyond the power of vain regrets.

Alvin scarcely noticed the curious or horrified glances of his fellow citizens as he and his retinue made their way through the familiar streets. He was marshaling the arguments he might have to use, and arranging his story in the form most favorable to himself. From time to time he assured himself that he was not in the least alarmed and that he was still master of the situation.

They waited only a few minutes in the anteroom, but it was long enough for Alvin to wonder why, if he was unafraid, his legs felt so curiously weak. He had known this sensation before when he had forced himself up the last slopes of that distant hill in Lys, where Hilvar had shown him the waterfall from whose summit they had seen the explosion of light that had drawn them to Shalmirane. He wondered what Hilvar was doing now, and if they would ever meet again. It was suddenly very important to him that they should.

The great doors dilated, and he followed Jeserac into the Council Chamber. The twenty members were already seated around their crescent-shaped table, and Alvin felt flattered as he noticed that there were no empty places. This must be the first time for many centuries that the entire Council had been gathered together without a single abstention. Its rare meetings were usually a complete formality, all ordinary business being dealt with by a few visiphone calls and, if necessary, an interview between the President and the Central Computer.

Alvin knew by sight most of the members of the Council, and felt reassured by the presence of so many familiar faces. Like Jeserac, they did not seem unfriendly—merely anxious and puzzled. They were, after all, reasonable men. They might be annoyed that someone had proved them wrong, but Alvin did not believe that they would bear him any resentment. Once this would have been a very rash assumption, but human nature had improved in some respects.

They would give him a fair hearing, but what they thought was not all-important. His judge now would not be the Council. It would be the Central Computer.

SIXTEEN

There were no formalities. The President declared the meeting open and then turned to Alvin.

"Alvin," he said, kindly enough, "we would like you to tell us what has happened to you since you disappeared ten days ago."

The use of the word "disappeared," thought Alvin, was highly significant. Even now, the Council was reluctant to admit that he had really gone outside Diaspar. He wondered if they knew that there had been strangers in the city, and rather doubted it. In that event, they would have shown considerably more alarm.

He told his story clearly and without any dramatics. It was strange and unbelievable enough to their ears, and needed no embellishment. Only at one place did he depart from strict accuracy, for he said nothing about the manner of his escape from Lys. It seemed more than likely that he might want to use the same method again.

It was fascinating to watch the way in which the attitude of the Council members altered during the course of his narrative. At first they were skeptical, refusing to accept the denial of all that they had believed, the violation of their deepest prejudices. When Alvin told them of his passionate desire to explore the world beyond the city, and his irrational conviction that such a world did exist, they stared at him as if he was some strange and incomprehensible animal. To their minds, indeed, he was. But finally they were compelled to admit that he had been right, and that they had been mistaken. As Alvin's story unfolded, any doubts they may have had slowly dissolved. They might not like what he had told them, but they could no longer deny its truth. If they felt tempted to do so, they had only to look at Alvin's silent companion.

There was only one aspect of his tale that roused their indignation—and then it was not directed toward him. A buzz of annoyance went around the chamber as Alvin explained the anxiety of Lys to avoid contamination with Diaspar, and the steps that Seranis had taken to prevent such a catastrophe. The city was proud of its culture, and with good reason. That anyone should regard them as inferiors was more than the Council members could tolerate.

Alvin was very careful not to give offense in anything he said; he wanted, as far as possible, to win the Council to his side. Throughout, he tried to give the impression that he had seen nothing wrong in what he had done, and that he expected praise rather than censure for his discoveries. It was the best policy he could have adopted, for it disarmed most of his would-be critics in advance. It also had the effect—though he had not intended this—of transferring any blame to the vanished Khedron. Alvin himself, it was clear to his listeners, was too young to see any danger in what he was doing. The Jester, however, should certainly have known better and had acted in a thoroughly irresponsible fashion. They did not yet know how fully Khedron himself had agreed with them.

Jeserac, as Alvin's tutor, was also deserving of some censure, and from time to time several of the councilors gave him thoughtful glances. He did not seem to mind, though he was perfectly well aware of what they were thinking. There was a certain honor in having instructed the most original mind that had come into Diaspar since the Dawn Ages, and nothing could rob Jeserac of that.

Not until Alvin had finished the factual account of his adventures did he attempt a little persuasion. Somehow, he would have to convince these men of the truths that he had learned in Lys, but how could he make them really understand something that they had never seen and could hardly imagine?

"It seems a great tragedy," he said, "that the two surviving branches of the human race should have become separated for such an enormous period of time. One day, perhaps, we may know how it happened, but it is more important now to repair the break—to prevent it happening again. When I was in Lys I protested against their view that they were superior to us; they may have much to teach us, but we also have much to teach them. If we both believe that we have nothing to learn from the other, is it not obvious that we will *both* be wrong?"

He looked expectantly along the line of faces, and was encouraged to go on.

"Our ancestors," he continued, "built an empire that reached to the stars. Men came and went at will among all those worlds—and now their descendants are afraid to stir beyond the walls of their city. *Shall I tell you why?*" He paused; there was no movement at all in the great, bare room.

"It is because we are afraid—afraid of something that happened at the beginning of history. I was told the truth in Lys, though I guessed it long ago. Must we always hide like cowards in Diaspar, pretending that nothing else exists—because a billion years ago the Invaders drove us back to Earth?"

He had put his finger on their secret fear—the fear that he had never shared and whose power he could therefore never fully understand. Now let them do what they pleased; he had spoken the truth as he saw it.

The President looked at him gravely.

"Have you anything more to say," he asked, "before we consider what is to be done?"

"Only one thing. I would like to take this robot to the Central Computer."

"But why? You know that the Computer is already aware of everything that has happened in this room."

"I still wish to go," replied Alvin politely but stubbornly. "I ask permission both of the Council and the Computer."

Before the President could reply, a clear, calm voice sounded through the chamber. Alvin had never heard it before in his life, but he knew what it was that spoke. The information machines, which were no more than outlying fragments of this great intelligence, could speak to men—but they did not possess this unmistakable accent of wisdom and authority.

"Let him come to me," said the Central Computer.

Alvin looked at the President. It was to his credit that he did not attempt to exploit his victory. He merely asked, "Have I your permission to leave?"

The President looked around the Council Chamber, saw no disagreement there, and replied a little helplessly: "Very well. The proctors will accompany you, and will bring you back here when we have finished our discussion."

Alvin gave a slight bow of thanks, the great doors expanded before him, and he walked slowly out of the chamber. Jeserac had accompanied him, and when the doors had closed once more, he turned to face his tutor.

"What do you think the Council will do now?" he asked anxiously. Jeserac smiled.

"Impatient as ever, aren't you?" he said. "I do not know what my guess is worth, but I imagine that they will decide to seal the Tomb of Yarlan Zey so that no one can ever again make your journey. Then Diaspar can continue as before, undisturbed by the outside world."

"That is what I am afraid of," said Alvin bitterly.

"And you still hope to prevent it?"

Alvin did not at once reply; he knew that Jeserac had read his intentions, but at least his tutor could not foresee his plans, for he had none. He had come to the stage when he could only improvise and meet each new situation as it arose.

"Do you blame me?" he said presently, and Jeserac was surprised by the new note in his voice. It was a hint of humility, the barest suggestion that for the first time Alvin sought the approval of his fellow men. Jeserac was touched by it, but he was too wise to take it very seriously. Alvin was under a considerable strain, and it would be unsafe to assume that any improvement in his character was permanent.

"That is a very hard question to answer," said Jeserac slowly. "I am tempted to say that all knowledge is valuable, and it cannot be denied that you have added much to our knowledge. But you have also added to our dangers, and in the long run which will be more important? How often have you stopped to consider that?"

For a moment master and pupil regarded each other pensively, each perhaps seeing the other's point of view more clearly than ever before in his life. Then, with one impulse, they turned together down the long passage from the Council Chamber, with their escort still following patiently in the rear.

This world, Alvin knew, had not been made for man. Under the glare of the fierce blue lights—so dazzling that they pained the eyes—the long, broad corridors seemed to stretch to infinity. Down these great passageways the robots of Diaspar must come and go throughout their endless lives, yet not once in centuries did they echo to the sound of human feet.

Here was the underground city, the city of machines without which Diaspar could not exist. A few hundred yards ahead, the corridor would open into a circular chamber more than a mile across, its roof supported by great columns that must also bear the unimaginable weight of Power Center. Here, according to the maps, the Central Computer brooded eternally over the fate of Diaspar.

The chamber was there, and it was even vaster than Alvin had dared imagine—but where was the Computer? Somehow he had expected to meet a single huge machine, naïve though he knew that this conception was. The tremendous but meaningless panorama beneath him made him pause in wonder and uncertainty.

The corridor along which they had come ended high in the wall of the chamber—surely the largest cavity ever built by man—and on either side long ramps swept down to the distant floor. Covering the whole of that brilliantly lit expanse were hundreds of great white structures, so unexpected that for a moment Alvin thought he must be looking down upon a subterranean city. The impression was startlingly vivid, and it was one that he never wholly lost. Nowhere at all was the sight he had expected—the familiar gleam of metal which since the beginning of time man had learned to associate with his servants.

Here was the end of an evolution almost as long as Man's. Its beginnings were lost in the mists of the Dawn Ages, when humanity had first learned the use of power and sent its noisy engines clanking about the world. Steam, water, wind—all had been harnessed for a little while and then abandoned. For centuries the energy of matter had run the world until it too had been superseded, and with each change the old machines were forgotten and new ones took their place. Very slowly, over thousands of years, the ideal of the perfect machine was approached—that ideal which had once been a dream, then a distant prospect, and at last reality:

No machine may contain any moving parts.

Here was the ultimate expression of that ideal. Its achievement had taken Man perhaps a hundred million years, and in the moment of his triumph he had turned his back upon the machine forever. It had reached finality, and thenceforth could sustain itself eternally while serving him.

Alvin no longer asked himself which of these silent white presences was the Central Computer. He knew that it comprised them all—and that it extended far beyond this chamber, including within its being all the countless other machines in Diaspar, whether they were mobile or motionless. As his own brain was the sum of many billion separate cells, arrayed throughout a volume of space a few inches across, so the physical elements of the Central Computer were scattered throughout the length and breadth of Diaspar. This chamber might hold no more than the switching system whereby all these dispersed units kept in touch with one another.

Uncertain where to go next, Alvin stared down the great sweeping ramps and across the silent arena. The Central Computer must know that he was here, as it knew everything that was happening in Diaspar. He could only wait for its instructions.

The now-familiar yet still awe-inspiring voice was so quiet and so close to him that he did not believe that his escort could also hear it. "Go down the left-hand ramp," it said. "I will direct you from there."

He walked slowly down the slope, the robot floating above him. Neither Jeserac nor the proctors followed; he wondered if they had received orders to remain here, or whether they had decided that they could supervise him just as well from their vantage point without the bother of making this long descent. Or perhaps they had come as close to the central shrine of Diaspar as they cared to approach.

At the foot of the ramp, the quiet voice redirected Alvin, and he walked between an avenue of sleeping titan shapes. Three times the voice spoke to him again, until presently he knew that he had reached his goal.

The machine before which he was standing was smaller than most of its companions, but he felt dwarfed as he stood beneath it. The five tiers with their sweeping horizontal lines gave the impression of some crouching beast, and looking from it to his own robot Alvin found it hard to believe that both were products of the same evolution, and both described by the same word.

About three feet from the ground a wide transparent panel ran the whole length of the structure. Alvin pressed his forehead against the smooth, curiously warm material and peered into the machine. At first he saw nothing; then, by shielding his eyes, he could distinguish thousands of faint points of light hanging in nothingness. They were ranged one beyond the other in a three-dimensional lattice, as strange and as meaningless to him as the stars must have been to ancient man. Though he watched for many minutes, forgetful of the passage of time, the colored lights never moved from their places and their brilliance never changed.

If he could look into his own brain, Alvin realized, it would mean as little to him. The machine seemed inert and motionless because he could not see its thoughts.

For the first time, he began to have some dim understanding of the powers and forces that sustained the city. All his life he had accepted without question the miracle of the synthesizers, which age after age provided in an unending stream all the needs of Diaspar. Thousands of times he had watched that act of creation, seldom remembering that somewhere must exist the prototype of that which he had seen come into the world.

As a human mind may dwell for a little while upon a single thought, so the infinitely greater brains which were but a portion of the Central Computer could grasp and hold forever the most intricate ideas. The patterns of all created things were frozen in these eternal minds, needing only the touch of a human will to make them reality.

The world had indeed gone far since, hour upon hour, the first cavemen had patiently chipped their arrowheads and knives from the stubborn stone.

Alvin waited, not caring to speak until he had received some further sign of recognition. He wondered how the Central Computer was aware of his presence, and could see him and hear his voice. Nowhere were there any signs of sense organs—none of the grilles or screens or emotionless crystal eyes through which robots normally had knowledge of the world around them.

"State your problem," said the quiet voice in his ear. It seemed strange that this overwhelming expanse of machinery should sum up its thoughts so softly. Then Alvin realized that he was flattering himself; perhaps not even a millionth part of the Central Computer's brain was dealing with him. He was just one of the innumerable incidents that came to its simultaneous attention as it watched over Diaspar.

It was hard to talk to a presence who filled the whole of the space around you. Alvin's words seemed to die in the empty air as soon as he had uttered them.

"What am I?" he asked.

If he had put that question to one of the information machines in the city, he knew what the reply would have been. Indeed, he had often done so, and they had always answered, "You are a Man." But now he was dealing with an intelligence of an altogether different order, and there was no need for painstaking semantic accuracy. The Central Computer would know what he meant, but that did not mean that it would answer him.

Indeed, the reply was exactly what Alvin had feared.

"I cannot answer that question. To do so would be to reveal the purpose of my builders, and hence to nullify it."

"Then my role was planned when the city was laid down?"

"That can be said of all men."

This reply made Alvin pause. It was true enough; the human inhabitants of Diaspar had been designed as carefully as its machines. The fact that he was a Unique gave Alvin rarity, but there was no necessary virtue in that.

He knew that he could learn nothing further here regarding the mystery of his origin. It was useless to try to trick this vast intelligence, or to hope that it would disclose information it had been ordered to conceal. Alvin was not unduly disappointed; he felt that he had already begun to glimpse the truth, and in any case this was not the main purpose of his visit.

He looked at the robot he had brought from Lys, and wondered how to make his next step. It might react violently if it knew what he was planning, so it was essential that it should not overhear what he intended to say to the Central Computer.

"Can you arrange a zone of silence?" he asked.

Instantly, he sensed the unmistakable "dead" feeling, the total blanketing of all sounds, which descended when one was inside such a zone. The voice of the Computer, now curiously flat and sinister, spoke to him: "No one can hear us now. Say what you wish."

Alvin glanced at the robot; it had not moved from its position. Perhaps it suspected nothing, and he had been quite wrong in ever imagining that it had plans of its own. It might have followed him into Diaspar like a faithful, trusting servant, in which case what he was planning now seemed a particularly churlish trick.

"You have heard how I met this robot," Alvin began. "It must possess priceless knowledge about the past, going back to the days before the city as we know it existed. It may even be able to tell us about other worlds than Earth, since it followed the Master on his travels. Unfortunately, its speech circuits are blocked. I do not know how effective that block is, but I am asking you to clear it."

His voice sounded dead and hollow as the zone of silence absorbed every word before it could form an echo. He waited, within that invisible and unreverberant void, for his request to be obeyed or rejected.

"Your order involves two problems," replied the Computer. "One is moral, one technical. This robot was designed to obey the orders of a certain man. What right have I to override them, even if I can?"

It was a question which Alvin had anticipated and for which he had prepared several answers.

"We do not know what exact form the Master's prohibition took," he replied. "If you can talk to the robot, you may be able to persuade it that the circumstances in which the block was imposed have now changed."

It was, of course, the obvious approach. Alvin had attempted it himself, without success, but he hoped that the Central Computer, with its infinitely greater mental resources, might accomplish what he had failed to do.

"That depends entirely upon the nature of the block," came the reply. "It is possible to set up a block which, if tampered with, will cause the contents of the memory cells to be erased. However, I think it unlikely that the Master possessed sufficient skill to do that; it requires somewhat specialized techniques. I will ask your machine if an erasing circuit has been set up in its memory units."

"But suppose," said Alvin in sudden alarm, "it causes erasure of memory merely to *ask* if an erasing circuit exists?"

"There is a standard procedure for such cases, which I shall follow. I shall set up secondary instructions, telling the machine to ignore my question if such a situation exists. It is then simple to insure that it will become involved in a logical paradox, so that whether it answers me or whether it says nothing it will be forced to disobey its instructions. In such an event all robots act in the same manner, for their own protection. They clear their input circuits and act as if no question has been asked."

Alvin felt rather sorry that he had raised the point, and after a moment's mental struggle decided that he too would adopt the same tactics and pretend that he had never asked the question. At least he was reassured on one point—the Central Computer was fully prepared to deal with any booby traps that might exist in the robot's memory units. Alvin had no wish to see the machine reduced to a pile of junk; rather than that, he would willingly return it to Shalmirane with its secrets still intact.

He waited with what patience he could while the silent, impalpable meeting of intellects took place. Here was an encounter between two minds, both of them created by human genius in the long-lost golden age of its greatest achievement. And now both were beyond the full understanding of any living man.

Many minutes later, the hollow, anechoic voice of the Central Computer spoke again.

"I have established partial contact," it said. "At least I know the nature of the block, and I think I know why it was imposed. There is only one way in which it can be broken. Not until the Great Ones come to Earth will this robot speak again."

"But that is nonsense!" protested Alvin. "The Master's other disciple believed in them, too, and tried to explain what they were like to us. Most of the time it was talking gibberish. The Great Ones never existed, and never will exist."

It seemed a complete impasse, and Alvin felt a sense of bitter, helpless disappointment. He was barred from the truth by the wishes of a man who had been insane, and who had died a billion years ago.

"You may be correct," said the Central Computer, "in saying that the Great Ones never existed. But that does not mean that they never will exist."

There was another long silence while Alvin considered the meaning of this remark, and while the minds of the two robots made their delicate contact again. And then, without any warning, he was in Shalmirane.

SEVENTEEN

It was just as he had last seen it, the great ebon bowl drinking the sunlight and reflecting none back to the eye. He stood among the ruins of the fortress, looking out across the lake, whose motionless waters showed that the giant polyp was now a dispersed cloud of animalcules and no longer an organized, sentient being.

The robot was still beside him, but of Hilvar there was no sign. He had no time to wonder what that meant, or to worry about his friend's absence, for almost at once there occurred something so fantastic that all other thoughts were banished from his mind.

The sky began to crack in two. A thin wedge of darkness reached from horizon to zenith, and slowly widened as if night and chaos were breaking in upon the Universe. Inexorably the wedge expanded until it embraced a quarter of the sky. For all his knowledge of the real facts of astronomy, Alvin could not fight against the overwhelming impression that he and his world lay beneath a great blue dome—and that *something* was now breaking through that dome from outside.

The wedge of night had ceased to grow. The powers that had made it were peering down into the toy universe they had discovered, perhaps conferring among themselves as to whether it was worth their attention. Underneath that cosmic scrutiny, Alvin felt no alarm, no terror. He knew that he was face to face with power and wisdom, before which a man might feel awe but never fear.

And now they had decided—they would waste some fragments of Eternity upon Earth and its peoples. They were coming through the window they had broken in the sky.

Like sparks from some celestial forge, they drifted down to Earth. Thicker and thicker they came, until a waterfall of fire was streaming down from heaven and splashing in pools of liquid light as it reached the ground. Alvin did not need the words that sounded in his ears like a benediction:

"The Great Ones have come."

The fire reached him, and it did not burn. It was everywhere, filling the great bowl of Shalmirane with its golden glow. As he watched in wonder, Alvin saw that it was not a featureless flood of light, but that it had form and structure. It began to resolve itself into distinct shapes, to gather into separate fiery whirlpools. The whirlpools spun more and more swiftly on their axes, their centers rising to form columns within which Alvin could glimpse mysterious evanescent shapes. From these glowing totem poles came a faint musical note, infinitely distant and hauntingly sweet.

"The Great Ones have come."

This time there was a reply. As Alvin heard the words: "The servants of the Master greet you. We have been waiting for your coming," he knew that the barriers were down. And in that moment, Shalmirane and its strange visitors were gone, and he was standing once more before the Central Computer in the depths of Diaspar.

It had all been illusion, no more real than the fantasy world of the sagas in which he had spent so many of the hours of his youth. But how had it been created; whence had come the strange images he had seen?

"It was an unusual problem," said the quiet voice of the Central Computer. "I knew that the robot must have some visual conception of the Great Ones in its mind. If I could convince it that the sense impressions it received coincided with that image, the rest would be simple."

"And how did you do that?"

"Basically, by asking the robot what the Great Ones were like, and then seizing the pattern it formed in its thoughts. The pattern was very incomplete, and I had to improvise a good deal. Once or twice the picture I created began to depart badly from the robot's conception, but when that happened I could sense the machine's growing perplexity and modify the image before it became suspicious. You will appreciate that I could employ hundreds of circuits where it could employ only one, and switch from one image to the other so quickly that the change could not be perceived. It was a kind of conjuring trick; I was able to saturate the robot's sensory circuits and also to overwhelm its critical faculties. What you saw was only the final, corrected image—the one which best fitted the Master's revelation. It was crude, but it sufficed. The robot was convinced of its genuineness long enough for the block to be lifted, and in that moment I was able to make complete contact with its mind. It is no longer insane; it will answer any questions you wish."

Alvin was still in a daze; the afterglow of that spurious apocalypse still burned in his mind, and he did not pretend fully to understand the Central Computer's explanation. No matter; a miracle of therapy had been accomplished, and the doors of knowledge had been flung open for him to enter.

Then he remembered the warning that the Central Computer had given him, and asked anxiously: "What about the moral objections you had to overriding the Master's orders?"

"I have discovered why they were imposed. When you examine his life story in detail, as you can now do, you will see that he claimed to have produced many miracles. His disciples believed him, and their conviction added to his power. But, of course, all those miracles had some simple explanation—when indeed they occurred at all. I find it surprising that otherwise intelligent men should have let themselves be deceived in such a manner."

"So the Master was a fraud?"

"No; it is not as simple as that. If he had been a mere impostor, he would never have achieved such success, and his movement would not have lasted so long. He was a good man, and much of what he taught was true and wise. In the end, he believed in his own miracles, but he knew that there was one witness who could refute them. The robot knew all his secrets; it was his mouthpiece and his colleague, yet if it was ever questioned too closely it could destroy the foundations of his power. So he ordered it never to reveal its memories until the last day of the Universe, when the Great Ones would come. It is hard to believe that such a mixture of deception and sincerity could exist in the same man, but such was the case."

Alvin wondered what the robot felt about this escape from its ancient bondage. It was, surely, a sufficiently complex machine to understand such emotions as resentment. It might be angry with the Master for having enslaved it—and equally angry with Alvin and the Central Computer for having tricked it back into sanity.

The zone of silence had been lifted; there was no further need for secrecy. The moment for which Alvin had been waiting had come at last. He turned to the robot, and asked it the question that had haunted him ever since he had heard the story of the Master's saga.

And the robot replied.

Jeserac and the proctors were still waiting patiently when he rejoined them. At the top of the ramp, before they entered the corridor, Alvin looked back across the cave, and the illusion was stronger than ever. Lying beneath him was a dead city of strange white buildings, a city bleached by a fierce light not meant for human eyes. Dead it might be, for it had never lived, but it pulsed with energies more potent than any that had ever quickened organic matter. While the world endured, these silent machines would still be here, never turning their minds from the thoughts that men of genius had given them long ago.

Though Jeserac tried to question Alvin on the way back to the Council Chamber, he learned nothing of his talk with the Central Computer. This was not merely discretion on Alvin's part; he was still too much lost in the wonder of what he had seen, too intoxicated with success, for any coherent conversation. Jeserac had to muster what patience he could, and hope that presently Alvin would emerge from his trance.

The streets of Diaspar were bathed with a light that seemed pale and wan after the glare of the machine city. But Alvin scarcely saw them; he had no regard for the familiar beauty of the great towers drifting past him, or the curious glances of his fellow citizens. It was strange, he thought, how everything that had happened to him led up to this moment. Since he had met Khedron, events seemed to have moved automatically toward a predetermined goal. The monitors—Lys—Shalmirane—at every stage he might have turned aside with unseeing eyes, but something had led him on. Was he the maker of his own destiny, or was he especially favored by Fate? Perhaps it was merely a matter of probabilities, of the operation of the laws of chance. Any man might have found the path his footsteps had traced, and countless times in the past ages others must have gone almost as far. Those earlier Uniques, for example—what had happened to them? Perhaps he was merely the first to be lucky.

All the way back through the streets, Alvin was establishing closer and closer rapport with the machine he had released from its age-long thralldom. It had always been able to receive his thoughts, but previously he had never known whether it would obey any orders he gave it. Now that uncertainty was gone; he could talk to it as he would to another human being, though since he was not alone he directed it not to use verbal speech but such simple thought images as he could understand. He sometimes resented the fact that robots could talk freely to one another on the telepathic level, whereas Man could not—except in Lys. Here was another power that Diaspar had lost or deliberately set aside.

He continued the silent but somewhat one-sided conversation while they were waiting in the anteroom of the Council Chamber. It was impossible not to compare his present situation with that in Lys, when Seranis and her colleagues had tried to bend him to their wills. He hoped that there would be no need for another conflict, but if one should arise he was now far better prepared for it.

His first glance at the faces of the Council members told Alvin what their decision had been. He was neither surprised nor particularly disappointed, and he showed none of the emotion the Councilors might have expected as he listened to the President's summing-up.

"Alvin," began the President, "we have considered with great care the situation which your discovery has brought about, and we have reached this unanimous decision. Because no one wishes any change in our way of life, and because only once in many millions of years is anyone born who is capable of leaving Diaspar even if the means exists, the tunnel system to Lys is unnecessary and may well be a danger. The entrance to the chamber of the moving ways has therefore been sealed.

"Moreover, since it is possible that there may be other ways of leaving the city, a search will be made of the monitor memory units. That search has already begun.

"We have also considered what action, if any, need be taken with regard to you. In view of your youth, and the peculiar circumstances of your origin, it is felt that you cannot be censured for what you have done. Indeed, by disclosing a potential danger to our way of life, you have done the city a service, and we record our appreciation of that fact."

There was a murmur of applause, and expressions of satisfaction spread across the faces of the Councilors. A difficult situation had been speedily dealt with, they had avoided the necessity of reprimanding Alvin, and now they could go their ways again feeling that they, the chief citizens of

Diaspar, had done their duty. With reasonably good fortune, it might be centuries before the need arose again.

The President looked expectantly at Alvin; perhaps he hoped that Alvin would reciprocate and express his appreciation of the Council for letting him off so lightly. He was disappointed.

"May I ask one question?" said Alvin politely.

"Of course."

"The Central Computer, I take it, approved of your action?"

In the ordinary way, this would have been an impertinent question to ask. The Council was not supposed to justify its decisions or explain how it had arrived at them. But Alvin himself had been taken into the confidence of the Central Computer, for some strange reason of its own. He was in a privileged position.

The question clearly caused some embarrassment, and the reply came rather reluctantly.

"Naturally we consulted with the Central Computer. It told us to use our own judgment."

Alvin had expected as much. The Central Computer would have been conferring with the Council at the same moment as it was talking to him—at the same moment, in fact, as it was attending to a million other tasks in Diaspar. It knew, as did Alvin, that any decision the Council now made was of no importance. The future had passed utterly beyond its control at the very moment when, in happy ignorance, it had decided that the crisis had been safely dealt with.

Alvin felt no sense of superiority, none of the sweet anticipation of impending triumph, as he looked at these foolish old men who thought themselves the rulers of Diaspar. He had seen the real ruler of the city, and had spoken to it in the grave silence of its brilliant, buried world. That was an encounter which had burned most of the arrogance out of his soul, but enough was left for a final venture that would surpass all that had gone before.

As he took leave of the Council, he wondered if they were surprised at his quiet acquiescence, his lack of indignation at the closing of the path to Lys. The proctors did not accompany him; he was no longer under observation, at least in so open a manner. Only Jeserac followed him out of the Council Chamber and into the colored, crowded streets.

"Well, Alvin," he said. "You were on your best behavior, but you cannot deceive me. What are you planning?"

Alvin smiled.

"I knew that you would suspect something; if you will come with me, I will show you why the subway to Lys is no longer important. And there is another experiment I want to try; it will not harm you, but you may not like it."

"Very well. I am still supposed to be your tutor, but it seems that the roles are now reversed. Where are you taking me?"

"We are going to the Tower of Loranne, and I am going to show you the world outside Diaspar."

Jeserac paled, but he stood his ground. Then, as if not trusting himself with words, he gave a stiff little nod and followed Alvin out onto the smoothly gliding surface of the moving way.

Jeserac showed no fear as they walked along the tunnel through which that cold wind blew forever into Diaspar. The tunnel had changed now; the stone grille that had blocked access to the outer world was gone. It served no structural purpose, and the Central Computer had removed it without comment at Alvin's request. Later, it might instruct the monitors to remember the grille again and bring it back into existence. But for the moment the tunnel gaped unfenced and unguarded in the sheer outer wall of the city.

Not until Jeserac had almost reached the end of the air shaft did he realize that the outer world was now upon him. He looked at the widening circle of sky, and his steps became more and more uncertain until they finally slowed to a halt. Alvin remembered how Alystra had turned and fled from this same spot, and he wondered if he could induce Jeserac to go any further.

"I am only asking you to *look*," he begged, "not to leave the city. Surely you can manage to do that!"

In Airlee, during his brief stay, Alvin had seen a mother teaching her child to walk. He was irresistibly reminded of this as he coaxed Jeserac along the corridor, making encouraging remarks as his tutor advanced foot by reluctant foot. Jeserac, unlike Khedron, was no coward. He was prepared to fight against his compulsion, but it was a desperate struggle. Alvin was almost as exhausted as the older man by the time he had succeeded in getting Jeserac to a point where he could see the whole, uninterrupted sweep of the desert.

Once there, the interest and strange beauty of the scene, so alien to all that Jeserac had ever known in this or any previous existence, seemed to overcome his fears. He was clearly fascinated by the immense vista of the rolling sand dunes and the far-off, ancient hills. It was late afternoon, and in a little while all this land would be visited by the night that never came to Diaspar.

"I asked you to come here," said Alvin, speaking quickly as if he could hardly control his impatience, "because I realize that you have earned more right than anyone to see where my travels have led me. I wanted you to see the desert, and I also want you to be a witness, so that the Council will know what I have done.

"As I told the Council, I brought this robot home from Lys in the hope that the Central Computer would be able to break the block that had been imposed on its memories by the man known as the Master. By a trick which I still don't fully understand, the Computer did that. Now I have access to all the memories in this machine, as well as to the special skills that had been designed into it. I'm going to use one of those skills now. Watch."

On a soundless order which Jeserac could only guess, the robot floated out of the tunnel entrance, picked up speed, and within seconds was no more than a distant metallic gleam in the sunlight. It was flying low over the desert, across the sand dunes that lay crisscrossed like frozen waves. Jeserac had the unmistakable impression that it was searching—though for what, he could not imagine.

Then, abruptly, the glittering speck soared away from the desert and came to rest a thousand feet above the ground. At the same moment, Alvin gave an explosive sigh of satisfaction and relief. He glanced quickly at Jeserac, as if to say: "This is it!"

At first, not knowing what to expect, Jeserac could see no change. Then, scarcely believing his eyes, he saw that a cloud of dust was slowly rising from the desert.

Nothing is more terrible than movement where no movement should ever be again, but Jeserac was beyond surprise or fear as the sand dunes began to slide apart. Beneath the desert something was stirring like a giant awakening from its sleep, and presently there came to Jeserac's ears the rumble of falling earth and the shriek of rock split asunder by irresistible force. Then, suddenly, a great geyser of sand erupted hundreds of feet into the air and the ground was hidden from sight.

Slowly the dust began to settle back into a jagged wound torn across the face of the desert. But Jeserac and Alvin still kept their eyes fixed steadfastly upon the open sky, which a little while ago had held only the waiting robot. Now at last Jeserac knew why Alvin had seemed so indifferent to the decision of the Council, why he had shown no emotion when he was told that the subway to Lys had been closed.

The covering of earth and rock could blur but could not conceal the proud lines of the ship still ascending from the riven desert. As Jeserac watched, it slowly turned toward them until it had foreshortened to a circle. Then, very leisurely, the circle started to expand.

Alvin began to speak, rather quickly, as if the time were short.

"This robot was designed to be the Master's companion and servant—and, above all, the pilot of his ship. Before he came to Lys, he landed at the Port of Diaspar, which now lies out there beneath those sands. Even in his day, it must have been largely deserted; I think that the Master's ship was one of the last ever to reach Earth. He lived for a while in Diaspar before he went to Shalmirane; the way must still have been open in those days. But he never needed the ship again, and all these ages it has been waiting out there beneath the sands. Like Diaspar itself, like this robot—like everything that the builders of the past considered really important—it was preserved by its own eternity circuits. As long as it had a source of power, it could never wear out or be destroyed; the image carried in its memory cells would never fade, and that image controlled its physical structure."

The ship was now very close, as the controlling robot guided it toward the tower. Jeserac could see that it was about a hundred feet long and sharply pointed at both ends. There appeared to be no windows or other openings, though the thick layer of earth made it impossible to be certain of this.

Suddenly they were spattered with dirt as a section of the hull opened outward, and Jeserac caught a glimpse of a small, bare room with a second door at its far end. The ship was hanging only a foot away from the mouth of the air vent, which it had approached very cautiously like a sensitive, living thing.

"Good-by, Jeserac," said Alvin. "I cannot go back into Diaspar to say farewell to my friends: please do that for me. Tell Eriston and Etania that I hope to return soon; if I do not, I am grateful for all that they did. And I am grateful to you, even though you may not approve of the way I have applied your lessons.

"And as for the Council—tell it that a road that has once been opened cannot be closed again merely by passing a resolution."

The ship was now only a dark stain against the sky, and of a sudden Jeserac lost it altogether. He never saw its going, but presently there echoed down from the heavens the most awe-inspiring of all the sounds that Man had ever made—the long-drawn thunder of air falling, mile after mile, into a tunnel of vacuum drilled suddenly across the sky.

Even when the last echoes had died away into the desert, Jeserac never moved. He was thinking of the boy who had gone—for to Jeserac, Alvin would always be a child, the only one to come into Diaspar since the cycle of birth and death had been broken, so long ago. Alvin would never grow up; to him the whole Universe was a plaything, a puzzle to be unraveled for his own amusement. In his play he had now found the ultimate, deadly toy which might wreck what was left of human civilization—but whatever the outcome, to him it would still be a game.

The sun was now low on the horizon, and a chill wind was blowing from the desert. But Jeserac still waited, conquering his fears; and presently for the first time in his life he saw the stars.

EIGHTEEN

Even in Diaspar, Alvin had seldom seen such luxury as that which lay before him when the inner door of the air lock slid aside. Whatever else he had been, at least the Master was no ascetic. Not until some time later did it occur to Alvin that all this comfort might be no vain extravagance; this little world must have been the Master's only home on many long journeys among the stars.

There were no visible controls of any kind, but the large, oval screen which completely covered the far wall showed that this was no ordinary room. Ranged in a half circle before it were three low couches; the rest of the cabin was occupied by two small tables and a number of padded chairs —some of them obviously not designed for human occupants.

When he had made himself comfortable in front of the screen, Alvin looked around for the robot. To his surprise, it had disappeared; then he located it, neatly stowed away in a recess beneath the curved ceiling. It had brought the Master across space to Earth and then, as his servant, followed him into Lys. Now it was ready, as if the intervening aeons had never been, to carry out its old duties once again.

Alvin threw it an experimental command, and the great screen shivered into life. Before him was the Tower of Loranne, curiously foreshortened and apparently lying on its side. Further trials gave him views of the sky, of the city, and of great expanses of desert. The definition was brilliantly, almost unnaturally, clear, although there seemed to be no actual magnification. Alvin experimented for a little while until he could obtain any view he wished; then he was ready to start.

"Take me to Lys." The command was a simple one, but how could the ship obey it when he himself had no idea of the direction? Alvin had not considered this, and when it did occur to him the machine was already moving across the desert at a tremendous speed. He shrugged his shoulders, accepting thankfully the fact that he now had servants wiser than himself.

It was difficult to judge the scale of the picture racing up the screen, but many miles must be passing every minute. Not far from the city the color of the ground had changed abruptly to a dull gray, and Alvin knew that he was now passing over the bed of one of the lost oceans. Once Diaspar must have been very near the sea, though there had never been any hint of this even in the most ancient records. Old though the city was, the oceans must have passed away long before its founding.

Hundreds of miles later, the ground rose sharply and the desert returned. Once Alvin halted his ship above a curious pattern of intersecting lines, showing faintly through the blanket of sand. For a moment it puzzled him; then he realized that he was looking down upon the ruins of some forgotten city. He did not stay for long; it was heartbreaking to think that billions of men had left no other trace of their existence save these furrows in the sand.

The smooth curve of the horizon was breaking up at last, crinkling into mountains that were beneath him almost as soon as they were glimpsed. The machine was slowing now, slowing and falling to earth in a great arc a hundred miles in length. And then below him was Lys, its forests and endless rivers forming a scene of such incomparable beauty that for a while he could go no further. To the east, the land was shadowed and the great lakes floated upon it like pools of darker night. But toward the sunset, the waters danced and sparkled with light, throwing back toward him such colors as he had never imagined.

It was not difficult to locate Airlee—which was fortunate, for the robot could guide him no further. Alvin had expected this, and felt a little glad to have discovered some limits to its powers. It was unlikely that it would ever have heard of Airlee, so the position of the village would never have been stored in its memory cells.

After a little experimenting, Alvin brought his ship to rest on the hillside that had given him his first glimpse of Lys. It was quite easy to control the machine; he had only to indicate his general desires and the robot attended to the details. It would, he imagined, ignore dangerous or impossible orders, though he had no intention of giving any if he could avoid it. Alvin was fairly certain that no one could have seen his arrival. He thought this rather important, for he had no desire to engage in mental combat with Seranis again. His plans were still somewhat vague, but he was running no risks until he had established friendly relations. The robot could act as his ambassador, while he remained safely in the ship.

He met no one on the road to Airlee. It was strange to sit in the spaceship while his field of vision moved effortlessly along the familiar path, and the whispering of the forest sounded in his ears. As yet he was unable to identify himself fully with the robot, and the strain of controlling it was still considerable.

It was nearly dark when he reached Airlee, and the little houses were floating in pools of light. Alvin kept to the shadows and had almost reached Seranis's home before he was discovered. Suddenly there was an angry, high-pitched buzzing and his view was blocked by a flurry of wings. He recoiled involuntarily before the onslaught; then he realized what had happened. Krif was once again expressing his resentment of anything that flew without wings.

Not wishing to hurt the beautiful but stupid creature, Alvin brought the robot to a halt and endured as best he could the blows that seemed to be raining upon him. Though he was sitting in comfort a mile away, he could not avoid flinching and was glad when Hilvar came out to investigate.

At his master's approach Krif departed, still buzzing balefully. In the silence that followed, Hilvar stood looking at the robot for a while. Then he smiled.

"Hello, Alvin," he said. "I'm glad you've come back. Or are you still in Diaspar?"

Not for the first time, Alvin felt an envious admiration for the speed and precision of Hilvar's mind.

"No," he said, wondering as he did so how clearly the robot echoed his voice. "I'm in Airlee, not very far away. But I'm staying here for the present."

Hilvar laughed.

"I think that's just as well. Seranis has forgiven you, but as for the Assembly—well, that is another matter. There is a conference going on here at the moment—the first we have ever had in Airlee."

"Do you mean," asked Alvin, "that your councilors have actually come here? With your telepathic powers, I should have thought that meetings weren't necessary."

"They are rare, but there are times when they are felt desirable. I don't know the exact nature of the crisis, but three Senators are already here and the rest are expected soon."

Alvin could not help smiling at the way in which events in Diaspar had been mirrored here. Wherever he went, he now seemed to be leaving a trail of consternation and alarm behind him.

"I think it would be a good idea," he said, "if I could talk to this Assembly of yours—as long as I can do so in safety."

"It would be safe for you to come here yourself," said Hilvar, "if the Assembly promises not to try and take over your mind again. Otherwise, I should stay where you are. I'll lead your robot to the Senators—they'll be rather upset to see it."

Alvin felt again that keen but treacherous sense of enjoyment and exhilaration as he followed Hilvar into the house. He was meeting the rulers of Lys on more equal terms now; though he felt no rancor against them, it was very pleasant to know that he was now master of the situation, and in command of powers which even yet he had not fully turned to account.

The door of the conference room was locked, and it was some time before Hilvar could attract attention. The minds of the Senators, it seemed, were so completely engaged that it was difficult to break into their deliberations. Then the walls slid reluctantly aside, and Alvin moved his robot swiftly forward into the chamber.

The three Senators froze in their seats as he floated toward them, but only the slightest flicker of surprise crossed Seranis's face. Perhaps Hilvar had already sent her a warning, or perhaps she had expected that, sooner or later, Alvin would return.

"Good evening," he said politely, as if this vicarious entry were the most natural thing in the world. "I've decided to come back."

Their surprise certainly exceeded his expectations. One of the Senators, a young man with graying hair, was the first to recover.

"How did you get here?" he gasped.

The reason for his astonishment was obvious. Just as Diaspar had done, so Lys must also have put the subway out of action.

"Why, I came here just as I did last time," said Alvin, unable to resist amusing himself at their expense.

Two of the Senators looked fixedly at the third, who spread his hands in a gesture of baffled resignation. Then the young man who had addressed him before spoke again.

"Didn't you have any—difficulty?" he asked.

"None at all," said Alvin, determined to increase their confusion. He saw that he had succeeded.

"I've come back," he continued, "under my own free will, and because I have some important news for you. However, in view of our previous disagreement I'm remaining out of sight for the moment. If I appear personally, will you promise not to try to restrict my movements again?"

No one said anything for a while, and Alvin wondered what thoughts were being silently interchanged. Then Seranis spoke for them all.

"We won't attempt to control you again—though I don't think we were very successful before."

"Very well," replied Alvin. "I will come to Airlee as quickly as I can."

He waited until the robot had returned; then, very carefully, he gave the machine its instructions and made it repeat them back to him. Seranis, he was quite sure, would not break her word; nevertheless he preferred to safeguard his line of retreat.

The air lock closed silently behind him as he left the ship. A moment later there was a whispering "hiss . . ." like a long-drawn gasp of surprise, as the air made way for the rising ship. For an instant a dark shadow blotted out the stars; then the ship was gone.

Not until it had vanished did Alvin realize that he had made a slight but annoying miscalculation of the kind that could bring the best-laid plans to disaster. He had forgotten that the robot's senses were more acute than his own, and the night was far darker than he had expected. More than once he lost the path completely, and several times he barely avoided colliding with trees. It was almost pitch-black in the forest, and once something quite large came toward him through the undergrowth. There was the faintest crackling of twigs, and two emerald eyes were looking steadfastly at him from the level of his waist. He called softly, and an incredibly long tongue rasped across his hand. A moment later a powerful body rubbed affectionately against him and departed without a sound. He had no idea what it could be.

Presently the lights of the village were shining through the trees ahead, but he no longer needed their guidance for the path beneath his feet had now become a river of dim blue fire. The moss upon which he was walking was luminous, and his footprints left dark patches which slowly disappeared behind him. It was a beautiful and entrancing sight, and when Alvin stooped to pluck some of the strange moss it glowed for minutes in his cupped hands before its radiance died.

Hilvar met him for the second time outside the house, and for the second time introduced him to Seranis and the Senators. They greeted him with a kind of wary and reluctant respect; if they wondered where the robot had gone, they made no comment.

"I'm very sorry," Alvin began, "that I had to leave your country in such an undignified fashion. It may interest you to know that it was nearly as difficult to escape from Diaspar." He let that remark sink in, then added quickly, "I have told my people all about Lys, and I did my best to give a favorable impression. But Diaspar will have nothing to do with you. In spite of all I could say, it wishes to avoid contamination with an inferior culture."

It was most satisfying to watch the Senators' reactions, and even the urbane Seranis colored slightly at his words. If he could make Lys and Diaspar sufficiently annoyed with each other, thought Alvin, his problem would be more than half solved. Each would be so anxious to prove the superiority of its way of life that the barriers between them would soon go down.

"Why have you come back to Lys?" asked Seranis.

"Because I want to convince you, as well as Diaspar, that you have made a mistake." He did not add his other reason—that in Lys was the only friend of whom he could be certain and whose help he now needed.

The Senators were still silent, waiting for him to continue, and he knew that looking through their eyes and listening through their ears were many other unseen intelligences. He was the representative of Diaspar, and the whole of Lys was judging him by what he might say. It was a great responsibility, and he felt humbled before it. He marshaled his thoughts and then began to speak.

His theme was Diaspar. He painted the city as he had last seen it, dreaming on the breast of the desert, its towers glowing like captive rainbows against the sky. From the treasure house of memory he recalled the songs that the poets of old had written in praise of Diaspar, and he spoke of the countless men who had spent their lives to increase its beauty. No one, he told them, could ever exhaust the city's treasures, however long they lived; always there would be something new. For a while he described some of the wonders which the men of Diaspar had wrought; he tried to make them catch a glimpse at least of the loveliness that the artists of the past had created for men's eternal admiration. And he wondered a little wistfully if it were indeed true that the music of Diaspar was the last sound that Earth had ever broadcast to the stars.

They heard him to the end without interruption or questioning. When he had finished it was very late, and Alvin felt more tired than he could ever before remember. The strain and excitement of the long day had told on him at last, and quite suddenly he was asleep.

When he awoke, he was in an unfamiliar room and it was some moments before he remembered that he was no longer in Diaspar. As consciousness returned, so the light grew around him, until presently he was bathed in the soft, cool radiance of the morning sun, streaming through the now transparent walls. He lay in drowsy half-awareness, recalling the events of the previous day and wondering what forces he had now set in motion.

With a soft, musical sound, one of the walls began to pleat itself up in a manner so complicated that it eluded the eye. Hilvar stepped through the opening that had been formed and looked at Alvin with an expression half of amusement, half of serious concern.

"Now that you're awake, Alvin," he said, "perhaps you'll at least tell me what your next move is, and how you managed to return here. The Senators are just leaving to look at the subway; they can't understand how you managed to come back through it. Did you?"

Alvin jumped out of bed and stretched himself mightily.

"Perhaps we'd better overtake them," he said. "I don't want to make them waste their time. As for the question you asked me—in a little while I'll show you the answer to that."

They had almost reached the lake before they overtook the three Senators, and both parties exchanged slightly self-conscious greetings. The Committee of Investigation could see that Alvin knew where it was going, and the unexpected encounter had clearly put it somewhat at a loss.

"I'm afraid I misled you last night," said Alvin cheerfully. "I didn't come to Lys by the old route, so your attempt to close it was quite unnecessary. As a matter of fact, the Council of Diaspar also closed it at their end, with equal lack of success."

The Senators' faces were a study in perplexity as one solution after another chased through their brains.

"Then how *did* you get here?" said the leader. There was a sudden, dawning comprehension in his eyes, and Alvin could tell that he had begun to guess the truth. He wondered if he had intercepted the command his mind had just sent winging across the mountains. But he said nothing, and merely pointed in silence to the northern sky.

Too swiftly for the eye to follow, a needle of silver light arced across the mountains, leaving a mile-long trail of incandescence. Twenty thousand feet above Lys, it stopped. There was no deceleration, no slow braking of its colossal speed. It came to a halt instantly, so that the eye that had been following it moved on across a quarter of the heavens before the brain could arrest its motion. Down from the skies crashed a mighty peal of thunder, the sound of air battered and smashed by the violence of the ship's passage. A little later the ship itself, gleaming splendidly in the sunlight, came to rest upon the hillside a hundred yards away.

It was difficult to say who was the most surprised, but Alvin was the first to recover. As they walked—very nearly running—toward the spaceship, he wondered if it normally traveled in this meteoric fashion. The thought was disconcerting, although there had been no sensation of movement on his first voyage. Considerably more puzzling, however, was the fact that a day ago this resplendent creature had been hidden beneath a thick layer of iron-hard rock—the coating it had still retained when it had torn itself loose from the desert. Not until Alvin had reached the ship, and burned his fingers by incautiously resting them on the hull, did he understand what had happened. Near the stern there were still traces of earth, but it had been fused into lava. All the rest had been swept away, leaving uncovered the stubborn shell which neither time nor any natural force could ever touch.

With Hilvar by his side, Alvin stood in the open door and looked back at the silent Senators. He wondered what they were thinking—what, indeed, the whole of Lys was thinking. From their expressions, it almost seemed as if they were beyond thought.

"I am going to Shalmirane," said Alvin, "and I will be back in Airlee within an hour or so. But that is only a beginning, and while I am away, there is a thought I would leave with you.

"This is no ordinary flyer of the kind in which men traveled over the Earth. It is a spaceship, one of the fastest ever built. If you want to know where I found it, you will find the answer in Diaspar. But you will have to go there, for Diaspar will never come to you."

He turned to Hilvar, and gestured to the door. Hilvar hesitated for a moment only, looking back once at the familiar scenes around him. Then he stepped forward into the air lock.

The Senators watched until the ship, now moving quite slowly—for it had only a little way to go—had disappeared into the south. Then the gray-haired young man who led the group shrugged his shoulders philosophically and turned to one of his colleagues.

"You've always opposed us for wanting change," he said, "and so far you have won. But I don't think the future lies with either of our groups now. Lys and Diaspar have both come to the end of an era, and we must make the best of it."

"I am afraid you are right," came the gloomy reply. "This is a crisis, and Alvin knew what he was saying when he told us to go to Diaspar. They know about us now, so there is no further purpose in concealment. I think we had better get in touch with our cousins—we may find them more anxious to co-operate now."

"But the subway is closed at both ends!"

"We can open ours; it will not be long before Diaspar does the same."

The minds of the Senators, those in Airlee and those scattered over the whole width of Lys, considered the proposal and disliked it heartily. But they saw no alternative.

Sooner than he had any right to expect, the seed that Alvin had planted was beginning to flower.

The mountains were still swimming in shadow when they reached Shalmirane. From their height the great bowl of the fortress looked very small; it seemed impossible that the fate of Earth had once depended on that tiny ebon circle.

When Alvin brought the ship to rest among the ruins by the lakeside, the desolation crowded in upon him, chilling his soul. He opened the air lock, and the stillness of the place crept into the ship. Hilvar, who had scarcely spoken during the entire flight, asked quietly: "Why have you come here again?"

Alvin did not answer until they had almost reached the edge of the lake. Then he said: "I wanted to show you what this ship was like. And I also hoped that the polyp might be in existence once more; I feel I owe it a debt, and I want to tell it what I've discovered."

"In that case," replied Hilvar, "you will have to wait. You have come back much too soon."

Alvin had expected that; it had been a remote chance and he was not disappointed that it had failed. The waters of the lake were perfectly still, no longer beating with that steady rhythm that had so puzzled them on their first visit. He knelt down at the water's edge and peered into the cold, dark depths.

Tiny translucent bells, trailing almost invisible tentacles, were drifting to and fro beneath the surface. Alvin plunged in his hand and scooped one up. He dropped it at once, with a slight exclamation of annoyance. It had stung him.

Some day—perhaps years, perhaps centuries in the future—these mindless jellies would reassemble and the great polyp would be reborn as its memories linked together and its consciousness flashed into existence once again. Alvin wondered how it would receive the discoveries he had made; it might not be pleased to learn the truth about the Master. Indeed, it might refuse to admit that all its ages of patient waiting had been in vain.

Yet had they? Deluded though these creatures might have been, their long vigil had at last brought its reward. As if by a miracle, they had saved from the past knowledge that else might have been lost forever. Now they could rest at last, and their creed could go the way of a million other faiths that had once thought themselves eternal.

NINETEEN

Hilvar and Alvin walked in reflective silence back to the waiting ship, and presently the fortress was once more a dark shadow among the hills. It dwindled swiftly until it became a black and lidless eye, staring up forever into space, and soon they lost it in the great panorama of Lys.

Alvin did nothing to check the machine; still they rose until the whole of Lys lay spread beneath them, a green island in an ocher sea. Never before had Alvin been so high; when finally they came to rest the whole crescent of the Earth was visible below. Lys was very small now, only an emerald stain against the rusty desert—but far around the curve of the globe something was glittering like a man-colored jewel. And so for the first time, Hilvar saw the city of Diaspar.

They sat for a long while watching the Earth turn beneath them. Of all Man's ancient powers, this surely was the one he could least afford to lose. Alvin wished he could show the world as he saw it now to the rulers of Lys and Diaspar.

"Hilvar," he said at last, "do you think that what I'm doing is right?"

The question surprised Hilvar, who did not suspect the sudden doubts that sometimes overwhelmed his friend, and still knew nothing of Alvin's meeting with the Central Computer and the impact which that had had upon his mind. It was not an easy question to answer dispassionately; like Khedron, though with less cause, Hilvar felt that his own character was becoming submerged. He was being sucked helplessly into the vortex which Alvin left behind him on his way through life.

"I believe you are right," Hilvar answered slowly. "Our two peoples have been separated for long enough." That, he thought, was true, though he knew that his own feelings must bias his reply. But Alvin was still worried.

"There's one problem that bothers me," he said in a troubled voice, "and that's the difference in our life spans." He said no more, but each knew what the other was thinking.

"I've been worried about that as well," Hilvar admitted, "but I think the problem will solve itself in time when our people get to know each other again. We can't *both* be right—our lives may be too short, and yours are certainly far too long. Eventually there will be a compromise."

Alvin wondered. That way, it was true, lay the only hope, but the ages of transition would be hard indeed. He remembered again those bitter words of Seranis: *"Both he and I will have been dead for centuries while you are still a young man."* Very well; he would accept the conditions. Even in Diaspar all friendships lay under the same shadow; whether it was a hundred or a million years away made little difference at the end.

Alvin knew, with a certainty that passed all logic, that the welfare of the race demanded the mingling of these two cultures; in such a cause individual happiness was unimportant. For a moment Alvin saw humanity as something more than the living background of his own life, and he accepted without flinching the unhappiness his choice must one day bring.

Beneath them the world continued on its endless turning. Sensing his friend's mood, Hilvar said nothing, until presently Alvin broke the silence.

"When I first left Diaspar," he said, "I did not know what I hoped to find. Lys would have satisfied me once—more than satisfied me—yet now everything on Earth seems so small and unimportant. Each discovery I've made has raised bigger questions, and opened up wider horizons. I wonder where it will end. . . ."

Hilvar had never seen Alvin in so thoughtful a mood, and did not wish to interrupt his soliloquy. He had learned a great deal about his friend in the last few minutes.

"The robot told me," Alvin continued, "that this ship can reach the Seven Suns in less than a day. Do you think I should go?"

"Do you think I could stop you?" Hilvar replied quietly.

Alvin smiled.

"That's no answer," he said. "Who knows what lies out there in space? The Invaders may have left the Universe, but there may be other intelligences unfriendly to man."

"Why should there be?" Hilvar asked. "That's one of the questions our philosophers have been debating for ages. A truly intelligent race is not likely to be unfriendly."

"But the Invaders—?"

"They are an enigma, I admit. If they were really vicious, they must have destroyed themselves by now. And even if they have not—" Hilvar pointed to the unending deserts below. "Once we had an Empire. What have we now that they would covet?"

Alvin was a little surprised that anyone else shared this point of view, so closely allied to his own.

"Do all your people think this way?" he asked.

"Only a minority. The average person doesn't worry about it, but would probably say that if the Invaders really wanted to destroy Earth, they'd have done it ages ago. I don't suppose anyone is actually afraid of them."

"Things are very different in Diaspar," said Alvin. "My people are great cowards. They are terrified of leaving their city, and I don't know what will happen when they hear that I've located a spaceship. Jeserac will have told the Council by now, and I would like to know what it is doing."

"I can tell you that. It is preparing to receive its first delegation from Lys. Seranis has just told me."

Alvin looked again at the screen. He could span the distance between Lys and Diaspar in a single glance; though one of his aims had been achieved, that seemed a small matter now. Yet he was very glad; now, surely, the long ages of sterile isolation would be ending.

The knowledge that he had succeeded in what had once been his main mission cleared away the last doubts from Alvin's mind. He had fulfilled his purpose here on Earth, more swiftly and more thoroughly than he had dared to hope. The way lay clear ahead for what might be his last, and would certainly be his greatest, adventure.

"Will you come with me, Hilvar?" he said, all too conscious of what he was asking.

Hilvar looked at him steadfastly.

"There was no need to ask that, Alvin," he said. "I told Seranis and all my friends that I was leaving with you—a good hour ago."

They were very high when Alvin gave the robot its final instructions. The ship had come almost to rest and the Earth was perhaps a thousand miles below, nearly filling the sky. It looked very uninviting; Alvin wondered how many ships in the past had hovered here for a little while and then continued on their way.

There was an appreciable pause, as if the robot was checking controls and circuits that had not been used for geological ages. Then came a very faint sound, the first that Alvin had ever heard from a machine. It was a tiny humming, which soared swiftly octave by octave until it was lost at the edge of hearing. There was no sense of change or motion, but suddenly he noticed that the stars were drifting across the screen. The Earth reappeared, and rolled past—then appeared again, in a slightly different position. The ship was "hunting," swinging in space like a compass needle seeking the north. For minutes the skies turned and twisted around them, until at last the ship came to rest, a giant projectile aimed at the stars.

Centered in the screen the great ring of the Seven Suns lay in its rainbow-hued beauty. A little of Earth was still visible as a dark crescent edged with the gold and crimson of the sunset. Something was happening now, Alvin knew, beyond all his experience. He waited, gripping his seat, while the seconds drifted by and the Seven Suns glittered on the screen.

There was no sound, only a sudden wrench that seemed to blur the vision—but Earth had vanished as if a giant hand had whipped it away. They were alone in space, alone with the stars and a strangely shrunken sun. Earth was gone as though it had never been.

Again came that wrench, and with it now the faintest murmur of sound, as if for the first time the generators were exerting some appreciable fraction of their power. Yet for a moment it seemed that nothing had happened; then Alvin realized that the sun itself was gone and that the stars were creeping slowly past the ship. He looked back for an instant and saw—nothing. All the heavens behind had vanished utterly, obliterated by a hemisphere of night. Even as he watched, he could see the stars plunge into it, to disappear like sparks falling upon water. The ship was traveling far faster than light, and Alvin knew that the familiar space of Earth and sun held him no more.

When that sudden, vertiginous wrench came for the third time, his heart almost stopped beating. The strange blurring of vision was unmistakable now: for a moment his surroundings seemed distorted out of recognition. The meaning of that distortion came to him in a flash of insight he could not explain. *It was real, and no delusion of his eyes.* Somehow he was catching, as he passed through the thin film of the Present, a glimpse of the changes that were occurring in the space around him.

At the same instant the murmur of the generators rose to a roar that shook the ship—a sound doubly impressive for it was the first cry of protest that Alvin had ever heard from a machine. Then it was all over, and the sudden silence seemed to ring in his ears. The great generators had done their work; they would not be needed again until the end of the voyage. The stars ahead flared blue-white and vanished into the ultraviolet. Yet by some magic of Science or Nature the Seven Suns were still visible, though now their positions and colors were subtly changed. The ship was hurtling toward them along a tunnel of darkness, beyond the boundaries of space and time, at a velocity too enormous for the mind to contemplate.

It was hard to believe that they had now been flung out of the Solar System at a speed which unless it were checked would soon take them through the heart of the Galaxy and into the greater emptiness beyond. Neither Alvin nor Hilvar could conceive the real immensity of their journey; the great sagas of exploration had completely changed Man's outlook toward the Universe and even now, millions of centuries later, the ancient traditions had not wholly died. There had once been a ship, legend whispered, that had circumnavigated the Cosmos between the rising and the setting of the sun. The billions of miles between the stars meant nothing before such speeds. To Alvin this voyage was very little greater, and perhaps less dangerous, than his first journey to Lys.

It was Hilvar who voiced both their thoughts as the Seven Suns slowly brightened ahead.

"Alvin," he remarked, "that formation can't possibly be natural."

The other nodded.

"I've thought that for years, but it still seems fantastic."

"The system may not have been built by Man," agreed Hilvar, "but intelligence must have created it. Nature could never have formed that perfect circle of stars, all equally brilliant. And there's nothing else in the visible Universe like the Central Sun."

"Why should such a thing have been made, then?"

"Oh, I can think of many reasons. Perhaps it's a signal, so that any strange ship entering our Universe will know where to look for life. Perhaps it marks the center of galactic administration. Or perhaps—and somehow I feel that this is the real explanation—it's simply the greatest of all works of art. But it's foolish to speculate now. In a few hours we shall know the truth."

"*We shall know the truth.*" Perhaps, thought Alvin—but how much of it shall we ever know? It seemed strange that now, while he was leaving Diaspar, and indeed Earth itself, at a speed beyond all comprehension, his mind should turn once more to the mystery of his origin. Yet perhaps it was not so surprising; he had learned many things since he had first arrived in Lys, but until now he had had not a single moment for quiet reflection.

There was nothing he could do now but sit and wait; his immediate future was controlled by the wonderful machine—surely one of the supreme engineering achievements of all time—that was now carrying him into the heart of the Universe. Now was the moment for thought and reflection, whether he wished it or not. But first he would tell Hilvar all that had happened to him since their hasty parting only two days before.

Hilvar absorbed the tale without comment and without asking for any explanations; he seemed to understand at once everything that Alvin described, and showed no signs of surprise even when he heard of the meeting with the Central Computer and the operation it had performed upon the robot's mind. It was not that he was incapable of wonder, but that the history of the past was full of marvels that could match anything in Alvin's story.

"It's obvious," he said, when Alvin had finished talking, "that the Central Computer must have received special instructions regarding you when it was built. By now, you must have guessed why."

"I think so. Khedron gave me part of the answer when he explained how the men who designed Diaspar had taken steps to prevent it becoming decadent."

"Do you think you—and the other Uniques before you—are part of the social mechanism which prevents complete stagnation? So that whereas the Jesters are short-term correcting factors, you and your kind are long-term ones?"

Hilvar had expressed the idea better than Alvin could, yet this was not exactly what he had in mind.

"I believe the truth is more complicated than that. It almost looks as if there was a conflict of opinion when the city was built, between those who wanted to shut it off completely from the outside world, and those who wanted to maintain some contacts. The first faction won, but the others did not admit defeat. I think Yarlan Zey must have been one of their leaders, but he was not powerful enough to act openly. He did his best, by leaving the subway in existence and by insuring that at long intervals someone would come out of the Hall of Creation who did not share the fears of all his fellow men. In fact, I wonder—" Alvin paused, and his eyes veiled with thought so that for a moment he seemed oblivious of his surroundings.

"What are you thinking now?" asked Hilvar.

"It's just occurred to me—perhaps *I* am Yarlan Zey. It's perfectly possible. He may have fed his personality into the Memory Banks, relying on it to break the mold of Diaspar before it was too firmly established. One day I must discover what happened to those earlier Uniques; that may help to fill in the gaps in the picture."

"And Yarlan Zey—or whoever it was—also instructed the Central Computer to give special assistance to the Uniques, whenever they were created," mused Hilvar, following this line of logic.

"That's right. The ironic thing is that I could have got all the information I needed direct from the Central Computer, without any assistance from poor Khedron. It would have told me more than it ever told him. But there's no doubt that he saved me a good deal of time, and taught me much that I could never have learned by myself."

"I think your theory covers all the known facts," said Hilvar cautiously. "Unfortunately, it still leaves wide open the biggest problem of all—the original purpose of Diaspar. Why did your people try to pretend that the outer world didn't exist? *That's* a question I'd like to see answered."

"It's a question I intend to answer," replied Alvin. "But I don't know when—or how."

So they argued and dreamed, while hour by hour the Seven Suns drifted apart until they had filled that strange tunnel of night in which the ship was riding. Then, one by one, the six outer stars vanished at the brink of darkness and at last only the Central Sun was left. Though it could no longer be fully in their space, it still shone with the pearly light that marked it out from all other stars. Minute by minute its brilliance increased, until presently it was no longer a point but a tiny disc. And now the disc was beginning to expand before them.

There was the briefest of warnings: for a moment a deep, bell-like note vibrated through the room. Alvin clenched the arms of his chair, though it was a futile enough gesture.

Once again the great generators exploded into life, and with an abruptness that was almost blinding, the stars reappeared. The ship had dropped back into space, back into the Universe of suns and planets, the natural world where nothing could move more swiftly than light.

They were already within the system of the Seven Suns, for the great ring of colored globes now dominated the sky. And what a sky it was! All the stars they had known, all the familiar constellations, had gone. The Milky Way was no longer a faint band of mist far to one side of the heavens; they were now at the center of creation, and its great circle divided the Universe in twain.

The ship was still moving very swiftly toward the Central Sun, and the six remaining stars of the system were colored beacons ranged around the sky. Not far from the nearest of them were the tiny sparks of circling planets, worlds that must have been of enormous size to be visible over such a distance.

The cause of the Central Sun's nacreous light was now clearly visible. The great star was shrouded in an envelope of gas which softened its radiation and gave it its characteristic color. The surrounding nebula could only be seen indirectly, and it was twisted into strange shapes that eluded the eye. But it was there, and the longer one stared the more extensive it seemed to be.

"Well, Alvin," said Hilvar, "we have a good many worlds to take our choice from. Or do you hope to explore them all?"

"It's lucky that won't be necessary," admitted Alvin. "If we can make contact anywhere, we'll get the information we need. The logical thing would be to head for the largest planet of the Central Sun."

"Unless it's too large. Some planets, I've heard, were so big that human life could not exist on them—men would be crushed under their own weight."

"I doubt if that will be true here, since I'm sure this system is entirely artificial. In any case, we'll be able to see from space whether there are any cities and buildings."

Hilvar pointed to the robot.

"Our problem has been solved for us. Don't forget—our guide has been here before. He is taking us home—and I wonder what he thinks about it?"

That was something that Alvin had also wondered. But was it accurate—did it make any sense at all—to imagine that the robot felt anything resembling human emotions now that it was returning to the ancient home of the Master, after so many aeons?

In all his dealings with it, since the Central Computer had released the blocks that made it mute, the robot had never shown any sign of feelings or emotion. It had answered his questions and obeyed his commands, but its real personality had proved utterly inaccessible to him. That it had a personality Alvin was sure; otherwise he would not have felt that obscure sense of guilt which afflicted him when he recalled the trick he had played upon it—and upon its now dormant companion.

It still believed in everything that the Master had taught it; though it had seen him fake his miracles and tell lies to his followers, these inconvenient facts did not affect its loyalty. It was able, as had many humans before it, to reconcile two conflicting sets of data.

Now it was following its immemorial memories back to their origin. Almost lost in the glare of the Central Sun was a pale spark of light, with around it the fainter gleams of yet smaller worlds. Their enormous journey was coming to its end; in a little while they would know if it had been in vain.

TWENTY

The planet they were approaching was now only a few million miles away, a beautiful sphere of multicolored light. There could be no darkness anywhere upon its surface, for as it turned beneath the Central Sun, the other stars would march one by one across its skies. Alvin now saw very clearly the meaning of the Master's dying words: *"It is lovely to watch the colored shadows on the planets of eternal light."*

Now they were so close that they could see continents and oceans and a faint haze of atmosphere. Yet there was something puzzling about its markings, and presently they realized that the divisions between land and water were curiously regular. This planet's continents were not as Nature had left them—but how small a task the shaping of a world must have been to those who built its suns!

"Those aren't oceans at all!" Hilvar exclaimed suddenly. "Look—you can see markings in them!"

Not until the planet was nearer could Alvin see clearly what his friend meant. Then he noticed faint bands and lines along the continental borders, well inside what he had taken to be the limits of the sea. The sight filled him with a sudden doubt, for he knew too well the meaning of those lines. He had seen them once before in the desert beyond Diaspar, and they told him that his journey had been in vain.

"This planet is as dry as Earth," he said dully. "Its water has all gone—those markings are the salt beds where the seas have evaporated."

"They would never have let that happen," replied Hilvar. "I think that, after all, we are too late."

His disappointment was so bitter that Alvin did not trust himself to speak again but stared silently at the great world ahead. With impressive slowness the planet turned beneath the ship, and its surface rose majestically to meet them. Now they could see buildings—minute white incrustations everywhere save on the ocean beds themselves.

Once this world had been the center of the Universe. Now it was still, the air was empty and on the ground were none of the scurrying dots that spoke of life. Yet the ship was still sliding purposefully over the frozen sea of stone—a sea which here and there had gathered itself into great waves that challenged the sky.

Presently the ship came to rest, as if the robot had at last traced its memories to their source. Below them was a column of snow-white stone springing from the center of an immense marble amphitheater. Alvin waited for a little while; then, as the machine remained motionless, he directed it to land at the foot of the pillar.

Even until now, Alvin had half hoped to find life on this planet. That hope vanished instantly as the air lock opened. Never before in his life, even in the desolation of Shalmirane, had he been in utter silence. On Earth there was always the murmur of voices, the stir of living creatures, or the sighing of the wind. Here were none of these, nor ever would be again.

"Why did you bring us to this spot?" asked Alvin. He felt little interest in the answer, but the momentum of his quest still carried him on even when he had lost all heart to pursue it further.

"The Master left from here," replied the robot.

"I thought that would be the explanation," said Hilvar. "Don't you see the irony of all this? He fled from this world in disgrace—now look at the memorial they built for him!"

The great column of stone was perhaps a hundred times the height of a man, and was set in a circle of metal slightly raised above the level of the plain. It was featureless and bore no inscription. For how many thousands or millions of years, wondered Alvin, had the Master's disciples gathered here to do him honor? And had they ever known that he died in exile on distant Earth?

It made no difference now. The Master and his disciples alike were buried in oblivion.

"Come outside," urged Hilvar, trying to jolt Alvin out of his mood of depression. "We have traveled halfway across the Universe to see this place. At least you can make the effort to step outdoors."

Despite himself, Alvin smiled and followed Hilvar through the air lock. Once outside, his spirits began to revive a little. Even if this world was dead, it must contain much of interest, much that would help him to solve some of the mysteries of the past.

The air was musty, but breathable. Despite the many suns in the sky, the temperature was low. Only the white disc of the Central Sun provided any real heat, and that seemed to have lost its strength in its passage through the nebulous haze around the star. The other suns gave their quota of color, but no warmth.

It took only a few minutes to make sure that the obelisk could tell them nothing. The stubborn material of which it was made showed definite signs of age; its edges were rounded, and the metal on which it was standing had been worn away by the feet of generations of disciples and visitors. It was strange to think that they might be the last of many billions of human beings ever to stand upon this spot.

Hilvar was about to suggest that they should return to the ship and fly across to the nearest of the surrounding buildings when Alvin noticed a long, narrow crack in the marble floor of the amphitheater. They walked along it for a considerable distance, the crack widening all the time until presently it was too broad for a man's legs to straddle.

A moment later they stood beside its origin. The surface of the arena had been crushed and splintered into an enormous shallow depression, more than a mile long. No intelligence, no imagination was needed to picture its cause. Ages ago—though certainly long after this world had been deserted—an immense cylindrical shape had rested here, then lifted once more into space and left the planet to its memories.

Who had they been? Where had they come from? Alvin could only stare and wonder. He would never know if he had missed these earlier visitors by a thousand or a million years.

They walked in silence back to their own ship (how tiny that would have looked beside the monster which once had rested here!) and flew slowly across the arena until they came to the most impressive of the buildings flanking it. As they landed in front of the ornate entrance, Hilvar pointed out something that Alvin had noticed at the same moment.

"These buildings don't look safe. See all that fallen stone over there—it's a miracle they're still standing. If there were any storms on this planet, they would have been flattened ages ago. I don't think it would be wise to go inside any of them."

"I'm not going to; I'll send the robot—it can travel far faster than we can, and it won't make any disturbance which might bring the roof crashing down on top of it."

Hilvar approved of this precaution, but he also insisted on one which Alvin had overlooked. Before the robot left on its reconnaissance, Alvin made it pass on a set of instructions to the almost equally intelligent brain of the ship, so that whatever happened to their pilot they could at least return safely to Earth.

It took little time to convince both of them that this world had nothing to offer. Together they watched miles of empty, dust-carpeted corridors and passageways drift across the screen as the robot explored these empty labyrinths. All buildings designed by intelligent beings, whatever form their bodies may take, must comply with certain basic laws, and after a while even the most alien forms of architecture or design fail to evoke surprise, and the mind becomes hypnotized by sheer repetition, incapable of absorbing any more impressions. These buildings, it seemed, had been purely residential, and the beings who had lived in them had been approximately human in size. They might well have been men; it was true that there were a surprising number of rooms and enclosures that could be entered only by flying creatures, but that did not mean that the builders of this city were winged. They could have used the personal antigravity devices that had once been in common use but of which there was now no trace in Diaspar.

"Alvin," said Hilvar at last, "we could spend a million years exploring these buildings. It's obvious that they've not merely been abandoned—

they were carefully stripped of everything valuable that they possessed. We are wasting our time."

"Then what do you suggest?" asked Alvin.

"We should look at two or three other areas of this planet and see if they are the same—as I expect they are. Then we should make an equally quick survey of the other planets, and only land if they seem fundamentally different or we notice something unusual. That's all we can hope to do unless we are going to stay here for the rest of our lives."

It was true enough; they were trying to contact intelligence, not to carry out archaeological research. The former task could be achieved in a few days, if it could be achieved at all. The latter would take centuries of labor by armies of men and robots.

They left the planet two hours later, and were thankful enough to go. Even when it had been bustling with life, Alvin decided, this world of endless buildings would have been very depressing. There were no signs of any parks, any open spaces where there could have been vegetation. It had been an utterly sterile world, and it was hard to imagine the psychology of the beings who had lived here. If the next planet was identical with this, Alvin decided, he would probably abandon the search there and then.

It was not; indeed, a greater contrast would have been impossible to imagine.

This planet was nearer the sun, and even from space it looked hot. It was partly covered with low clouds, indicating that water was plentiful, but there were no signs of any oceans. Nor was there any sign of intelligence; they circled the planet twice without glimpsing a single artifact of any kind. The entire globe, from poles down to the equator, was clothed with a blanket of virulent green.

"I think we should be very careful here," said Hilvar. "This world is alive—and I don't like the color of that vegetation. It would be best to stay in the ship, and not to open the air lock at all."

"Not even to send out the robot?"

"No, not even that. You have forgotten what disease is, and though my people know how to deal with it, we are a long way from home and there may be dangers here which we cannot see. I think this is a world that has run amok. Once it may have been all one great garden or park, but when it was abandoned Nature took over again. It could never have been like this while the system was inhabited."

Alvin did not doubt that Hilvar was right. There was something evil, something hostile to all the order and regularity on which both Lys and Diaspar were based, in the biological anarchy below. Here a ceaseless battle had raged for a billion years; it would be well to be wary of the survivors.

They came cautiously down over a great level plain, so uniform that its flatness posed an immediate problem. The plain was bordered by higher ground, completely covered with trees whose height could only be guessed —they were so tightly packed, and so enmeshed with undergrowth, that their trunks were virtually buried. There were many winged creatures flying among their upper branches, though they moved so swiftly that it was impossible to tell whether they were birds or insects—or neither.

Here and there a forest giant had managed to climb a few scores of feet above its battling neighbors, who had formed a brief alliance to tear it down and destroy the advantage it had won. Despite the fact that this was a silent war, fought too slowly for the eye to see, the impression of merciless, implacable conflict was overwhelming.

The plain, by comparison, appeared placid and uneventful. It was flat, to within a few inches, right out to the horizon, and seemed to be covered with a thin, wiry grass. Though they descended to within fifty feet of it, there was no sign of any animal life, which Hilvar found somewhat surprising. Perhaps, he decided, it had been scared underground by their approach.

They hovered just above the plain while Alvin tried to convince Hilvar that it would be safe to open the air lock, and Hilvar patiently explained such conceptions as bacteria, fungi, viruses, and microbes—ideas which Alvin found hard to visualize, and harder still to apply to himself. The argument had been in progress for some minutes before they noticed a peculiar fact. The vision screen, which a moment ago had been showing the forest ahead of them, had now become blank.

"Did you turn that off?" said Hilvar, his mind, as usual, just one jump ahead of Alvin's.

"No," replied Alvin, a cold shiver running down his spine as he thought of the only other explanation. "Did *you* turn it off?" he asked the robot.

"No," came the reply, echoing his own.

With a sigh of relief, Alvin dismissed the idea that the robot might have started to act on its own volition—that he might have a mechanical mutiny on his hands.

"Then why is the screen blank?" he asked.

"The image receptors have been covered."

"I don't understand," said Alvin, forgetting for a moment that the robot would only act on definite orders or questions. He recovered himself quickly and asked: "What's covered the receptors?"

"I do not know."

The literal-mindedness of robots could sometimes be as exasperating as the discursiveness of humans. Before Alvin could continue the interrogation, Hilvar interrupted.

"Tell it to lift the ship—slowly," he said, and there was a note of urgency in his voice.

Alvin repeated the command. There was no sense of motion; there never was. Then, slowly, the image re-formed on the vision screen, though for a moment it was blurred and distorted. But it showed enough to end the argument about landing.

The level plain was level no longer. A great bulge had formed immediately below them—a bulge which was ripped open at the top where the ship had torn free. Huge pseudopods were waving sluggishly across the gap, as if trying to recapture the prey that had just escaped from their clutches. As he stared in horrified fascination, Alvin caught a glimpse of a pulsing scarlet orifice, fringed with whiplike tentacles which were beating in unison, driving anything that came into their reach down into that gaping maw.

Foiled of its intended victim, the creature sank slowly into the ground—and it was then that Alvin realized that the plain below was merely the thin scum on the surface of a stagnant sea.

"What was that—*thing?*" he gasped.

"I'd have to go down and study it before I could tell you that," Hilvar replied matter-of-factly. "It may have been some form of primitive animal—perhaps even a relative of our friend in Shalmirane. Certainly it was not intelligent, or it would have known better than to try to eat a spaceship."

Alvin felt shaken, though he knew that they had been in no possible danger. He wondered what else lived down there beneath that innocent sward, which seemed to positively invite him to come out and run upon its springy surface.

"I could spend a lot of time here," said Hilvar, obviously fascinated by what he had just seen. "Evolution must have produced some very interesting results under these conditions. Not only evolution, but *devolution* as well, as higher forms of life regressed when the planet was deserted. By now equilibrium must have been reached and—you're not leaving already?" His voice sounded quite plaintive as the landscape receded below them.

"I am," said Alvin. "I've seen a world with no life, and a world with too much, and I don't know which I dislike more."

Five thousand feet above the plain, the planet gave them one final surprise. They encountered a flotilla of huge, flabby balloons drifting down the wind. From each semitransparent envelope, clusters of tendrils dangled to form what was virtually an inverted forest. Some plants, it seemed, in the effort to escape from the ferocious conflict on the surface had learned to conquer the air. By a miracle of adaptation, they had managed to prepare hydrogen and store it in bladders, so that they could lift themselves into the comparative peace of the lower atmosphere.

Yet it was not certain that even here they had found security. Their downward-hanging stems and leaves were infested with an entire fauna of spidery animals, which must spend their lives floating far above the surface of the globe, continuing the universal battle for existence on their lonely aerial islands. Presumably they must from time to time have some contact with the ground; Alvin saw one of the great balloons suddenly collapse and fall out of the sky, its broken envelope acting as a crude parachute. He wondered if this was an accident, or part of the life cycle of these strange entities.

Hilvar slept while they waited for the next planet to approach. For some reason which the robot could not explain to them, the ship traveled slowly—at least by comparison with its Universe-spanning haste—now that it was within a Solar System. It took almost two hours to reach the world that Alvin had chosen for his third stop, and he was a little surprised that any mere interplanetary journey should last so long.

He woke Hilvar as they dropped down into the atmosphere.

"What do you make of *that?*" he asked, pointing to the vision screen.

Below them was a bleak landscape of blacks and grays, showing no sign of vegetation or any other direct evidence of life. But there was indirect evidence; the low hills and shallow valleys were dotted with perfectly formed hemispheres, some of them arranged in complex, symmetrical patterns.

They had learned caution on the last planet, and after carefully considering all the possibilities remained poised high in the atmosphere while they sent the robot down to investigate. Through its eyes, they saw one of the hemispheres approach until the robot was floating only a few feet away from the completely smooth, featureless surface.

There was no sign of any entrance, nor any hint of the purpose which the structure served. It was quite large—over a hundred feet high; some of the other hemispheres were larger still. If it was a building, there appeared to be no way in or out.

After some hesitation, Alvin ordered the robot to move forward and touch the dome. To his utter astonishment, it refused to obey him. This indeed was mutiny—or so at first sight it seemed.

"Why won't you do what I tell you?" asked Alvin, when he had recovered from his astonishment.

"It is forbidden," came the reply.

"Forbidden by whom?"

"I do not know."

"Then how—no, cancel that. Was the order built into you?"

"No."

That seemed to eliminate one possibility. The builders of these domes might well have been the race who made the robot, and might have included this taboo in the machine's original instructions.

"When did you receive the order?" asked Alvin.

"I received it when I landed."

Alvin turned to Hilvar, the light of a new hope burning in his eyes.

"There's intelligence here! Can you sense it?"

"No," Hilvar replied. "This place seems as dead to me as the first world we visited."

"I'm going outside to join the robot. Whatever spoke to it may speak to me."

Hilvar did not argue the point, though he looked none too happy. They brought the ship to earth a hundred feet away from the dome, not far from the waiting robot, and opened the air lock.

Alvin knew that the lock could not be opened unless the ship's brain had already satisfied itself that the atmosphere was breathable. For a moment he thought it had made a mistake—the air was so thin and gave such little sustenance to his lungs. Then, by inhaling deeply, he found that he could grasp enough oxygen to survive, though he felt that a few minutes here would be all that he could endure.

Panting hard, they walked up to the robot and to the curving wall of the enigmatic dome. They took one more step—then stopped in unison as if hit by the same sudden blow. In their minds, like the tolling of a mighty gong, had boomed a single message:

DANGER. COME NO CLOSER.

That was all. It was a message not in words, but in pure thought. Alvin was certain that any creature, whatever its level of intelligence, would receive the same warning, in the same utterly unmistakable fashion—deep within its mind.

It was a warning, not a threat. Somehow they knew that it was not directed *against* them; it was for their own protection. Here it seemed to say, is something intrinsically dangerous, and we, its makers, are anxious that no one shall be hurt through blundering ignorantly into it.

Alvin and Hilvar stepped back several paces, and looked at each other, each waiting for the other to say what was in his mind. Hilvar was the first to sum up the position.

"I was right, Alvin," he said. "There is no intelligence here. That warning is automatic—triggered by our presence when we get too close."

Alvin nodded in agreement.

"I wonder what they were trying to protect," he said. "There could be buildings—anything—under these domes."

"There's no way we can find out, if all the domes warn us off. It's interesting—the difference between the three planets we've visited. They took everything away from the first—they abandoned the second without bothering about it—but they went to a lot of trouble here. Perhaps they expected to come back some day, and wanted everything to be ready for them when they returned."

"But they never did—and that was a long time ago."

"They may have changed their minds."

It was curious, Alvin thought, how both he and Hilvar had unconsciously started using the word "they." Whoever or whatever "they" had been, their presence had been strong on that first planet—and was even stronger here. This was a world that had been carefully wrapped up, and put away until it might be needed again.

"Let's go back to the ship," panted Alvin. "I can't breathe properly here."

As soon as the air lock had closed behind them, and they were at ease once more, they discussed their next move. To make a thorough investigation, they should sample a large number of domes, in the hope that they might find one that had no warning and which could be entered. If that failed—but Alvin would not face that possibility until he had to.

He faced it less than an hour later, and in a far more dramatic form than he would have dreamed. They had sent the robot down to half a dozen domes, always with the same result, when they came across a scene that was badly out of place on this tidy, neatly packaged world.

Below them was a broad valley, sparsely sprinkled with the tantalizing, impenetrable domes. At its center was the unmistakable scar of a great explosion—an explosion that had thrown debris for miles in all directions and burned a shallow crater in the ground.

And beside the crater was the wreckage of a spaceship.

TWENTY-ONE

They landed close to the scene of this ancient tragedy, and walked slowly, conserving their breath, toward the immense, broken hull towering above them. Only a short section—either the prow or the stern—of the ship remained; presumably the rest had been destroyed in the explosion. As they approached the wreck, a thought slowly dawned in Alvin's mind, becoming stronger and stronger until it attained the status of certainty.

"Hilvar," he said, finding it hard to talk and walk at the same time, "I believe this is the ship that landed on the first planet we visited."

Hilvar nodded, preferring not to waste air. The same idea had already occurred to him. It was a good object lesson, he thought, for incautious visitors. He hoped it would not be lost on Alvin.

They reached the hull and stared up into the exposed interior of the ship. It was like looking into a huge building that had been roughly sliced in two; floors and walls and ceilings, broken at the point of the explosion, gave a distorted chart of the ship's cross section. What strange beings, wondered Alvin, still lay where they had died in the wreckage of their vessel?

"I don't understand this," said Hilvar suddenly. "This portion of the ship is badly damaged, but it's still fairly intact. Where's the rest of it? Did it break in two out in space, and this part crash here?"

Not until they had sent the robot exploring again, and had themselves examined the area around the wreckage, did they learn the answer. There was no shadow of doubt; any reservations they might have had were banished when Alvin found the line of low mounds, each ten feet long, on the little hill beside the ship.

"So they landed here," mused Hilvar, "and ignored the warning. They were inquisitive, just as you are. They tried to open that dome."

He pointed to the other side of the crater, to the smooth, still unmarked shell within which the departed rulers of this world had sealed their treasures. But it was no longer a dome: it was now an almost complete sphere, for the ground in which it had been set had been blasted away.

"They wrecked their ship, and many of them were killed. Yet despite that, they managed to make repairs and leave again, cutting off this section and stripping out everything of value. What a task that must have been!"

Alvin scarcely heard him. He was looking at the curious marker that had first drawn him to this spot—the slim shaft ringed by a horizontal circle a third of the way down from its tip. Alien and unfamiliar though it was, he could respond to the mute message it had carried down the ages.

Underneath those stones, if he cared to disturb them, was the answer to one question at least. It could remain unanswered; whatever these creatures might have been, they had earned their right to rest.

Hilvar scarcely heard the words Alvin whispered as they walked slowly back to the ship.

"I hope they got home," he said.

"And where now?" asked Hilvar, when they were once more out in space.

Alvin stared thoughtfully at the screen before replying.

"Do you think I should go back?" he said.

"It would be the sensible thing to do. Our luck may not hold out much longer, and who knows what other surprises these planets may have waiting for us?"

It was the voice of sanity and caution, and Alvin was now prepared to give it greater heed than he would have done a few days before. But he had come a long way, and waited all his life, for this moment; he would not turn back while there was still so much to see.

"We'll stay in the ship from now on," he said, "and we won't touch surface anywhere. That should be safe enough, surely."

Hilvar shrugged his shoulders, as if refusing to accept any responsibility for what might happen next. Now that Alvin was showing a certain amount of caution, he thought it unwise to admit that he was equally anxious to continue their exploring, though he had long ago abandoned all hope of meeting intelligent life upon any of these planets.

A double world lay ahead of them, a great planet with a smaller satellite beside it. The primary might have been the twin of the second world they had visited; it was clothed in that same blanket of livid green. There would be no point in landing here; this was a story they already knew.

Alvin brought the ship low over the surface of the satellite; he needed no warning from the complex mechanisms which protected him to know that there was no atmosphere here. All shadows had a sharp, clean edge, and there were no gradations between night and day. It was the first world on which he had seen something approaching night, for only one of the more distant suns was above the horizon in the area where they made first contact. The landscape was bathed in a dull red light, as though it had been dipped in blood.

For many miles they flew low above mountains that were still as jagged and sharp as in the distant ages of their birth. This was a world that had never known change or decay, had never been scoured by winds and rains. No eternity circuits were needed here to preserve objects in their pristine freshness.

But if there was no air, then there could have been no life—or could there have been?

"Of course," said Hilvar, when Alvin put the question to him, "there's nothing biologically absurd in the idea. Life can't originate in airless space—but it can evolve forms that will survive in it. It must have happened millions of times, whenever an inhabited planet lost its atmosphere."

"But would you expect *intelligent* life forms to exist in a vacuum? Wouldn't they have protected themselves against the loss of their air?"

"Probably, if it occurred *after* they achieved enough intelligence to stop it happening. But if the atmosphere went while they were still in the primitive state, they would have to adapt or perish. After they had adapted, they might then develop a very high intelligence. In fact, they probably would—the incentive would be so great."

The argument, decided Alvin, was a purely theoretical one, as far as this planet was concerned. Nowhere was there any sign that it had ever borne life, intelligent or otherwise. But in that case, what was the purpose of this world? The entire multiple system of the Seven Suns, he was now certain, was artificial, and this world must be part of its grand design.

It could, conceivably, be intended purely for ornament—to provide a moon in the sky of its giant companion. Even in that case, however, it seemed likely that it would be put to *some* use.

"Look," said Hilvar, pointing to the screen. "Over there, on the right."

Alvin changed the ship's course, and the landscape tilted around them. The red-lit rocks blurred with the speed of their motion; then the image stabilized, and sweeping below was the unmistakable evidence of life.

Unmistakable—yet also baffling. It took the form of a wide-spaced row of slender columns, each a hundred feet from its neighbor and twice as high. They stretched into the distance, dwindling in hypnotic perspective, until the far horizon swallowed them up.

Alvin swung the ship to the right, and began to race along the line of columns, wondering as he did so what purpose they could ever have served. They were absolutely uniform, marching in an unbroken file over hills and down into valleys. There was no sign that they had ever supported anything; they were smooth and featureless, tapering very slightly toward the top.

Quite abruptly, the line changed its course, turning sharply through a right angle. Alvin overshot by several miles before he reacted and was able to swing the ship around in the new direction.

The columns continued with the same unbroken stride across the landscape, their spacing perfectly regular. Then, fifty miles from the last change of course, they turned abruptly through another right angle. At this rate, thought Alvin, we will soon be back where we started.

The endless sequence of columns had so mesmerized them that when it was broken they were miles past the discontinuity before Hilvar cried out and made Alvin, who had noticed nothing, turn the ship back. They descended slowly, and as they circled above what Hilvar had found, a fantastic suspicion began to dawn in their minds—though at first neither dared mention it to the other.

Two of the columns had been broken off near their bases, and lay stretched out upon the rocks where they had fallen. Nor was that all; the two columns adjoining the gap had been bent outward by some irresistible force.

There was no escape from the awesome conclusion. Now Alvin knew what they had been flying over; it was something he had seen often enough in Lys, but until this moment the shocking change of scale had prevented recognition.

"Hilvar," he said, still hardly daring to put his thoughts into words, "do you know what this is?"

"It seems hard to believe, but we've been flying around the edge of a corral. This thing is a fence—a fence that hasn't been strong enough."

"People who keep pets," said Alvin, with the nervous laugh men sometimes use to conceal their awe, "should make sure they know how to keep them under control."

Hilvar did not react to his forced levity; he was staring at the broken barricade, his brow furrowed with thought.

"I don't understand it," he said at last. "Where could it have got food on a planet like this? And why did it break out of its pen? I'd give a lot to know what kind of animal it was."

"Perhaps it was left here, and broke out because it was hungry," Alvin surmised. "Or something may have made it annoyed."

"Let's go lower," said Hilvar. "I want to have a look at the ground."

They descended until the ship was almost touching the barren rock, and it was then that they noticed that the plain was pitted with innumerable small holes, no more than an inch or two wide. Outside the stockade, however, the ground was free from these mysterious pockmarks; they stopped abruptly at the line of the fence.

"You are right," said Hilvar. "It was hungry. But it wasn't an animal: it would be more accurate to call it a plant. It had exhausted the soil inside its pen, and had to find fresh food elsewhere. It probably moved quite slowly; perhaps it took years to break down those posts."

Alvin's imagination swiftly filled in the details he could never know with certainty. He did not doubt that Hilvar's analysis was basically correct, and that some botanical monster, perhaps moving too slowly for the eye to see, had fought a sluggish but relentless battle against the barriers that hemmed it in.

It might still be alive, even after all these ages, roving at will over the face of this planet. To look for it, however, would be a hopeless task, since it would mean quartering the surface of an entire globe. They made a desultory search in the few square miles around the gap, and located one great circular patch of pockmarks, almost five hundred feet across, where the creature had obviously stopped to feed—if one could apply that word to an organism that somehow drew its nourishment from solid rock.

As they lifted once more into space, Alvin felt a strange weariness come over him. He had seen so much, yet learned so little. There were many wonders on all these planets, but what he sought had fled them long ago. It would be useless, he knew, to visit the other worlds of the Seven Suns. Even if there was still intelligence in the Universe, where could he seek it now? He looked at the stars scattered like dust across the vision screen, and knew that what was left of time was not enough to explore them all.

A feeling of loneliness and oppression such as he had never before experienced seemed to overwhelm him. He could understand now the fear of Diaspar for the great spaces of the Universe, the terror that had made his people gather in the little microcosm of their city. It was hard to believe that, after all, they had been right.

He turned to Hilvar for support. But Hilvar was standing, fists tightly clenched and with a glazed look in his eyes. His head was tilted on one side; he seemed to be listening, straining every sense into the emptiness around them.

"What is it?" said Alvin urgently. He had to repeat the question before Hilvar showed any sign of hearing it. He was still staring into nothingness when he finally replied.

"There's something coming," he said slowly. "Something that I don't understand."

It seemed to Alvin that the cabin had suddenly become very cold, and the racial nightmare of the Invaders reared up to confront him in all its terror. With an effort of will that sapped his strength, he forced his mind away from panic.

"Is it friendly?" he asked. "Shall I run for Earth?"

Hilvar did not answer the first question—only the second. His voice was very faint, but showed no sign of alarm or fear. It held rather a vast astonishment and curiosity, as if he had encountered something so surprising that he could not be bothered to deal with Alvin's anxious query.

"You're too late," he said. "It's already here."

The Galaxy had turned many times on its axis since consciousness first came to Vanamonde. He could recall little of those first aeons and the creatures who had tended him then—but he could remember still his desolation when they had gone and left him alone among the stars. Down the ages since, he had wandered from sun to sun, slowly evolving and increasing his powers. Once he had dreamed of finding again those who had attended his birth, and though the dream had faded now, it had never wholly died.

On countless worlds he had found the wreckage that life had left behind, but intelligence he had discovered only once—and from the Black Sun he had fled in terror. Yet the Universe was very large, and the search had scarcely begun.

Far away though it was in space and time, the great burst of power from the heart of the Galaxy beckoned to Vanamonde across the light-years. It was utterly unlike the radiation of the stars, and it had appeared in his field of consciousness as suddenly as a meteor trail across a cloudless sky. He moved through space and time toward it, to the latest moment of its existence, sloughing from him in the way he knew the dead, unchanging pattern of the past.

The long metal shape, with its infinite complexities of structure, he could not understand, for it was as strange to him as almost all the things of the physical world. Around it still clung the aura of power that had drawn him across the Universe, but that was of no interest to him now. Carefully, with the delicate nervousness of a wild beast half poised for flight, he reached out toward the two minds he had discovered.

And then he knew that his long search was ended.

Alvin grasped Hilvar by the shoulders and shook him violently, trying to drag him back to a greater awareness of reality.

"Tell me what's happening!" he begged. "What do you want me to do?"

The remote, abstracted look slowly faded from Hilvar's eyes.

"I still don't understand," he said, "but there's no need to be frightened—I'm sure of that. Whatever it is, it won't harm us. It seems simply —interested."

Alvin was about to reply when he was suddenly overwhelmed by a sensation unlike any he had ever known before. A warm, tingling glow seemed to spread through his body; it lasted only a few seconds, but when it was gone he was no longer merely Alvin. Something was sharing his brain, overlapping it as one circle may partly cover another. He was conscious, also, of Hilvar's mind close at hand, equally entangled in whatever creature had descended upon them. The sensation was strange rather than unpleasant, and it gave Alvin his first glimpse of true telepathy—the power which in his people had so degenerated that it could now be used only to control machines.

Alvin had rebelled at once when Seranis had tried to dominate his mind, but he did not struggle against this intrusion. It would have been useless, and he knew that this creature, whatever it might be, was not unfriendly. He let himself relax, accepting without resistance the fact that an infinitely greater intelligence than his own was exploring his mind. But in that belief, he was not wholly right.

One of these minds, Vanamonde saw at once, was more sympathetic and accessible than the other. He could tell that both were filled with wonder at his presence, and that surprised him greatly. It was hard to believe that they could have forgotten; forgetfulness, like mortality, was beyond the comprehension of Vanamonde.

Communication was very difficult; many of the thought-images in their minds were so strange that he could hardly recognize them. He was puzzled and a little frightened by the recurrent fear pattern of the Invaders; it reminded him of his own emotions when the Black Sun first came into his field of knowledge.

But they knew nothing of the Black Sun, and now their own questions were beginning to form in his mind.

"What are you?"

He gave the only reply he could.

"I am Vanamonde."

There came a pause (how long the pattern of their thoughts took to form!) and then the question was repeated. They had not understood; that was strange, for surely their kind had given him his name for it to be among the memories of his birth. Those memories were very few, and they began strangely at a single point in time, but they were crystal clear.

Again their tiny thoughts struggled up into his consciousness.

"Where are the people who built the Seven Suns? What happened to them?"

He did not know; they could scarcely believe him, and their disappointment came sharp and clear across the abyss separating their minds from his. But they were patient and he was glad to help them, for their quest was the same as his and they gave him the first companionship he had ever known.

As long as he lived, Alvin did not believe he would ever again undergo so strange an experience as this soundless conversation. It was hard to believe that he could be little more than a spectator, for he did not care to admit, even to himself, that Hilvar's mind was in some ways so much more capable than his own. He could only wait and wonder, half dazed by the torrent of thought just beyond the limits of his understanding.

Presently Hilvar, rather pale and strained, broke off the contact and turned to his friend.

"Alvin," he said, his voice very tired. "There's something strange here. I don't understand it at all."

The news did a little to restore Alvin's self-esteem, and his face must have shown his feelings for Hilvar gave a sudden, sympathetic smile.

"I can't discover what this–Vanamonde–is," he continued. "It's a creature of tremendous knowledge, but it seems to have very little intelligence. Of course," he added, "its mind may be of such a different order that we can't understand it–yet somehow I don't believe that is the right explanation."

"Well, what *have* you learned?" asked Alvin with some impatience. "Does it know anything about the Seven Suns?"

Hilvar's mind still seemed very far away.

"They were built by many races, including our own," he said absently. "It can give me facts like that, but it doesn't seem to understand their meaning. I believe it's conscious of the past, without being able to interpret it. Everything that's ever happened seems jumbled together in its mind."

He paused thoughtfully for a moment; then his face lightened.

"There's only one thing to do; somehow or other, we must get Vanamonde to Earth so that our philosophers can study him."

"Would that be safe?" asked Alvin.

"Yes," answered Hilvar, thinking how uncharacteristic his friend's remark was. "Vanamonde is friendly. More than that, in fact, he seems almost affectionate."

And quite suddenly the thought that all the while had been hovering at the edge of Alvin's consciousness came clearly into view. He remembered Krif and all the small animals that were constantly escaping, to the annoyance or alarm of Hilvar's friends. And he recalled—how long ago that seemed!—the zoological purpose behind their expedition to Shalmirane.

Hilvar had found a new pet.

TWENTY-TWO

How completely unthinkable, Jeserac mused, this conference would have seemed only a few short days ago. The six visitors from Lys sat facing the Council, along a table placed across the open end of the horseshoe. It was ironic to remember that not long ago Alvin had stood at that same spot and heard the Council rule that Diaspar must be closed again from the world. Now the world had broken in upon it with a vengeance—and not only the world, but the Universe.

The Council itself had already changed. No less than five of its members were missing. They had been unable to face the responsibilities and problems now confronting them, and had followed the path that Khedron had already taken. It was, thought Jeserac, proof that Diaspar had failed if so many of its citizens were unable to face their first real challenge in millions of years. Many thousands of them had already fled into the brief oblivion of the Memory Banks, hoping that when they awoke the crisis would be past and Diaspar would be its familiar self again. They would be disappointed.

Jeserac had been co-opted to fill one of the vacant places on the Council. Though he was under something of a cloud, owing to his position as Alvin's tutor, his presence was so obviously essential that no one had suggested excluding him. He sat at one end of the horseshoe-shaped table—a position which gave him several advantages. Not only could he study the profiles of the visitors, but he could also see the faces of his fellow Councilors—and their expressions were sufficiently instructive.

There was no doubt that Alvin had been right, and the Council was slowly realizing the unpalatable truth. The delegates from Lys could think far more swiftly than the finest minds in Diaspar. Nor was that their only advantage, for they also showed an extraordinary degree of co-ordination which Jeserac guessed must be due to their telepathic powers. He wondered if they were reading the Councilors' thoughts, but decided that they would not have broken the solemn assurance without which this meeting would have been impossible.

Jeserac did not think that much progress had been made; for that matter, he did not see how it could have been made. The Council, which had barely accepted the existence of Lys, still seemed incapable of realizing what had happened. But it was clearly frightened—and so, he guessed, were the visitors, though they managed to conceal the fact better.

Jeserac himself was not as terrified as he had expected; his fears were still there, but he had faced them at last. Something of Alvin's own recklessness—or was it courage?—had begun to change his outlook and give him new horizons. He did not believe he would ever be able to set foot beyond the walls of Diaspar, but now he understood the impulse that had driven Alvin to do so.

The President's question caught him unawares, but he recovered himself quickly.

"I think," he said, "that it was sheer chance that this situation never arose before. We know that there were fourteen earlier Uniques, and there must have been some definite plan behind their creation. That plan, I believe, was to insure that Lys and Diaspar would not remain apart forever. Alvin has seen to that, but he has also done something which I do not imagine was ever in the original scheme. Could the Central Computer confirm that?"

The impersonal voice replied at once.

"The Councilor knows that I cannot comment on the instructions given to me by my designers."

Jeserac accepted the mild reproof.

"Whatever the cause, we cannot dispute the facts. Alvin has gone out into space. When he returns, you may prevent him leaving again—though I doubt if you will succeed, for he may have learned a great deal by then. And if what you fear has happened, there is nothing any of us can do about it. Earth is utterly helpless—as she has been for millions of centuries."

Jeserac paused and glanced along the tables. His words had pleased no one, nor had he expected them to do so.

"Yet I don't see why we should be alarmed. Earth is in no greater danger now than she has always been. Why should two men in a single small ship bring the wrath of the Invaders down upon us again? If we'll be honest with ourselves, we must admit that the Invaders could have destroyed our world ages ago."

There was a disapproving silence. This was heresy—and once Jeserac himself would have condemned it as such.

The President interrupted, frowning heavily.

"Is there not a legend that the Invaders spared Earth itself only on condition that Man never went into space again? And have we not now broken those conditions?"

"A legend, yes," said Jeserac. "We accept many things without question, and this is one of them. However, there is no proof of it. I find it hard to believe that anything of such importance would not be recorded in the memories of the Central Computer, yet it knows nothing of this pact. I have asked it, though only through the information machines. The Council may care to ask the question directly."

Jeserac saw no reason why he should risk a second admonishment by trespassing on forbidden territory, and waited for the President's reply.

It never came, for in that moment the visitors from Lys suddenly started in their seats, while their faces froze in simultaneous expressions of incredulity and alarm. They seemed to be listening while some faraway voice poured its message into their ears.

The Councilors waited, their own apprehension growing minute by minute as the soundless conversation proceeded. Then the leader of the delegation shook himself free from his trance, and turned apologetically to the President.

"We have just had some very strange and disturbing news from Lys," he said.

"Has Alvin returned to Earth?" asked the President.

"No—not Alvin. Something else."

As he brought his faithful ship down in the glade of Airlee, Alvin wondered if ever in human history any ship had brought such a cargo to Earth—if, indeed, Vanamonde was located in the physical space of the machine. There had been no sign of him on the voyage; Hilvar believed, and his knowledge was more direct, that only Vanamonde's sphere of attention could be said to have any position in space. Vanamonde himself was not located anywhere—perhaps not even *anywhen*.

Seranis and five Senators were waiting for them as they emerged from the ship. One of the Senators Alvin had already met on his last visit; the other two from that previous meeting were, he gathered, now in Diaspar. He wondered how the delegation was faring, and how the city had reacted to the presence of the first intruders from outside in so many millions of years.

"It seems, Alvin," said Seranis dryly, after she had greeted her son, "that you have a genius for discovering remarkable entities. Still, I think it will be some time before you can surpass your present achievement."

For once, it was Alvin's turn to be surprised.

"Then Vanamonde's arrived?"

"Yes, hours ago. Somehow he managed to trace the path your ship made on its outward journey—a staggering feat in itself, and one which raises interesting philosophical problems. There is some evidence that he reached Lys at the moment you discovered him, so that he is capable of infinite speeds. And that is not all. In the last few hours he has taught us more of history than we thought existed."

Alvin looked at her in amazement. Then he understood; it was not hard to imagine what the impact of Vanamonde must have been upon this people, with their keen perceptions and their wonderfully interlocking minds. They had reacted with surprising speed, and he had a sudden incongruous picture of Vanamonde, perhaps a little frightened, surrounded by the eager intellects of Lys.

"Have you discovered what he is?" Alvin asked.

"Yes. That was simple, though we still don't know his origin. He's a pure mentality and his knowledge seems to be unlimited. But he's childish, and I mean that quite literally."

"Of course!" cried Hilvar. "I should have guessed!"

Alvin looked puzzled, and Seranis took pity on him.

"I mean that although Vanamonde has a colossal, perhaps an infinite mind, he's immature and undeveloped. His actual intelligence is less than that of a human being"—she smiled a little wryly—"though his thought processes are much faster and he learns very quickly. He also has some powers we do not yet understand. The whole of the past seems open to his mind, in a way that's difficult to describe. He may have used that ability to follow your path back to Earth."

Alvin stood in silence, for once somewhat overcome. He realized how right Hilvar had been to bring Vanamonde to Lys. And he knew how lucky he had been ever to outwit Seranis; that was not something he would do twice in a lifetime.

"Do you mean," he asked, "that Vanamonde has only just been born?"

"By his standards, yes. His actual age is very great, though apparently less than Man's. The extraordinary thing is that he insists that *we* created him, and there's no doubt that his origin is bound up with all the great mysteries of the past."

"What's happening to Vanamonde now?" asked Hilvar in a slightly possessive voice.

"The historians of Grevarn are questioning him. They are trying to map out the main outlines of the past, but the work will take years. Vanamonde can describe the past in perfect detail, but as he doesn't understand what he sees it's very difficult to work with him."

Alvin wondered how Seranis knew all this; then he realized that probably every waking mind in Lys was watching the progress of the great research. He felt a sense of pride in the knowledge that he had now made as great a mark on Lys as on Diaspar, yet with that pride was mingled frustration. Here was something that he could never fully share nor understand: the direct contact even between human minds was as great a mystery to him as music must be to a deaf man or color to a blind one. Yet the people of Lys were now exchanging thoughts with this unimaginably alien being, whom he had led to Earth but whom he could never detect with any sense that he possessed.

There was no place for him here; when the inquiry was finished, he would be told the answers. He had opened the gates of infinity, and now felt awe—even fear—for all that he had done. For his own peace of mind, he must return to the tiny, familiar world of Diaspar, seeking its shelter while he came to grips with his dreams and his ambition. There was irony here; the one who had spurned the city to venture out among the stars was coming home as a frightened child runs back to its mother.

TWENTY-THREE

Diaspar was none too pleased to see Alvin again. The city was still in a ferment, like a giant beehive that had been violently stirred with a stick. It was still reluctant to face reality, but those who refused to admit the existence of Lys and the outside world no longer had a place to hide. The Memory Banks had ceased to accept them; those who tried to cling to their dreams, and to seek refuge in the future, now walked in vain into the Hall of Creation. The dissolving, heatless flame refused to greet them; they no longer awoke, their minds washed clean, a hundred thousand years further down the river of time. No appeal to the Central Computer was of any avail, nor would it explain the reason for its actions. The intended refugees had to turn sadly back into the city, to face the problems of their age.

Alvin and Hilvar had landed at the periphery of the park, not far from Council Hall. Until the last moment, Alvin was not certain that he could bring the ship into the city, through whatever screens fenced its sky from the outer world. The firmament of Diaspar, like all else about it, was artificial, or at least partly so. Night, with its starry reminder of all that Man had lost, was never allowed to intrude upon the city; it was protected also from the storms that sometimes raged across the desert and filled the sky with moving walls of sand.

The invisible guardians let Alvin pass, and as Diaspar lay spread out beneath him, he knew that he had come home. However much the Universe and its mysteries might call him, this was where he was born and where he belonged. It would never satisfy him, yet always he would return. He had gone halfway across the Galaxy to learn this simple truth.

The crowds had gathered even before the ship landed, and Alvin wondered how his fellow citizens would receive him now that he had returned. He could read their faces easily enough, as he watched them through the viewing screen before he opened the air lock. The dominant emotion seemed to be curiosity—in itself something new in Diaspar. Mingled with that was apprehension, while here and there were unmistakable signs of fear. No one, Alvin thought a little wistfully, seemed glad to see him back.

The Council, on the other hand, positively welcomed him—though not out of pure friendship. Though he had caused this crisis, he alone could give the facts on which future policy must be based. He was listened to with deep attention as he described his flight to the Seven Suns and his meeting with Vanamonde. Then he answered innumerable questions, with a patience which probably surprised his interrogators. Uppermost in their minds, he quickly discovered, was the fear of the Invaders, though they never mentioned the name and were clearly unhappy when he broached the subject directly.

"If the Invaders are still in this Universe," Alvin told the Council, "then surely I should have met them at its very center. But there is no intelligent life among the Seven Suns; we had already guessed that before Vanamonde confirmed it. I believe that the Invaders departed ages ago; certainly Vanamonde, who appears to be at least as old as Diaspar, knows nothing of them."

"I have a suggestion," said one of the Councilors suddenly. "Vanamonde may be a descendant of the Invaders, in some way beyond our present understanding. He has forgotten his origin, but that does not mean that one day he may not be dangerous again."

Hilvar, who was present merely as a spectator, did not wait for permission to speak. It was the first time that Alvin had ever seen him angry.

"Vanamonde has looked into my mind," he said, "and I have glimpsed something of his. My people have already learned much about him, though they have not yet discovered what he is. But one thing is certain—he is friendly, and was glad to find us. We have nothing to fear from him."

There was a brief silence after this outburst, and Hilvar relaxed with a somewhat embarrassed expression. It was noticeable that the tension in the Council Chamber lessened from then on, as if a cloud had lifted from the spirits of those present. Certainly the President made no attempt, as he was supposed to do, to censure Hilvar for his interruption.

It was clear to Alvin, as he listened to the debate, that three schools of thought were represented on the Council. The conservatives, who were in a minority, still hoped that the clock could be turned back and that the old order could somehow be restored. Against all reason, they clung to the hope that Diaspar and Lys could be persuaded to forget each other again.

The progressives were an equally small minority; the fact that there were any on the Council at all pleased and surprised Alvin. They did not exactly welcome this invasion of the outer world, but they were determined to make the best of it. Some of them went so far as to suggest that there might be a way of breaking through the psychological barriers which for so long had sealed Diaspar even more effectively than the physical ones.

Most of the Council, accurately reflecting the mood of the city, had adopted an attitude of watchful caution, while they waited for the pattern of the future to emerge. They realized that they could make no general plans, nor try to carry out any definite policy, until the storm had passed.

Jeserac joined Alvin and Hilvar when the session was over. He seemed to have changed since they had last met—and last parted—in the Tower of Loranne, with the desert spread out beneath them. The change was not one that Alvin had expected, though it was one that he was to encounter more and more often in the days to come.

Jeserac seemed younger, as if the fires of life had found fresh fuel and were burning more brightly in his veins. Despite his age, he was one of those who could accept the challenge that Alvin had thrown to Diaspar.

"I have some news for you, Alvin," he said. "I think you know Senator Gerane."

Alvin was puzzled for a moment; then he remembered.

"Of course—he was one of the first men I met in Lys. Isn't he a member of their delegation?"

"Yes; we have grown to know each other quite well. He is a brilliant man, and understands more about the human mind than I would have believed possible—though he tells me that by the standards of Lys he is only a beginner. While he is here, he is starting a project which will be very close to your heart. He is hoping to analyze the compulsion which keeps us in the city, and he believes that once he has discovered how it was imposed, he will be able to remove it. About twenty of us are already co-operating with him."

"And you are one of them?"

"Yes," replied Jeserac, showing the nearest approach to bashfulness that Alvin had ever seen or ever would see. "It is not easy, and certainly not pleasant—but it is stimulating."

"How does Gerane work?"

"He is operating through the sagas. He has had a whole series of them constructed, and studies our reactions when we are experiencing them. I never thought, at my age, that I should go back to my childhood recreations again!"

"What are the sagas?" asked Hilvar.

"Imaginary dream worlds," explained Alvin. "At least, most of them are imaginary, though some are probably based on historical facts. There are millions of them recorded in the memory cells of the city; you can take your choice of any kind of adventure or experience you wish, and it will seem utterly real to you while the impulses are being fed into your mind." He turned to Jeserac.

"What kind of sagas does Gerane take you into?"

"Most of them are concerned, as you might expect, with leaving Diaspar. Some have taken us back to our very earliest lives, to as near to the founding of the city as we can get. Gerane believes that the closer he can get to the origin of this compulsion, the more easily he will be able to undermine it."

Alvin felt very encouraged by this news. His work would be merely half accomplished if he had opened the gates of Diaspar—only to find that no one would pass through them.

"Do you *really* want to be able to leave Diaspar?" asked Hilvar shrewdly.

"No," replied Jeserac, without hesitation. "I am terrified of the idea. But I realize that we were completely wrong in thinking that Diaspar was all the world that mattered, and logic tells me that something has to be done to rectify the mistake. Emotionally, I am still quite incapable of leaving the city; perhaps I always shall be. Gerane thinks he can get some of us to come to Lys, and I am willing to help him with the experiment—even though half the time I hope that it will fail."

Alvin looked at his old tutor with a new respect. He no longer discounted the power of suggestion, nor underestimated the forces which could compel a man to act in defiance of logic. He could not help comparing Jeserac's calm courage with Khedron's panic flight into the future—though with his new understanding of human nature he no longer cared to condemn the Jester for what he had done.

Gerane, he was certain, would accomplish what he had set out to do. Jeserac might be too old to break the pattern of a lifetime, however willing he might be to start afresh. That did not matter, for others would succeed, with the skilled guidance of the psychologists of Lys. And once a few had escaped from their billion-year-old mold, it would only be a question of time before the remainder could follow.

He wondered what would happen to Diaspar—and to Lys—when the barriers were fully down. Somehow, the best elements of both must be saved, and welded into a new and healthier culture. It was a terrifying task, and would need all the wisdom and all the patience that each could bring to bear.

Some of the difficulties of the forthcoming adjustments had already been encountered. The visitors from Lys had, politely enough, refused to live in the homes provided for them in the city. They had set up their own temporary accommodation in the park, among surroundings which reminded them of Lys. Hilvar was the only exception; though he disliked living in a house with indeterminate walls and ephemeral furniture, he bravely accepted Alvin's hospitality, reassured by the promise that they would not stay here for long.

Hilvar had never felt lonely in his life, but he knew loneliness in Diaspar. The city was stranger to him than Lys had been to Alvin, and he was oppressed and overwhelmed by its infinite complexity and by the myriads of strangers who seemed to crowd every inch of space around him. He knew, if only in a tenuous manner, everyone in Lys, whether he had met them or not. In a thousand lifetimes he could never know everyone in Diaspar, and though he realized that this was an irrational feeling, it left him vaguely depressed. Only his loyalty to Alvin held him here in a world that had nothing in common with his own.

He had often tried to analyze his feelings toward Alvin. His friendship sprang, he knew, from the same source that inspired his sympathy for all small and struggling creatures. This would have astonished those who thought of Alvin as willful, stubborn, and self-centered, needing no affection from anyone and incapable of returning it even if it was offered.

Hilvar knew better than this; he had sensed it instinctively even from the first. Alvin was an explorer, and all explorers are seeking something they have lost. It is seldom that they find it, and more seldom still that the attainment brings them greater happiness than the quest.

What Alvin was seeking, Hilvar did not know. He was driven by forces that had been set in motion ages before, by the men of genius who planned Diaspar with such perverse skill—or by the men of even greater genius who had opposed them. Like every human being, Alvin was in some measure a machine, his actions predetermined by his inheritance. That did not alter his need for understanding and sympathy, nor did it render him immune to loneliness or frustration. To his own people, he was so unaccountable a creature that they sometimes forgot that he still shared their emotions. It needed a stranger from a totally different environment to see him as another human being.

Within a few days of arriving in Diaspar, Hilvar had met more people than in his entire life. Met them—and had grown to know practically none. Because they were so crowded together, the inhabitants of the city maintained a reserve that was hard to penetrate. The only privacy they knew was that of the mind, and they still clung to this even as they made their way through the endless social activities of Diaspar. Hilvar felt sorry for them, though he knew that they felt no need for his sympathy. They did not realize what they were missing—they could not understand the warm sense of community, the feeling of *belonging*, which linked everyone together in the telepathic society of Lys. Indeed, though they were polite enough to try to conceal it, it was obvious that most of the people he spoke to looked upon him pityingly as leading an incredibly dull and drab existence.

Eriston and Etania, Alvin's guardians, Hilvar quickly dismissed as kindly but totally baffled nonentities. He found it very confusing to hear Alvin refer to them as his father and mother—words which in Lys still retained their ancient biological meaning. It required a continual effort of imagination to remember that the laws of life and death had been repealed by the makers of Diaspar, and there were times when it seemed to Hilvar that despite all the activity around him, the city was half empty because it had no children.

He wondered what would happen to Diaspar now that its long isolation was over. The best thing the city could do, he decided, was to destroy the Memory Banks which had held it entranced for so many ages. Miraculous though they were—perhaps the supreme triumph of the science that had produced them—they were the creations of a sick culture, a culture that had been afraid of many things. Some of those fears had been based on reality, but others, it now seemed, lay only in the imagination. Hilvar knew a little of the pattern that was beginning to emerge from the exploration of Vanamonde's mind. In a few days, Diaspar would know it too—and would discover how much of its past had been a myth.

Yet if the Memory Banks were destroyed, within a thousand years the city would be dead, since its people had lost the power to reproduce themselves. That was the dilemma that had to be faced, but already Hilvar had glimpsed one possible solution. There was always an answer to any technical problem, and his people were masters of the biological sciences. What had been done could be undone, if Diaspar so wished.

First, however, the city would have to learn what it had lost. Its education would take many years—perhaps many centuries. But it was beginning; very soon the impact of the first lesson would shake Diaspar as profoundly as had contact with Lys itself.

It would shake Lys too. For all the difference between the two cultures, they had sprung from the same roots—and they had shared the same illusions. They would both be healthier when they looked once more, with a calm and steadfast gaze, into the past which they had lost.

TWENTY-FOUR

The amphitheater had been designed to hold the entire waking population of Diaspar, and scarcely one of its ten million places was empty. As he looked down the great curving sweep from his vantage point high up the slope, Alvin was irresistibly reminded of Shalmirane. The two craters were of the same shape, and almost the same size. If one packed the crater of Shalmirane with humanity, it would look very much like this.

There was, however, one fundamental difference between the two. The great bowl of Shalmirane existed; this amphitheater did not. Nor had it ever done so; it was merely a phantom, a pattern of electronic charges, slumbering in the memory of the Central Computer until the need came to call it forth. Alvin knew that in reality he was still in his room, and that all the myriads of people who appeared to surround him were equally in their own homes. As long as he made no attempt to move from this spot, the illusion was perfect. He could believe that Diaspar had been abolished and that all its citizens had been assembled here in this enormous concavity.

Not once in a thousand years did the life of the city stop so that all its people could meet in Grand Assembly. In Lys also, Alvin knew, the equivalent of this gathering was taking place. There it would be a meeting of minds, but perhaps associated with it would be an apparent meeting of bodies, as imaginary yet as seemingly real as this.

He could recognize most of the faces around him, out to the limits of unaided vision. More than a mile away, and a thousand feet below, was the little circular stage upon which the attention of the entire world was now fixed. It was hard to believe that he could see anything from such a distance, but Alvin knew that when the address began, he would hear and observe everything that happened as clearly as anyone else in Diaspar.

The stage filled with mist; the mist became Callitrax, leader of the group whose task it had been to reconstruct the past from the information which Vanamonde had brought to Earth. It had been a stupendous, almost an impossible undertaking, and not merely because of the spans of time involved. Only once, with the mental help of Hilvar, had Alvin been given a brief glimpse into the mind of the strange being they had discovered—or who had discovered them. To Alvin, the thoughts of Vanamonde were as meaningless as a thousand voices shouting together in some vast, echoing cave. Yet the men of Lys could disentangle them, could record them to be analyzed at leisure. Already, so it was rumored—though Hilvar would neither deny nor confirm this—what they had discovered was so strange that it bore scarcely any resemblance to the history which all the human race had accepted for a billion years.

Callitrax began to speak. To Alvin, as to everyone else in Diaspar, the clear, precise voice seemed to come from a point only a few inches away. Then, in a manner that was hard to define, just as the geometry of a dream defies logic yet rouses no surprise in the mind of the dreamer, Alvin was standing beside Callitrax while at the same time he retained his position high up on the slope of the amphitheater. The paradox did not puzzle him; he simply accepted it without question, like all the other masteries over time and space which science had given him.

Very briefly, Callitrax ran through the accepted history of the race. He spoke of the unknown peoples of the Dawn Civilizations, who had left behind them nothing but a handful of great names and the fading legends of the Empire. Even at the beginning, so the story went, Man had desired the stars—and had at last attained them. For millions of years he had expanded across the Galaxy, gathering system after system beneath his sway. Then, out of the darkness beyond the rim of the Universe, the Invaders had struck and wrenched from him all that he had won.

The retreat to the Solar System had been bitter and must have lasted many ages. Earth itself was barely saved by the fabulous battles that raged around Shalmirane. When all was over, Man was left with only his memories and the world on which he had been born.

Since then, all else had been long-drawn anticlimax. As an ultimate irony, the race that had hoped to rule the Universe had abandoned most of its own tiny world, and had split into the two isolated cultures of Lys and Diaspar—oases of life in a desert that sundered them as effectively as the gulfs between the stars.

Callitrax paused; to Alvin, as to everyone in the great assembly, it seemed that the historian was looking directly at him with eyes that had witnessed things which even now they could not wholly credit.

"So much," said Callitrax, "for the tales we have believed since our records began. I must tell you now that they are false—false in every detail—*so false that even now we have not fully reconciled them with the truth.*"

He waited for the full meaning of his words to strike home. Then, speaking slowly and carefully, he gave to both Lys and Diaspar the knowledge that had been won from the mind of Vanamonde.

It was not even true that Man had reached the stars. The whole of his little empire was bounded by the orbits of Pluto and Persephone, for interstellar space proved a barrier beyond his power to cross. His entire civilization was huddled around the sun, and was still very young when—the stars reached him.

The impact must have been shattering. Despite his failures, Man had never doubted that one day he would conquer the depths of space. He believed too that if the Universe held his equals, it did not hold his superiors. Now he knew that both beliefs were wrong, and that out among the stars were minds far greater than his own. For many centuries, first in the ships of other races and later in machines built with borrowed knowledge, Man had explored the Galaxy. Everywhere he found cultures he could understand but could not match, and here and there he encountered minds which would soon have passed altogether beyond his comprehension.

The shock was tremendous, but it proved the making of the race. Sadder and infinitely wiser, Man had returned to the Solar System to brood upon the knowledge he had gained. He would accept the challenge, and slowly he evolved a plan which gave hope for the future.

Once the physical sciences had been Man's greatest interest. Now he turned even more fiercely to genetics and the study of the mind. Whatever the cost, he would drive himself to the limits of his evolution.

The great experiment had consumed the entire energies of the race for millions of years. All that striving, all that sacrifice and toil, became only a handful of words in Callitrax's narrative. It had brought Man his greatest victories. He had banished disease; he could live forever if he wished, and in mastering telepathy he had bent the most subtle of all powers to his will.

He was ready to go out again, relying upon his own resources, into the great spaces of the Galaxy. He would meet as an equal the races of the worlds from which he had once turned aside. And he would play his full part in the story of the Universe.

These things he did. From this age, perhaps the most spacious of all history, came the legends of the Empire. It had been an Empire of many races, but this had been forgotten in the drama, too tremendous for tragedy, in which it had come to its end.

The Empire had lasted for at least a million years. It must have known many crises, perhaps even wars, but all these were lost in the sweep of great races moving together toward maturity.

"We can be proud," continued Callitrax, "of the part our ancestors played in this story. Even when they had reached their cultural plateau, they lost none of their initiative. We deal now with conjecture rather than proved fact, but it seems certain that the experiments which were at once the Empire's downfall and its crowning glory were inspired and directed by Man.

"The philosophy underlying these experiments appears to have been this. Contact with other species had shown Man how profoundly a race's world-picture depended upon its physical body and the sense organs with which it was equipped. It was argued that a true picture of the Universe could be attained, if at all, only by a mind that was free from such physical limitations—a pure mentality, in fact. This was a conception common among many of Earth's ancient religious faiths, and it seems strange that an idea which had no rational origin should finally become one of the greatest goals of science.

"No disembodied intelligence had ever been encountered in the natural Universe; the Empire set out to create one. We have forgotten, with so much else, the skills and knowledge that made this possible. The scientists of the Empire had mastered all the forces of Nature, all the secrets of time and space. As our minds are the by-product of an immensely intricate arrangement of brain cells, linked together by the network of the nervous system, so they strove to create a brain whose components were not material, but patterns embossed upon space itself. Such a brain, if one can call it that, would use electrical or yet higher forces for its operation, and would be completely free from the tyranny of matter. It could function with far greater speed than any organic intelligence; it could endure as long as there was an erg of free energy left in the Universe, and no limit could be seen for its powers. Once created, it would develop potentialities which even its makers could not foresee.

"Largely as a result of the experience gained in his own regeneration, Man suggested that the creation of such beings should be attempted. It was the greatest challenge ever thrown out to intelligence in the Universe, and after centuries of debate it was accepted. All the races of the Galaxy joined together in its fulfillment.

"More than a million years were to separate the dream from the reality. Civilizations were to rise and fall, again and yet again the age-long toil of worlds was to be lost, but the goal was never forgotten. One day we may know the full story of this, the greatest sustained effort in all history. Today we only know that its ending was a disaster that almost wrecked the Galaxy.

"Into this period Vanamonde's mind refuses to go. There is a narrow region of time which is blocked to him; but only, we believe, by his own fears. At its beginning we can see the Empire at the summit of its glory, taut with the expectation of coming success. At its end, only a few thousand years later, the Empire is shattered and the stars themselves are dimmed as though drained of their power. Over the Galaxy hangs a pall of fear, a fear with which is linked the name: 'The Mad Mind.'

"What must have happened in that short period is not hard to guess. The pure mentality had been created, but it was either insane or, as seems more likely from other sources, was implacably hostile to matter. For centuries it ravaged the Universe until brought under control by forces at which we cannot guess. Whatever weapon the Empire used in its extremity squandered the resources of the stars; from the memories of that conflict spring some, though not all, of the legends of the Invaders. But of this I shall presently say more.

"The Mad Mind could not be destroyed, for it was immortal. It was driven to the edge of the Galaxy and there imprisoned in a way we do not understand. Its prison was a strange artificial star known as the Black Sun, and there it remains to this day. When the Black Sun dies, it will be free again. How far in the future that day lies there is no way of telling."

Callitrax became silent, as if lost in his own thoughts, utterly unconscious of the fact that the eyes of all the world were upon him. In the long silence, Alvin glanced over the packed multitude around him, seeking to read their minds as they faced this revelation—and this unknown threat which must now replace the myth of the Invaders. For the most part, the faces of his fellow citizens were frozen in disbelief; they were still struggling to reject their false past, and could not yet accept the yet stranger reality that had superseded it.

Callitrax began to speak again in a quiet, more subdued voice as he described the last days of the Empire. This was the age, Alvin realized as the picture unfolded before him, in which he would have liked to have lived. There had been adventure then, and a superb and dauntless courage —the courage that could snatch victory from the teeth of disaster.

"Though the Galaxy had been laid waste by the Mad Mind, the resources of the Empire were still enormous, and its spirit was unbroken. With a courage at which we can only marvel, the great experiment was resumed and a search made for the flaw that had caused the catastrophe. There were now, of course, many who opposed the work and predicted further disasters, but they were overruled. The project went ahead and, with the knowledge so bitterly gained, this time it succeeded.

"The new race that was born had a potential intellect that could not even be measured. But it was completely infantile; we do not know if this was expected by its creators, but it seems likely that they knew it to be inevitable. Millions of years would be needed before it reached maturity, and nothing could be done to hasten the process. Vanamonde was the first of these minds; there must be others elsewhere in the Galaxy, but we believe that only a very few were created, for Vanamonde has never encountered any of his fellows.

"The creation of the pure mentalities was the greatest achievement of Galactic civilization; in it Man played a major and perhaps a dominant part. I have made no reference to Earth itself, for its story is merely a tiny thread in an enormous tapestry. Since it had always been drained of its most adventurous spirits, our planet had inevitably become highly conservative, and in the end it opposed the scientists who created Vanamonde. Certainly it played no part at all in the final act.

"The work of the Empire was now finished; the men of that age looked around at the stars they had ravaged in their desperate peril, and they made their decision. They would leave the Universe to Vanamonde.

"There is a mystery here—a mystery we may never solve, for Vanamonde cannot help us. All we know is that the Empire made contact with—something—very strange and very great, far away around the curve of the Cosmos, at the other extremity of space itself. What it was we can only guess, but its call must have been of immense urgency, and immense promise. Within a very short period of time our ancestors and their fellow races have gone upon a journey which we cannot follow. Vanamonde's thoughts seem to be bounded by the confines of the Galaxy, but through his mind we have watched the beginnings of this great and mysterious adventure. Here is the image that we have reconstructed; now you are going to look more than a billion years into the past—"

A pale wraith of its former glory, the slowly turning wheel of the Galaxy hung in nothingness. Throughout its length were the great empty rents which the Mad Mind had torn—wounds that in ages to come the drifting stars would fill. But they would never replace the splendor that had gone.

Man was about to leave his Universe, as long ago he had left his world. And not only Man, but the thousand other races that had worked with him to make the Empire. They were gathered together, here at the edge of the Galaxy, with its whole thickness between them and the goal they would not reach for ages.

They had assembled a fleet before which imagination quailed. Its flagships were suns, its smallest vessels, planets. An entire globular cluster, with all its solar systems and all their teeming worlds, was about to be launched across infinity.

The long line of fire smashed through the heart of the Universe, leaping from star to star. In a moment of time a thousand suns had died, feeding their energies to the monstrous shape that had torn along the axis of the Galaxy, and was now receding into the abyss. . . .

"So the Empire left our Universe, to meet its destiny elsewhere. When its heirs, the pure mentalities, have reached their full stature, it may return again. But that day must still lie far ahead.

"This, in its briefest and most superficial outlines, is the story of Galactic civilization. Our own history, which to us seems so important, is no more than a belated and trivial epilogue, though one so complex that we have not been able to unravel all its details. It seems that many of the older, less adventurous races refused to leave their homes; our direct ancestors were among them. Most of these races fell into decadence and are now extinct, though some may still survive. Our own world barely escaped the same fate. During the Transition Centuries—which actually lasted for millions of years—the knowledge of the past was lost or else deliberately destroyed. The latter, hard though it is to believe, seems more probable. For ages, Man sank into a superstitious yet still scientific barbarism during which he distorted history to remove his sense of impotence and failure. The legends of the Invader are completely false, although the desperate struggle against the Mad Mind undoubtedly contributed something to them. Nothing drove our ancestors back to Earth except the sickness in their souls.

"When we made this discovery, one problem in particular puzzled us in Lys. The Battle of Shalmirane never occurred—yet Shalmirane existed, and exists to this day. What is more, it was one of the greatest weapons of destruction ever built.

"It took us some time to resolve this puzzle, but the answer, once it was found, was very simple. Long ago our Earth had a single giant satellite, the Moon. When, in the tug of war between the tides and gravity, the Moon at last began to fall, it became necessary to destroy it. Shalmirane was built for that purpose, and around its use were woven the legends you all know."

Callitrax smiled a little ruefully at his immense audience.

"There are many such legends, partly true and partly false, and other paradoxes in our past which have not yet been resolved. That problem, though, is one for the psychologist rather than the historian. Even the records of the Central Computer cannot be wholly trusted, and bear clear evidence of tampering in the very remote past.

"On Earth, only Diaspar and Lys survived the period of decadence—Diaspar thanks to the perfection of its machines, Lys owing to its partial isolation and the unusual intellectual powers of its people. But both cultures, even when they had struggled back to their former level, were distorted by the fears and myths they had inherited.

"These fears need haunt us no longer. It is not my duty as a historian to predict the future, only to observe and interpret the past. But its lesson is clear enough; we have lived too long out of contact with reality, and now the time has come to rebuild our lives."

TWENTY-FIVE

Jeserac walked in silent wonder through the streets of a Diaspar he had never seen. So different was it, indeed, from the city in which he had passed all his lives that he would never have recognized it. Yet he knew that it was Diaspar, though *how* he knew, he did not pause to ask.

The streets were narrow, the buildings lower—and the park was gone. Or, rather, it did not yet exist. This was the Diaspar before the change, the Diaspar that had been open to the world and to the Universe. The sky above the city was pale blue and flecked with raveled wisps of cloud, slowly twisting and turning in the winds that blew across the face of this younger Earth.

Passing through and beyond the clouds were more substantial voyagers of the sky. Miles above the city, lacing the heavens with their silent tracery, the ships that linked Diaspar with the outer world came and went upon their business. Jeserac stared for a long time at the mystery and wonder of the open sky, and for a moment fear brushed against his soul. He felt naked and unprotected, conscious that this peaceful, blue dome above his head was no more than the thinnest of shells—that beyond it lay space, with all its mystery and menace.

The fear was not strong enough to paralyze his will. In part of his mind Jeserac knew that this whole experience was a dream, and a dream could not harm him. He would drift through it, savoring all that it brought to him, until he woke once more in the city that he knew.

He was walking into the heart of Diaspar, toward the point where in his own age stood the Tomb of Yarlan Zey. There was no tomb here, in this ancient city—only a low, circular building with many arched doorways leading into it. By one of those doorways a man was waiting for him.

Jeserac should have been overcome with astonishment, but nothing could surprise him now. Somehow it seemed right and natural that he should now be face to face with the man who had built Diaspar.

"You recognize me, I imagine," said Yarlan Zey.

"Of course; I have seen your statue a thousand times. You are Yarlan Zey, and this is Diaspar as it was a billion years ago. I know I am dreaming, and that neither of us is really here."

"Then you need not be alarmed at anything that happens. So follow me, and remember that nothing can harm you, since whenever you wish you can wake up in Diaspar—in your own age."

Obediently, Jeserac followed Yarlan Zey into the building, his mind a receptive, uncritical sponge. Some memory, or echo of a memory, warned him of what was going to happen next, and he knew that once he would have shrunk from it in horror. Now, however, he felt no fear. Not only did he feel protected by the knowledge that this experience was not real, but the presence of Yarlan Zey seemed a talisman against any dangers that might confront him.

There were few people drifting down the glideways that led into the depths of the building, and they had no other company when presently they stood in silence beside the long, streamlined cylinder which, Jeserac knew, could carry him out of the city on a journey that would once have shattered his mind. When his guide pointed to the open door, he paused for no more than a moment on the threshold, and then was through.

"You see?" said Yarlan Zey with a smile. "Now relax, and remember that you are safe—that nothing can touch you."

Jeserac believed him. He felt only the faintest tremor of apprehension as the tunnel entrance slid silently toward him, and the machine in which he was traveling began to gain speed as it hurtled through the depths of the earth. Whatever fears he might have had were forgotten in his eagerness to talk with this almost mythical figure from the past.

"Does it not seem strange to you," began Yarlan Zey, "that though the skies are open to us, we have tried to bury ourselves in the Earth? It is the beginning of the sickness whose ending you have seen in your age. Humanity is trying to hide; it is frightened of what lies out there in space, and soon it will have closed all the doors that lead into the Universe."

"But I saw spaceships in the sky above Diaspar," said Jeserac.

"You will not see them much longer. We have lost contact with the stars, and soon even the planets will be deserted. It took us millions of years to make the outward journey—but only centuries to come home again. And in a little while we will have abandoned almost all of Earth itself."

"Why did you do it?" asked Jeserac. He knew the answer, yet somehow felt impelled to ask the question.

"We needed a shelter to protect us from two fears—fear of death, and fear of space. We were a sick people, and wanted no further part in the Universe—so we pretended that it did not exist. We had seen chaos raging through the stars, and yearned for peace and stability. Therefore Diaspar had to be closed, so that nothing new could ever enter it.

"We designed the city that you know, and invented a false past to conceal our cowardice. Oh, we were not the first to do that—but we were the first to do it so thoroughly. And we redesigned the human spirit, robbing it of ambition and the fiercer passions, so that it would be contented with the world it now possessed.

"It took a thousand years to build the city and all its machines. As each of us completed his task, his mind was washed clean of its memories, the carefully planned pattern of false ones was implanted, and his identity was stored in the city's circuits until the time came to call it forth again.

"So at last there came a day when there was not a single man alive in Diaspar; there was only the Central Computer, obeying the orders which we had fed into it, and controlling the Memory Banks in which we were sleeping. There was no one who had any contact with the past—and so at this point, history began.

"Then, one by one, in a predetermined sequence, we were called out of the memory circuits and given flesh again. Like a machine that had just been built and was now set operating for the first time, Diaspar began to carry out the duties for which it had been designed.

"Yet some of us had had doubts even from the beginning. Eternity was a long time; we recognized the risks involved in leaving no outlet, and trying to seal ourselves completely from the Universe. We could not defy the wishes of our culture, so we worked in secret, making the modifications we thought necessary.

"The Uniques were our invention. They would appear at long intervals and would, if circumstances allowed them, discover if there was anything beyond Diaspar that was worth the effort of contacting. We never imagined that it would take so long for one of them to succeed—nor did we imagine that his success would be so great."

Despite that suspension of the critical faculties which is the very essence of a dream, Jeserac wondered fleetingly how Yarlan Zey could speak with such knowledge of things that had happened a billion years after his time. It was very confusing . . . he did not know where in time or space he was.

The journey was coming to an end; the walls of the tunnel no longer flashed past him at such breakneck speed. Yarlan Zey began to speak with an urgency, and an authority, which he had not shown before.

"The past is over; we did our work, for better or for ill, and that is finished with. When you were created, Jeserac, you were given that fear of the outer world, and that compulsion to stay within the city, that you share with everyone else in Diaspar. You know now that that fear was groundless, that it was artificially imposed on you. I, Yarlan Zey, who gave it to you, now release you from its bondage. Do you understand?"

With those last words, the voice of Yarlan Zey became louder and louder, until it seemed to reverberate through all of space. The subterranean carrier in which he was speeding blurred and trembled around Jeserac as if his dream was coming to an end. Yet as the vision faded, he could still hear that imperious voice thundering into his brain: "You are no longer afraid, Jeserac. *You are no longer afraid.*"

He struggled up toward wakefulness, as a diver climbs from the ocean depths back to the surface of the sea. Yarlan Zey had vanished, but there was a strange interregnum when voices which he knew but could not recognize talked to him encouragingly, and he felt himself supported by friendly hands. Then like a swift dawn reality came flooding back.

He opened his eyes, and saw Alvin and Hilvar and Gerane standing anxiously beside him. But he paid no heed to them; his mind was too filled with the wonder that now lay spread before him—the panorama of forests and rivers, and the blue vault of the open sky.

He was in Lys; and he was not afraid.

No one disturbed him as the timeless moment imprinted itself forever on his mind. At last, when he had satisfied himself that this indeed was real, he turned to his companions.

"Thank you, Gerane," he said. "I never believed you would succeed."

The psychologist, looking very pleased with himself, was making delicate adjustments to a small machine that hung in the air beside him.

"You gave us some anxious moments," he admitted. "Once or twice you started to ask questions that couldn't be answered logically, and I was afraid I would have to break the sequence."

"Suppose Yarlan Zey had not convinced me—what would you have done then?"

"We would have kept you unconscious, and taken you back to Diaspar where you could have waked up naturally, without ever knowing that you'd been to Lys."

"And that image of Yarlan Zey you fed into my mind—how much of what he said was the truth?"

"Most of it, I believe. I was much more anxious that my little saga should be convincing rather than historically accurate, but Callitrax has examined it and can find no errors. It is certainly consistent with all that we know about Yarlan Zey and the origins of Diaspar."

"So now we can really open the city," said Alvin. "It may take a long time, but eventually we'll be able to neutralize this fear so that everyone who wishes can leave Diaspar."

"It *will* take a long time," replied Gerane dryly. "And don't forget that Lys is hardly large enough to hold several hundred million extra people, if all your people decide to come here. I don't think that's likely, but it's possible."

"That problem will solve itself," answered Alvin. "Lys may be tiny, but the world is wide. Why should we let the desert keep it all?"

"So you are still dreaming, Alvin," said Jeserac with a smile. "I was wondering what there was left for you to do."

Alvin did not answer; that was a question which had become more and more insistent in his own mind during the past few weeks. He remained lost in thought, falling behind the others, as they walked down the hill toward Airlee. Would the centuries that lay ahead of him be one long anticlimax?

The answer lay in his own hands. He had discharged his destiny; now, perhaps, he could begin to live.

TWENTY-SIX

There is a special sadness in achievement, in the knowledge that a long-desired goal has been attained at last, and that life must now be shaped toward new ends. Alvin knew that sadness as he wandered alone through the forests and fields of Lys. Not even Hilvar accompanied him, for there are times when a man must be apart even from his closest friends.

He did not wander aimlessly, though he never knew which village would be his next port of call. He was seeking no particular place, but a mood, an influence—indeed, a way of life. Diaspar had no need of him now; the ferments he had introduced into the city were working swiftly, and nothing he could do would accelerate or retard the changes that were happening there.

This peaceful land would also change. Often he wondered if he had done wrong, in the ruthless drive to satisfy his own curiosity, by opening up the ancient way between the two cultures. Yet surely it was better that Lys should know the truth—that it also, like Diaspar, had been partly founded upon fears and falsehoods.

Sometimes he wondered what shape the new society would take. He believed that Diaspar must escape from the prison of the Memory Banks, and restore again the cycle of life and death. Hilvar, he knew, was sure that this could be done, though his proposals were too technical for Alvin to follow. Perhaps the time would come again when love in Diaspar was no longer completely barren.

Was *this,* Alvin wondered, what he had always lacked in Diaspar—what he had really been seeking? He knew now that when power and ambition and curiosity were satisfied, there still were left the longings of the heart. No one had really lived until they had achieved that synthesis of love and desire which he had never dreamed existed until he came to Lys.

He had walked upon the planets of the Seven Suns—the first man to do so in a billion years. Yet that meant little to him now; sometimes he thought he would give all his achievements if he could hear the cry of a newborn child, and know that it was his own.

In Lys, he might one day find what he wanted; there was a warmth and understanding about its people, which, he now realized, was lacking in Diaspar. But before he could rest, before he could find peace, there was one decision yet to be made.

Into his hands had come power; that power he still possessed. It was a responsibility he had once sought and accepted with eagerness, but now he knew that he could have no peace while it was still his. Yet to throw it away would be the betrayal of a trust.

He was in a village of tiny canals, at the edge of a wide lake, when he made his decision. The colored houses, which seemed to float at anchor upon the gentle waves, formed a scene of almost unreal beauty. There was life and warmth and comfort here—everything he had missed among the desolate grandeur of the Seven Suns.

One day humanity would once more be ready for space. What new chapter Man would write among the stars, Alvin did not know. That would be no concern of his; his future lay here on Earth.

But he would make one more flight before he turned his back upon the stars.

When Alvin checked the upward rush of the ascending ship, the city was too distant to be recognized as the work of Man, and the curve of the planet was already visible. Presently they could see the line of twilight, thousands of miles away on its unending march across the desert. Above and around were the stars, still brilliant for all the glory they had lost.

Hilvar and Jeserac were silent, guessing but not knowing with certainty why Alvin was making this flight, and why he had asked them to come with him. Neither felt like speech, as the desolate panorama unfolded below them. Its emptiness oppressed them both, and Jeserac felt a sudden contemptuous anger for the men of the past who had let Earth's beauty die through their own neglect.

He hoped that Alvin was right in dreaming that all this could be changed. The power and the knowledge still existed—it needed only the will to turn back the centuries and make the oceans roll again. The water was still there, deep down in the hidden places of the Earth; or if necessary, transmutation plants could be built to make it.

There was so much to do in the years that lay ahead. Jeserac knew that he stood between two ages; around him he could feel the pulse of mankind beginning to quicken again. There were great problems to be faced—but Diaspar would face them. The recharting of the past would take centuries, but when it was finished Man would have recovered almost all that he had lost.

Yet could he regain it all? Jeserac wondered. It was hard to believe that the Galaxy would be reconquered, and even if that were achieved, what purpose would it serve?

Alvin broke into his reverie, and Jeserac turned from the screen.

"I wanted you to see this," said Alvin quietly. "You may never have another chance."

"You're not leaving Earth?"

"No; I want nothing more of space. Even if any other civilizations still survive in this Galaxy, I doubt if they will be worth the effort of finding.

There is so much to do here; I know now that this is my home, and I am not going to leave it again."

He looked down at the great deserts, but his eyes saw instead the waters that would be sweeping over them a thousand years from now. Man had rediscovered his world, and he would make it beautiful while he remained upon it. And after that—

"We aren't ready to go out to the stars, and it will be a long time before we can face their challenge again. I have been wondering what I should do with this ship; if it stays here on Earth, I shall always be tempted to use it, and will never have any peace of mind. Yet I cannot waste it; I feel that it has been given into my trust, and I must use it for the benefit of the world.

"So this is what I have decided to do. I'm going to send it out of the Galaxy, with the robot in control, to discover what happened to our ancestors—and, if possible, *what* it was they left our Universe to find. It must have been something wonderful for them to have abandoned so much to go in search of it.

"The robot will never tire, however long the journey takes. One day our cousins will receive my message, and they'll know that we are waiting for them here on Earth. They will return, and I hope that by then we will be worthy of them, however great they have become."

Alvin fell silent, staring into a future he had shaped but which he might never see. While Man was rebuilding his world, this ship would be crossing the darkness between the galaxies, and in thousands of years to come it would return. Perhaps he would still be here to meet it, but if not, he was well content.

"I think you are wise," said Jeserac. Then, for the last time, the echo of an ancient fear rose up to plague him. "But suppose," he added, "the ship makes contact with something we do not wish to meet. . . ." His voice faded away as he recognized the source of his anxiety and he gave a wry, self-deprecatory smile that banished the last ghost of the Invaders.

"You forget," said Alvin, taking him more seriously than he expected, "that we will soon have Vanamonde to help us. We don't know what powers he possesses, but everyone in Lys seems to think they are potentially unlimited. Isn't that so, Hilvar?"

Hilvar did not reply at once. It was true that Vanamonde was the other great enigma, the question mark that would always lie across the future of humanity while it remained on Earth. Already, it seemed certain, Vanamonde's evolution toward self-consciousness had been accelerated by his contact with the philosophers of Lys. They had great hopes of future co-operation with the childlike supermind, believing that they could foreshorten the aeons which his natural development would require.

"I am not sure," confessed Hilvar. "Somehow, I don't think that we should expect too much from Vanamonde. We can help him now, but we will be only a brief incident in his total life span. I don't think that his ultimate destiny has anything to do with ours."

Alvin looked at him in surprise.

"Why do you feel that?" he asked.

"I can't explain it," said Hilvar. "It's just an intuition." He could have added more, but he kept his silence. These matters were not capable of communication, and though Alvin would not laugh at his dream, he did not care to discuss it even with his friend.

It was more than a dream, he was sure of that, and it would haunt him forever. Somehow it had leaked into his mind, during that indescribable and unsharable contact he had had with Vanamonde. Did Vanamonde himself know what his lonely destiny must be?

One day the energies of the Black Sun would fail and it would release its prisoner. And then, at the end of the Universe, as time itself was faltering to a stop, Vanamonde and the Mad Mind must meet each other among the corpses of the stars.

That conflict might ring down the curtain on Creation itself. Yet it was a conflict that had nothing to do with Man, and whose outcome he would never know. . . .

"Look!" said Alvin suddenly. "This is what I wanted to show you. Do you understand what it means?"

The ship was now above the Pole, and the planet beneath them was a perfect hemisphere. Looking down upon the belt of twilight, Jeserac and Hilvar could see at one instant both sunrise and sunset on opposite sides of the world. The symbolism was so perfect, and so striking, that they were to remember this moment all their lives.

In this universe the night was falling; the shadows were lengthening toward an east that would not know another dawn. But elsewhere the stars were still young and the light of morning lingered; and along the path he once had followed, Man would one day go again.

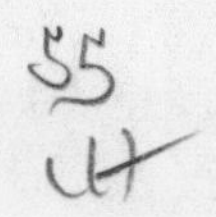